**ONE OF THE MOST POPULAR
AUTHORS OF OUR TIME!**
— Publishers Weekly

Jony spoke directly to the spacemen. "Now listen very carefully, both of you. I think this whole lab should be smashed. I don't like cages, and I don't like people who hurt my friends. Do you understand that?"

"We weren't hurting them—we were testing . . ." one of the Terrans returned.

"I have seen what happens to lab 'animals.' You believe these People are animals, don't you?" He bore in fiercely.

"But," protested the other human, "we have no intention of touching you or the children. Ask her—" he indicated Maba, "whether she has not been well treated."

"I don't doubt it in the least," Jony returned. "You accepted her as one of your own kind. But we do not accept you as one of us! We are of the People—" he motioned towards Yaa and Voak.

"You are human stock," the spacemen said hotly.

Jony replied firmly, "We are of the People."

IRON CAGE

Andre Norton

ace books
A Division of Charter Communications Inc.
1120 Avenue of the Americas
New York, N.Y. 10036

IRON CAGE

Copyright © 1974 by Andre Norton

All Rights Reserved

An Ace Book by arrangement with The Viking Press, Inc.

ANDRE NORTON, one of the Ace Books' most respected and prolific authors—with over fifty books and millions of copies in print—is world renowned for her uncanny ability to create tightly plotted action stories based on her extensive readings in travel, archeology, anthropology, natural history, folklore and psycho-esper research. With classic understatement belied by the enthusiastic critical reception of all her books, she has described herself as ". . . rather a very staid teller of old fashioned stories . . ."

Miss Norton began her literary career as an editor for her high school paper and quickly progressed to writing, publishing her first book before the age of twenty-one. After graduating from Western University, and working for the Library of Congress for a number of years, she began her writing career in earnest, consistently producing science fiction novels of the highest quality.

Miss Norton presently resides in Florida under the careful management of her feline associates.

There was once a time when many animals, including man, needed each other to survive the onslaughts of raging elements in a hostile world. Their affinity must have been very deep, involving senses and abilities long lost.

We have a tendency to patronize animals, to limit their abilities, to compare adversely their physical forms, minds, and lives with our high estate. But animals live in realms of their own, realms totally different and far older than ours. They dwell within the earth, in jungles and desert, in seas and the skies. They possess senses, and extensions of senses, we have lost or never attained. They see sights we shall never see. They hear sounds we shall never hear. They respond to terrestrial and cosmic rhythms and cycles that we have never charted.

If man could remove hate and fear from his heart, then might this fundamental bond of affinity and affection bring beneficent cooperation between all the kingdoms of Life.

—Vincent and Margaret Gaddis
The Strange World of Animals and Pets

"WHAT ARE YOU GOING TO DO WITH THE CAT?"

"Send her to the Humane Society. We certainly can't take her with us. And she's going to have kittens again."

"But what will Cathy—?"

"We've told her that we have found a good home for Bitsy. After all, they *do* find homes for some of them, don't they?"

"A female—and pregnant?"

"Well, there's nothing else to do. The Hawkins boy has promised to pick her up. There he is in the drive-way now. He'll run her over to the Humane Society. Just don't let Cathy know. She gets entirely too emotional about animals. Really, I don't know what I am going to do with that child! I've made up my mind about one thing—no more pets! Luckily we'll be in the new apartment where they aren't allowed."

The black and white cat crouched in the carton into which she had been unceremoniously thrust an hour earlier. Her protesting yowls had brought no escape, any more than her frenzied scratching, which only made the carton rock a little on the porch step. Fear possessed her now, though she could not understand the words muffled by the box, behind the screen door. She had been uneasy all morning, her time for kittening was very near. She must get *out,* find a safe place. Every instinct told her that; yet her utmost efforts had not brought freedom.

At the sound of the car pulling into the drive, she crouched even flatter. Then the box which held her was jerked up roughly, so she was shaken from side to side. Inside— She was inside the car. She yowled once again, despairingly, afraid, seeking the hands, the voice which always meant security and comfort. But there came no answer at all. In her nervous reaction she fouled the box with spray, which made her even more eager for freedom.

The car was stopping.

"What's the matter with you, man? How come you're so late?"

"Got an errand to run for the Stansons—they're moving tomorrow. Got to take their old cat to the Humane Society and dump her off."

"The Humane Society? You know where that is? About five miles away from here. And we're late now! Go all that way just to dump a cat—man, you're crazy!"

"So? What do I do then, smart brain?"

"She in that box? Phew, she's stinking up the car, too. You'd better get rid of her fast if you plan to take that Henslow chick out tonight. Cat stink like that stays forever. I'll tell you what to do, dumbhead. You drive out a little way along the highway; there's a woods on the second turn that's a real dump. See, it's going to rain—and you want to make time if you're still planning on going to the game."

"I guess that's all right."

"It sure is. Get rid of that old, stinking cat and get back here, but quick. We've still got to meet those chicks, and they aren't the kind you keep waiting."

The cat whimpered. Those harsh voices were only a noise, meaning nothing. She was gasping now, the evil smell of the box making her sick—if she could only get out!

Once more the car stopped, the box again caught up roughly. Thrust through an open window, it hit the ground hard, rolling down a slope to lie with the other illegally dumped trash. The cat, shaken, in pain, cried out again.

There came the sound of the car driving away— then nothing. Except the rain striking on the box. She fought once more for freedom with claws dragging down the carton side. Why was she here? Where was home?

The rough handling had started her labor. She writhed and cried sharply in pain. There was no room! The box shook under the pummeling of a rising storm. One kitten had come. The cat nosed it once, but made no effort to lick it into life. It was dead. She fought now with new frenzy at the side of the carton, and, softened by the rain, the heavy cardboard began to give. The chance at freedom made her wild and she worked at the hole until she had torn open a doorway. Rain beat in upon her, soaking her fur, making her cry aloud again.

Instinct ruled her. She must find shelter, a place— before . . . before . . .

Crying still, she pulled out of the box, looked around. There was the massive pile of dumped litter. Not too far away a refrigerator lay on its side, the door ripped off. Toward this small hope of shelter the cat dragged herself. She was inside when the next kitten came, feebly alive. And then there were two more. She had found shelter, but food, drink—she was too tired, too beaten by fear and shock to try to hunt for those. She lay on her side and whimpered a little as she slept.

"THIS IS THE MAUN FEMALE? WHAT WILL YOU DO WITH her? She is heavy with young."

"Worthless for our purpose. She is mad, also. When we took her last young for experiments, she turned dangerous. We bred her to the younger male, but she fought him badly. Luckily he was mind-controlled and, so, useful in such cases."

"It is odd, the mind-controls do not work evenly. There are reports—"

"Do not speak of reports! They pile in the reader, and when does one have a chance to really sort through them? Now, with Lllayron ordering this early take-off, a goodly number of the experiments will never be carried through. This female—we cannot space with her—she would never deliver living young. Not that that is of much interest, since she is plainly a reject. To dispose of her is best."

Rutee crouched in the cage, hunched over, her arms protectively around her bulging abdomen. A baby —another baby in this hellish place! She wished she could kill herself and the child before it was born! Only there was no way. If you did not eat they tied you down and force-fed you with their shots. Just as they had made her have—Rutee tried to close her mind to memory.

She was not mind-controlled as were most of the other experimental livestock. Bron had not been either. That was why they had killed him right at the start. That—that *thing* they had used to father what she now carried . . . No, *that* she must *not* remember.

The aliens were probably discussing her. But not one of her species had ever heard an alien speak. Either they were telepathic or their range of communication was above or below the power of her human ear. She could sense, however, that they were concerned with her. And she was smart enough to know that some event beyond the regular lab procedure was close at hand. They had been doing a lot of packing, putting things in special containers and sealing them. Was what she suspected the truth? Were they preparing to space again? Then—what of the baby?

She curled into a tighter ball, remembering what had happened to Luci who had been caged with her for a while right after they had all been captured. Luci had been pregnant, too. And in space she had died. Rutee tried to think clearly.

Over the months—how long had she been here? There was no way of reckoning time. But it had been long enough for her to learn that somehow she differed from most of the others. When they turned that controller thing on her, she felt only a prickling, not the compulsion which apparently gripped her fellow victims. Jony, he had not either!

She turned her head a little, trying to see down the line of cages.

"Jony!" she called softly. "Are you there, Jony?"

One of her discoveries had been that the aliens did not or could not hear her voice any more than she could theirs. It had given her one little ray of hope.

Perhaps now was the time to make the final effort.

"Jony?" she called again.

"Rutee," he answered her. Then he was still there! Each period of waking time she always feared he would not be.

"Jony," she picked her words carefully. "I think that something is going to happen. Do you remember what I told you—about the locks of the cage?"

"I've already done it, Rutee. When they brought the eating bowl a little while ago, I did it!" There was excited triumph in his reply.

Rutee drew a deep breath. Jony was almost alarmingly bright sometimes; he seemed able to sense things quickly. For a seven-year-old he was unusual. But then, he was Bron's own son. Bron's and hers, born out of their love and belief in each other and a future they had thought they had, when they had been colonists on that planet they had named Ishtar. No, this was no time to remember—it was a time to act.

She studied the aliens searchingly.

Their physical strangeness was so far removed from the norm her people had always considered "human" that she had never been able to think of them as anything but devilish nightmares—even apart from the treatment they accorded their unfortunate "specimens." Towering on their spindly legs far over the tallest man she had ever seen, they had round pouchy bodies and heads which appeared to rest on their narrow shoulders without benefit of neck. Their mouths were gaping slits, their eyes protruded like goggling globes. Their entire greenish-yellow bodies were entirely hairless.

And their minds—Rutee shuddered. She could not deny them mental process superior to her own species. To these monsters her flesh and blood were only animals—to be used as such and discarded.

One was coming now to unfasten the clamps which held her cage in a line with the rest. They—they were taking her away? Jony—no, no!

Rutee wanted to beat on the bars, tear at them. However, better act as if she were cowed. She did not want them to bring a pressure stick, give her jolts of pain.

"Jony, they are moving my cage. I do not know what they are going to do with me." She tried to make her message matter-of-fact.

"They are going to put you in the dump place," Jony's words startled her. "But they will not!"

The dump place—where the dead and the useless disappeared! Rutee wanted to scream aloud her fear, though that would do no good.

"They won't do it!" Jony repeated. Perhaps he did sense all she felt at that time. He had those odd flashes of empathy. "Wait for me, Rutee!"

"Jony!" Now she was suddenly more afraid for him than she was for herself. "Don't try anything—don't let them hurt you."

"They won't. Just wait, Rutee."

The alien had her cage freed and was carrying it beside his giant's body down the aisle. She clung to the bars, trying not to be hurled from side to side. They were close to the dump door now. Rutee hoped death came quickly on the other side.

But, to her amazement, they passed that. After Jony's words she had been so certain of her fate that she was a little dazed as they went out the lab door, down a corridor, only able to understand that death, apparently, had been put off for a little while. She was still puzzled as they came into the open, down the ramp of the ship which towered far above any building she had ever seen.

It was when they were on their way down the ramp she caught sight of Jony. Not in another cage, but slipping along the floor, progressing by quick darts, a few feet forward at a time, and then freezing into immobility before he made another dash. Jony had indeed triggered his lock; he was free. The wonder and hope of that filled her for a long moment with an emotion close to joy.

Jony never understood how he knew things. It was as if answers just came into his head. But while Rutee had sensed that change was coming, he had known it for certain. This place (Rutee said it was a spaceship) was going away, up into the sky. And Rutee—the Big Ones were going to get rid of Rutee. Perhaps he could get free, reach her cage and open it from the outside. He had to!

Moments earlier when he had been sure of what was

happening even as Rutee herself, he had balled up, his arms about his crooked knees, his chin resting on those same knees. Some time ago he had made his big discovery. Rutee had told him that he was not like the others, who did just what the Big Ones told them. Sometimes, if he tried very hard, he could make a Big One do just as he thought!

Now—now he must do that with the Big One who was standing in front of Rutee's cage. There was only one of the enemy, so he had a chance. Jony put to work all his power of concentration (which was such as would have astounded Rutee if she had known) into a single thought. Rutee—must—not—go—in—the—dump—place. Rutee—must—NOT—

He was startled out of that concentration by Rutee's call. However, after he had answered, his thoughts once more centered only on the Big One and Rutee's cage.

That was loose now, grasped in a single hand where the six digits were all small, boneless tentacles, yet with a power of grip his own five fingers could never possess. Jony thought—

The door to the dump place, the Big One had passed it! Jony unrolled in an instant, was out of his cage, clambering down the wire of the empty one below, making the last drop to the floor. Then he moved in small rushes from one hiding place he marked out ahead to the next. He reached the ramp to see the Big One with Rutee's cage stamping down ahead of him. Jony drew a deep breath and ran full speed. He flashed past the Big One, heading on into the open world beyond, expecting every moment that one of those great hands would reach from above, wrap its tentacles about him, take him prisoner again.

But, fear-ridden though he was, he turned when he was aware of cover over him. Throwing himself flat, he rolled back into the dim shadow of a towering bush. Once in that shadow, Jony drew several gasping breaths, hardly daring to believe he was still free. Then, resolutely, he wriggled forward to peer back at the only place he had ever known as a shelter.

He could see only a bit of it, the ramp, the hatch from which it sprang, then the rest towering up and up so it was hidden beyond his range of sight. The Big One had paused at the foot of the ramp. Jony sensed his bewilderment.

Once more Jony concentrated. The cage—put it over there.

Fiercely he aimed that thought at the enemy. There was still a feedback of confusion from the alien. However, he *was* moving forward away from the ramp, the cage in his hand.

Then the Big One stiffened, glancing back at the ramp as if he had been called by someone at its head. Jony shivered. There was no way of contacting the other now—he would return to the ship with Rutee and—

Only the alien did not. At least he did not take the cage. Instead he threw it from him, went pounding back up the ramp. Even as he reached the hatch, it began to close and the ramp was jerked in. The Big One was inside as the ship sealed itself.

Rutee—the cage— Jony scrambled from his hiding

hole, fought his way through brush which lashed his bare body, leaving long, smarting scratches.

"Rutee!" He cried aloud. Then his voice was swallowed up in a thunderous rumble of sound, so terrible he crouched against the side of a huge tree, his hands flying to his ears to keep out that deafening explosion of noise. There was a wind beating in to follow. Jony tried to make himself even smaller. Could he have dug his way into the root-bound ground beneath him he would have gladly done so.

For moments he only endured; his fear, filling all his mind, sent his body into convulsive shivering. He whimpered.

The wind died and the sound was gone. He took his hands from his ears, gulped in air. Tears streaked his scratched face. Still he shivered. It was cold here. And dark—the gloom in the brush was thick as it had never been in the cage room which was all he could remember.

"Rutee?" her name was a hissed whisper. Somehow he could not force his dry lips to make that any louder. He wanted Rutee! He must find her!

Blundering blindly on, Jony tunneled away through brush, twice coming up against growth which resisted his passage. He staggered along beside it until he could find some way to get through. His head was whirling and he could not think; he only knew that he must find Rutee!

The cage had arched through the air when the alien had thrown it. Rutee had had a moment or two of panic. Then she was shaken and bruised as her prison landed on a wall of brush, its weight bearing down the vegetation that acted as a brake for its descent. The smashing fall she had expected was eased by so much. Perhaps that had saved her life—for now.

She lay on the floor, broken branches spearing at her through the heavy wire mesh, threatening her. Both hands were pressed to her belly. Pain—the child—it must be coming. She was trapped in here . . .

She had a few moments to endure that fresh terror before the world went mad with sound. Then came a blast of wind. Only because she was lying on her side facing in the right direction did she see the rise of the ship which had been her prison. And that only briefly, for with the fantastic speed of the alien ships it vanished.

Jony—she had seen him run down the ramp; he had reached the outer world. "Jony," she whispered his name feebly, moaning as pain bore down upon her again relentlessly with an agony which filled the whole world for an endless moment.

When the thrust subsided Rutee moved, sat up. She crawled to the door of the cage, working her hands through the mesh to try to reach the latch, though she knew of old such action was useless. She was trapped as securely here as she had been in the lab. Only that stubborn will to live which had possessed her ever since her capture kept her fumbling away as best she could.

At length the pain hit again. She groveled and wept, hating herself for her own weakness. Jony—where was

Jony? It was getting much darker; clouds were gathering. Now rain began, and the chill of those pelting drops set her shivering.

Summoning all her strength as the pain ebbed again, Rutee screamed aloud into the storm:

"Jony!"

Her only answer was another gust of cold rain beating in upon her. She was so cold . . . cold . . . Never before she could remember being so cold. There should be clothing to put on, heat—protection against this cold. There had been once—when, where? Rutee wept. Her head hurt when she tried to remember. She was cold and she hurt—she needed to get to where it was warm, she must because . . . because . . . She could not remember the reason for that either, as pain came again to fill every inch of her with torment.

But Jony had heard that scream, even through the fury of the storm. He began to think again, stopped just running mindlessly seeking without a guide. Purposefully he turned, breaking a way to the right, refusing to accept the brush and the soaking vegetation as a barrier.

Rutee was ahead, somewhere. He must find Rutee. He concentrated on that one thought with the same intensity of purpose which had made the Big One do what *he* wished and not throw Rutee into the dump place. Mud plastered him almost knee high and his shivering never stopped. This was the first time in his life he had ever been Outside. But he did not even look around him with faint curiosity. All his will was directed toward one end: finding Rutee. She needed him. The wave of her need was so strong that it was like a pain, though he could not have put it into words; he could only feel it.

Twice he stopped short, his hands flying to his head, as they had by instinct tried to close his ears to the blast of the ship's lifting. There were—thoughts—feelings . . . Only these had nothing to do with Rutee. They were as strange as those he sometimes touched when the Big Ones gathered. At first he crept into the brush again, almost sure that one of the enemy hunted. But there was a difference . . . No, no Big One had come after him; the ship was safely gone.

The next time, and the next, that Jony felt the touch which he could not explain, he doggedly refused to think about it. He must hold Rutee in his mind, or he would never find her in this wild place.

Jony staggered, his bruised hand out to a tree trunk in support. Rutee! She was near and she hurt! She hurt so bad, Jony wanted to double up, as his nerves made instant sympathetic response. He had to wait for what seemed a long time, crying a little, his breath coming in harsh gasps which he felt but could not hear. Her pain had eased; he could go on.

He came to where even through the darkness of the storm he could see the bulk of the cage. It was not quite at ground level, being held up by a mass of crushed foliage and branches. Rutee was only a pale, small huddle within it. Jony knew he could open the lock—if he could reach it. Only that was well above his head, for as he neared the place he realized that the bottom of the cage itself was above him.

Somehow he would have to climb up over all the brush and the wire netting.

Twice he jumped, caught branches, teetered on rain-wet footing, and was spilled painfully, when they gave under his weight, slight as it was. But his determination never faltered; he only tried again. There was a deep, bleeding furrow down his leg where a splintered branch had gouged. And his arms and shoulders ached with the strain he put on them as he strove to pull up higher.

At last he worked his way up until he could catch at the wire. There he clung, speechless, caught in a spasm of the pain which radiated from Rutee, hanging on desperately because he must, until he dared move again. Too, as he climbed toward the locking device, his weight pulled the cage forward. That it might crash forward to crush him beneath it was not in Jony's thoughts now; he had only room for one thing: the belief that he must reach the lock—get Rutee out.

He heard her cries, and then his hand closed on the fastening, which she had been unable to touch. It went this way . . . One-handed, Jony held to his perch, flattened against the wire as the cage trembled. Yes—now *this* way!

Through the storm's sounds he could not hear the faint click of the released device. However, his weight against the door caused it to swing open and out. Jony dangled by one hand for a heart-thumping instant. Then his toes, his feet found anchorage on the wires;

his two arms wrapped in and around it. Only the cage was tipping more and more in his direction.

Fear froze him where he was, aware at last that all might crash down. Rutee was moving, crawling to the very edge of the doorway on her hands and knees.

She had been only half-aware of Jony's coming. But, after her last pain had ebbed, she knew at once his danger. He had paid no attention to her orders to get down and away, perhaps he never even heard them. Now he clung as if plastered to the door, suspended over a dark drop she did not know the extent of. She had now, not only to escape herself, but perhaps save Jony.

Cautiously she lowered her clumsy body half over the edge of the tilting cage, groping with her legs, her feet, for some means of support. Twice she kicked against the branches, but these gave too easily to pressure; she dared not trust her weight to such. A third time her right foot scraped painfully along something horizontal and then thumped home, with a jar that brought an agonized moan from her, on a surface which did not slip away or sway as she dared exert more pressure.

She must move now. The cage was certainly going to slide forward, and, if she remained where she was, it might mean that both she and Jony would be crushed. There was a lull in the rising of the wind, though the rain was still steady. Her first attempt at speech was a hoarse croak, but she tried again.

"Move, Jony, to the left." It was so hard to think.

Her mind seemed all fuzzy as it had when the aliens had experimented with her that first time. And she dared not linger where she was to see if Jony heard and obeyed. Her weight and his, both at the forepart of the cage, was pulling it out and down.

Now she had both her feet on that firm support; and she allowed her grasp on the cage itself to loosen, as she dropped one hand and the other to the unseen sturdy point she had found. When her grip on that was sure, she dared to look up.

Jony moved! He had dropped down to the bottom edge of the cage door, was feeling for footholds below. She wondered if she could reach him, but was sure she could not. Not when, as her pains hit once more, she could only cling with a death-tight grip to her own hold.

The cage was going; Jony knew it. He allowed his hold on the wire to loosen and, as he slipped, grabbed desperately. A slime of mashed leaves made the handfuls he grasped slippery and treacherous. Finally he thudded into a mass which swayed but did not spill him over. The cage fell, and Jony had all he could do to keep his small hold from being torn away by the resulting flailing of the broken brush.

He was shaking so hard now, not only from the chill of the beating rain, but also from the narrow margin of his escape, that he dared not move. But he screamed as something closed tightly about his ankle.

Just before he kicked out wildly and disastrously to free himself he heard Rutee:

"Jony!"

With a cry he lowered himself, felt her chill flesh against his as she held him tightly to her. They were closer than they had been for a long time. Close—and safe! He said her name over and over, burrowing his head against her shoulder.

But Rutee was not the same—she was hurt. Even as he clung to her, her body jerked and she cried out. He could again feel her pain.

"Rutee!" Fear was so strong in Jony it was as if he could taste it, a bitter taste in his mouth. "Rutee, you are hurt!"

"I—I must find a place, Jony—a safe place." her voice came in small spurts of words. "Soon—Jony—please—soon . . ."

But it was dark. And where were there any safe places in this *Outside?* Jony knew about the Outside, but only because Rutee had told him before the Big Ones had pulled him away from her long ago and put him in a cage by himself. The strangeness of Outside itself began to impress him as it had not when he had been so intent on finding Rutee.

"Jony—" Rutee's arm about his shoulders was so convulsively tight it hurt, but he did not fight against her hold. "You—you will have to help—help me—"

"Yes. We have to climb down, Rutee. It's hard . . ."

Jony could never remember the details of that descent. That they made it at all, he realized long afterwards, was a wonder. Even when they stood together on the muddy ground they were not safe. It was so dark that any distance away there were only thick shadows. Also they had to go slowly because Rutee hurt so. When those pains came, she was forced to stop and wait. The second time that happened Jony held her hand between his two.

"Rutee—let me go over there. You wait here. Maybe I can find a safe place . . ."

"No . . ."

However, Jony broke her attempt to hold him and ran across a small open space to the shadow he had chosen. He did not know just why he had picked that particular direction, but it seemed of utmost importance.

In the dusk he blundered into a dry pocket. Sometime in the far past a very giant among trees had fallen here. Its upended mass of roots towered skyward; and the cavity which held those was a deep hollow over which vines had crawled and intertwined to enmesh some nearby saplings, forming a roof, which, while not entirely waterproof, kept the worst of the wind and rain away. Drifted into the hollow was a mat of leaves, deep with numerous years of accumulation. Jony's feet sank almost ankle deep in their softness, as he explored swiftly with both hand and eye.

Rutee could come here; he would bring her. And . . . he was already running back to where she stood as a pale figure in the dusk, to catch her hand.

"Come, Rutee—come . . ." He led, half-supported her with all the wiry strength of his small body, toward the rude nest he had found.

RUTEE LAY MOANING ON THE LEAVES. JONY HAD TRIED to heap them up over her body, to keep her warmer. But she shoved them off, her swollen body twisting with each new pain. Jony crouched beside her, not knowing what he could do. Rutee—Rutee was hurting! He needed to help her, only he did not know how.

Twice he crawled to the edge of their poor shelter, gazed out into the dusk and the rain. There was no help to be found there. Only Rutee was hurting—bad! He could sense her pain in his own self.

Rutee was caught up in that world of agony. She no longer was aware of Jony, of where she lay, of anything but the pain which filled her tormented body.

Jony began to cry a little. He wanted to strike out— to hurt someone—something—as Rutee hurt. The Big Ones—they had done this! A small, cold seed of hatred lodged deep in him and took root in that moment of despair. Let the Big Ones come hunting them—just let them! Jony's hand closed upon a large stone, his fingers curled about it as he jerked it free from the leaves and the earth. He clutched the crude weapon to him, in his mind seeing the stone fly from his hand, strike full into the ugly face of a Big One—smash—smash—smash!

Yet that trick of mind which had set him apart from

the other young, the mind-controlled, also told him that he would fail in any such attempt. A Big One could crush him between wriggling fingers so there was nothing left at all.

"Rutee!" He leaned closer to her, called pleadingly, "Please, Rutee—"

A moan was his only answer. He had to do something—he had to! Jony crawled out into the open, unable to listen any more, his arm crooked over his eyes as if so he could erase the sight of Rutee which was burned into his mind.

He turned his face up into the rain and the wind, knowing in one part of him there was no one there to listen, to help, but saying because he had to:

"Please . . . help Rutee . . . please!"

Awareness— Jony spun around. In the dark he could not see, but he knew. Knew that someone, something, was back there in the shadows, watching—listening. But the mind he sensed was not that of a Big One. No, Jony scowled in perplexity for he could not understand the thought he had touched. This was as if something had flashed across his sight for a single instant and then was gone. He was certain of only one thing: whatever witnessed his misery did not mean him harm.

Drawing a deep breath, Jony made himself take one step and then two toward that gathering of shadows.

"You—please—can you help?" he spoke his plea aloud. For a moment or two he thought that the watcher was gone, had melted back into the unknown, for he could no longer pick up the sensation of a presence.

Then there was movement as a shape shambled forward. Though the light was poor Jony could see it was big (not as large as one of the Big Ones but still perhaps twice his own size). He caught his lower lip between his teeth and stood his ground. It—first it had wondered about him, he knew that, and now it was coming because it wanted to . . .

It wanted to help!

Jony was as sure of that as he was of his own misery or Rutee's pain.

"Please," he said uncertainly—perhaps it could not hear him, nor understand his words if it did. There was a sense of good will which enveloped him as it moved to stand—or hunker—directly before him.

No, this was not a Big One. In no way did the creature resemble those hated enemies. It had a roundish body covered with thick fur, the color marbled with strange patches of light and dark, so that Jony had to watch very carefully or it simply faded back to become a part of the brush again. The four limbs were thick and sturdy. The stranger squatted on the back two, the front ones dangling over its rounded belly. Those forefeet ended in paws which were oddly hand-like in outline, though the hairless skin on them was very dark. A round head crowned wide shoulders, with a short, thick neck between. The face was a muzzle, ending in a button of a nose. But the eyes above that were very large and luminous in the dark as they now regarded Jony.

He ventured to move, reaching out one of his own hands to touch the stranger on the forearm. The fur

beneath his fingers was damp but very soft. Jony had
no fear now; rather a feeling that help had come. He
closed his hold on that limb, though his small hand
could not span it. But he could feel the muscles strong
and hard under the furred skin.

"Rutee?" he said.

There was a queer whining noise from the other—
not words—but the sound did carry a message into
Jony's mind. Yes, this was help! He turned back to
the hollow. The strange creature arose on its hind legs
and shuffled along, towering well above the boy. One
of the dark-skinned hands rested on Jony's shoulder.
And he found the weight vastly comforting.

But there was so little room within the poor shelter
Jony had found he had to edge against the rotting roots
at the far end so that the stranger could crowd in. The
round head swung low, the muzzle nearly touching
Rutee, as the creature moved its nose slowly along the
woman's contorted body.

"Jony?" Rutee lay with her eyes wide open, but she
did not even try to see the boy. Nor when her gaze met
that of the sniffing stranger, did she show any surprise.
Her arm flailed out. Jony caught her wrist, held tightly,
quivering himself as her pain fed into his own body.

The beast was doing something with its black paw-
hands, Jony was not sure what. His faith in its help
was blind but continued. Rutee shrieked, the sound
she made tearing at his head, his mind. He cried out in
turn and closed his eyes. He would have put his hands
over his ears, but her hold had turned to meet his and
was merciless.

Then came another sound—a weak, wailing cry!
Jony, astounded, dared to look again. The black paw-
hands held the struggling thing which was making that
noise. Round head dropped, the nose sniffed carefully
along what the creature held as if it needed scent, more
than sight, for this matter of importance. Then it held
out to Jony the squirming thing. Rutee's hand had
dropped away. She lay breathing in long hard gasps.

Against his will Jony took the baby. The stranger
had turned back swiftly to Rutee, was again sniffing.
Again Rutee screamed weakly, her body jerking.

For the second time the paw-hands held another
baby, and the nose sniffed. But this time a long tongue
came out between strong teeth. Jony was jolted—it
was going to eat—! Before his protest formed in full,
he saw that the tongue was washing the baby,
thoroughly, from head to foot. Another sniffing examination followed before the child the stranger held was
placed gently down on the leaves beside Rutee.

Jony had hardly been aware of the baby in his own
hands though that was still crying, squirming against
his briar-scratched skin. The paw-hands reached out
and he surrendered the baby, to see it washed in turn
and then laid down.

Darkness gathered in the hollow, but not so much
that Jony could not see Rutee's eyes were closed. Her
head had fallen to one side. Frantically he aimed a
thought in the way which had been instinctive for him
ever since he could remember. No—there was no
blankness there. Rutee was alive!

The babies lay against her body, one on either side

as the stranger had so carefully placed them. Now the paw-hands raked through the leaves, drawing up bunches of them to place across both Rutee and the twins. Jony could understand. It was so cold, and some of the rain still sifted in. Rutee, the babies needed protection. He set to work on his side, hunting the driest handfuls to spread over the unconscious woman.

He sensed the approval of the stranger. This was right. When Rutee and the babies were covered, except for their faces, the furred one backed away.

"No!" Jony could not bear to be left alone. What if Rutee were sick—hurt again? And the babies—he did not know what to do for the babies! He was frantic in his need to keep the stranger with them.

Paw-hands fell on his shoulders, holding him very still, while those great luminous eyes stared straight into his. Jony wanted to turn his head, to avoid that level gaze, because in his head there was a swaying feeling as if he could not catch hold of an important thought, but only touch the edge of it fleetingly.

He calmed down. There was a purpose in the creature's going, something important to be done. Jony nodded as quickly as if he had been reassured in words familiar to him. He would not be alone except for a little. He had asked for help, there would be help.

Jony considered the thought of help. He had never asked for it since he had been taken forcibly from Rutee's cage and put by himself. Long before that had been done he had known, and Rutee had made it clear to him, that even those who were of his own kind, or at least looked like him, must never be trusted. They thought only the thoughts the Big Ones allowed them. Rutee was not like them, and he was not. He did not know why, only that the fact was important, Rutee had impressed on him. Never to be one who the Big Ones could use. This had been the main lesson of his childhood.

His world had been the cages and what he could see of the lab beyond their walls. However, Rutee had told of Outside. She had once lived Outside, before the Big Ones had come to put her and the others in cages. Jony now began to think back, as he had so many times, on what Rutee had taught him. When they had put him in a cage by himself, he had made himself remember all he could of what Rutee had said.

They were small and weak, and the Big Ones had ways of hurting and forcing them to be what the Big Ones wanted. But it had not been so with Rutee, or with Bron. Of course he could not remember Bron, though Rutee had talked of him so much that Jony sometimes believed he could.

Rutee, and Bron, and many people (far more than still lingered in the cages of the Big Ones) had lived Outside. Then the Big Ones had come with the smell-stuff which made people go to sleep, and picked up those they wanted. Rutee never knew what had happened to the rest of her people. The Big Ones had used what Rutee called their prisoners. Some—Bron was one and he had been put into the dump place. But most of the others became just what the Big Ones wanted after they were controlled.

Some were taken out of their cages while the Big Ones did horrible things to them. Mostly those ended in the dump place when the Big Ones were finished. But young ones such as Jony, and some of those like Rutee, they kept. To the Big Ones they were not people; they were things, just to use.

Rutee had told him over and over that he must never let them use him, that he was not a *thing*. He was Jony and there was no one else exactly like him, just as there was no one exactly like Rutee. Jony moved now, remembering that, looking more closely at the twins.

Their small, damp, wrinkled faces did not look like Rutee's. And there were two of them. Did that mean they *were* alike? Rutee's head turned restlessly on the leaves and Jony became instantly alert.

"Water—" she said faintly, but she did not open her eyes.

Water? There was plenty falling outside the hollow, but Jony did not see how he was going to bring any in. However, he crept out, noticing as he did so, that it _____ be lightening, but maybe that was only in _____ dusk of the hollow. Water?

_____ him. Not too far away was a plant _____ the width of Jony's hand or _____ loose, holding it with up- _____ poured off a vine _____ without spilling, _____ d a little,

seemed to _____
contrast to the _____
He looked about h _____
with big leaves, each one _____
more. He twisted one of them _____
curved edges where a trickle of ra _____
stem. When he had all he could s _____
he edged carefully in and rais _____

putting the tip of the leaf to her lips so the scant burden of moisture ran into her mouth. She swallowed desperately, and he made the trip again and again.

The last time he returned her eyes were open and looked at him as if she saw him, Jony.

"Jony?"

"Drink." He held the leaf for her. As she tried to raise her head higher, one of the babies whimpered. Startled, she looked down at its flushed face.

"Baby!" She raised her hand slowly, touched fingertip to the tiny cheek.

Jony jerked back, dropping the leaf. He did not know just why, but he felt lost when he saw the way Rutee looked at the newcomer. Rutee—she was the bigger part of Jony's life, she always had been. Now there were the two babies . . .

"You got two," he said harshly. "Two babies!"

Rutee looked surprised as her gaze followed his gesture to the other side.

"Two—?" she repeated wonderingly. "But, Jony—how . . . ?"

"It was the—the good thing who came . . . he answered in a rush of words, con—. . . . that Rutee . . . and not at either of was now looking straigh— —and helped . . ." He those intruders . . . cked the stranger had done, only that was — . . . de Rutee. the babies, bedding them down

. . . he good thing?" she repeated his words again. What do you mean, Jony?"

He used what words he could to describe the half-seen furred creature who had answered his cry for help.

"I don't understand," Rutee said when he had done. "You are sure, Jony, this isn't just something you thought about? Oh, Jony, what—who—could it have been? And—Jony!" Her eyes were big, frightened. She was no longer looking at Jony, but over his shoulder. A twitch of fear of the unknown arose in him to answer. He screwed his head far enough around to see outside.

The stranger was back, crouched down, peering in at them.

"It's the one, Rutee—the one who came to help!" Jony's fear was gone the moment he sighted those shining eyes.

However, the woman watched the creature warily. Slowly she began to sense the feeling it brought with it: comfort, help. And she, who had learned through terror, horror, and continued fear, to look upon the whole world as a potential enemy, relaxed. Rutee did not know what—who—this being was, but she was sure within her that the creature meant her and the children no harm, quite the reverse. Now she lay back weakly in her nest of leaves.

Though its body seemed soft action to it. its solid bulk, it moved briskly, perhaps because of sert itself into their refuge this ti. d not try to in- a mass which it had carried looped in'd not try to in- to its breast, shoving it at Jony. dropped Obedient to its manifest signal, the boy pu offering to him. Branches had been broken, leaving sharp, bark-peeled ends. But still clinging to those boughs were a number of bright green balls. The creature snapped a single one of those from the stem and put it into its gaping mouth. The meaning was plain: this was food.

Food to Jony had always been the squares of dull brown substance which the Big Ones had dropped into the feeding slot of his cage at regular intervals. Now, at the sight of the creature's eating, he was immediately aware that he was hungry. In fact his hunger was an ache which was close to pain. He grabbed at the nearest of the balls for himself.

"No, Jony!" Rutee protested. How could she make him understand that what might be meat or drink to an alien whose world this was, could in turn be deadly poison to someone from another planet? She should have warned him, she should have . . .

The globe was already in Jony's mouth. He bit down hard. A little juice dribbled from between his lips to glisten on his grimy chin. He swallowed before she could snatch it from him.

"Rutee—" he beamed at her. "Good! Better than cage food. Good!"

He was breaking balls recklessly from the branches, and those in one hand he forced upon her.

"Eat, Rutee!"

The woman looked longingly at the fruit. It had been a long time since she had tasted anything but the dry and flavorless rations which had kept her alive but had no savor in them. Now she resigned herself. There would be no more of those cakes given to the caged ones; the ship had taken off and they were here now. Either they could live on native food or they would starve. And she still had enough desire to live to make her take one of the fruits from Jony and bite into it slowly.

Sweet, and full of moisture which was even better for her dry mouth than the rainwater Jony had brought her. This was like—like what . . . Her mind summoned up dim memories of that life long ago. No, she could find nothing there to compare this to. The fruit appeared to have no pit or seed, was all edible. She swallowed and reached for more, the need in her very great.

Together she and Jony cleaned the branches of all the fruit. It was only when Rutee was sure that the last globe was gone she remembered the giver. The strange, heavy-looking creature still squatted there watching them. The rain had stopped; there was further lightening of the world without.

Jony straightened out one leg and gave a little gasp. Rutee saw the raw gouge in his skin; blood stood out in new drops when he moved.

"Jony—" She tried to lever herself up on her hands from out of the leaves. As she moved one of the babies wailed loudly. Rutee found the world swinging unsteadily around her dazed head.

She saw a large hand (or was it closer to a paw?) reach within their small shelter. The hand closed firmly about Jony's ankle and drew him away from her side.

The boy did not fight. Even when he lay across the outstretched arm of the creature, Jony had no fear. Nor did he experience the instant revulsion which had always arisen in him when he had been handled by the slimy hands of the Big Ones. He did not struggle as the stranger straightened out his leg, sniffed along the broken flesh as it had along Rutee's body.

But he was surprised as that long tongue came forth and touched the torn skin, rasped over his wound. Jony was held firmly so that his start did not send him rolling away, but kept him just the proper distance from the probing tongue. As the creature had earlier licked the babies from head to foot, so now it washed the gouge. Nor was Jony released at once when the other raised its head, snapped its tongue back between its jaws.

Instead he was held against a broad, furry chest, one massive arm both cradling and restraining him, as the stranger got to its feet, strode away from the tree shelter. Jony squirmed and would have fought then, for his freedom, to return to Rutee. But there was no way he could break the grip which held him prisoner.

They had not gone far before the stranger paused, reaching out with its free hand to tear up from the ground a long-leafed plant. The muzzle above Jony's head opened; teeth worried the top-most leaves free of their parent stem, chomped away.

Jony smelled a queer scent—saw a little dribble of juice at the corners of the full lips. Then the creature spat what it chewed into the palm of its hand as a thick glob of paste.

With the tip of its tongue it prodded what it held, seemed satisfied. Swiftly it applied the mass to the tear on Jony's skin. The boy tried to evade the plastering, for the stuff stung fiercely. But the stranger held him tightly until there was a thick smear covering the whole of the gouge. Now the stinging subsided, and with it vanished the smarting pain of which Jony had been only half aware during his anxiety over Rutee.

"Jony—Jony—what has that thing done!" Rutee had somehow reached the edge of the shelter, was looking up and out, her face very pale under the leaf dust. "Jony—!"

"It's all right," he roused to reassure her. "The good one just put some chewed leaves on my leg. See." He moved a little so he could show the plastered leg. "It hurt a little, just at first, but it is all right now."

Gently the stranger lowered Jony to the ground. He limped a little when he walked, yes, but the wound no longer smarted. Now he turned around, still favoring his leg, and looked all the way up to the muzzled face above him.

"Thank you . . ." Because words probably did not mean anything to the stranger, Jony concentrated, as fiercely as he had when he had saved Rutee from the dump place, on making his gratitude known.

Once he was sure that thought had touched thought, if very fleetingly, and that the stranger did understand. Then one of the babies began crying in loud wails.

Rutee drew back into her shelter, took them both up, one in each arm, and held them close to her, crooning softly until the crying died down into a small whimpering. Jony watched. Once more his faint resentment of Rutee's preoccupation with the little ones troubled him. Though he did not know why he wished these two interlopers gone.

There was a warm touch on his shoulder. He looked around. It seemed to him that the muzzle wore a smile, if those thick lips could ever move in a way to imitate his. Jony grinned and reached out to clasp one of the paw-hands, which closed very tight and protectingly around his own much smaller and weaker fist.

SUNLIGHT STRUCK BRIGHT ON THE SURFACE OF THE
stream which frothed from the edge of the small falls
on through the narrow valley. The same steady beams
heated the rocks, drying quickly any spatter of spray
that had reached this point. Jony lay belly down, his
head propped on arms folded before him so he could
watch where Maba and Geogee were diving back and
forth under the falling water, shrieking at each other
worse than a couple of vor birds.

They were not alone. Two of the People cublings
splashed around them. But Huuf and Uga were more
intent on a little fishing, trying to lever water-dwelling
tidbits out from under stream-bed stones.

In the brilliant sunlight the patchy coloring of the
People's fur, which gave them such good concealment
in the brush, looked ragged. There was no pattern to
the splotches of light and dark which dappled their
stocky bodies. The fur of all patches was a green-yellow
but in such a diversity of shades as to make their outlines almost indiscernible even here in the open. Only
on their round heads was the color laid in an even de-
sign of light on the muzzle, dark about their large eyes.

Jony and the twins were not so well provided with
body covering, to his resentment and disgust. He did

wear a kilt of drab, coarse stuff which was dabbled with berry and vine juice to resemble the People's shading. But, compared to the soft fur of his companions, he considered it highly inadequate, which it was.

Though he lay at ease, his mind was alert on sentry duty. For more seasons than he could now count, for he had never tried to keep track, they had shared the life of the People. Formidable as they were (even a second season cub could best Jony in a friendly strength-match) they had their enemies, also. And Jony had early discovered that that inner sense of his was, in its way, a more accurate warning than any the People possessed.

He tried now to count how many seasons it had been since Rutee had died of the coughing sickness. She had never been strong, Jony realized now, since the birth of the twins. But she had held on to life until they were almost as old as Jony had been when they had escaped from the Big Ones. In this time he had grown taller, taller than Rutee, nearly as tall as Voak who headed this clan of the People. It had been Voak's mate, Yaa, who had found them, saved Rutee and the babies, brought them back to be of the clan. When Rutee left them, Yaa had taken over the raising of Maba and Geogee as if they were her own cublings.

Jony sent out a questing thought. He detected nothing—save that which should be on wing or on paw, going about the normal business of living. He allowed his mind a chance to deal with his own present burning desire: further exploration.

The clan had their established hunting grounds. Mainly the People were vegetarians, with a liking for a water creature now and then, or thumb-thick grubs which could be found in the rotted wood of certain fallen trees. But last season there had been a drought in the section held loosely by Voak's and Yaa's kin. A drying land had forced them to move away into the hills, beyond which rose those mountains that held up the sky bowl.

Grumbling and snorting, they had come. The People were a settled lot who distrusted and disliked change. But Jony had welcomed the move. There was something which ever urged him on, a curiosity which was as much a part of him as the clubbed braid of his dark hair, his sun-browned skin. He wanted always to know what lay a little farther on.

During that journey they had come across a thing which astounded Jony by its very being. It was like the stream below, save it was not formed of water, but stone (or something as hard as the rock about Jony now). However, in the likeness of a stream, it ran as a narrow length from the lowlands up toward the hills. The top of it was uniformly smooth, though in places earth had drifted across its surface, even as sand bars pushed at the water of the stream.

Jony had run along that surface for a space, finding excitement in being able to move so quickly without stone or brush to impede his going. In the sign language of the People (Jony and his kind could not reproduce their grunting speech), he had tried to ask questions about this strange river of rock. He had been with Trush that day. Trush had been Yaa's cubling when she had come to Rutee's aid.

To Jony's vast surprise, Trush had turned away his head, started determinedly walking away from the rock river, refusing to answer any of Jony's questions, acting as if no one must see or speak of such a thing. His displeasure was enough to subdue Jony; and the boy had reluctantly joined in that retreat, though he had been plagued ever since by the memory of the strange thing and the need to know more.

By his People-trained ability of location he was certain that, had the river of rock really penetrated deeply into the hills, it could not lie far now from this present site. As soon as he could persuade Maba and Geogee to leave the water and see them back with the cubs to the clan campsite, he was going to do a little prowling on his own.

However, unless Jony wanted to arouse the only too annoying curiosity of the twins, he must do nothing to make them suspicious. Jony sighed. He considered that he was as cautious and reasonable as Voak, but the twins rushed madly into action without ever thinking. Also, they both lacked his own ability to sense danger, or to use the control he could hold by concentration upon some other minds.

Not that he could so influence the People. Their minds were too different. Jony had never been able to enter, let alone bend, any one of them to his will, as he had that Big One during the crucial moments of escape. Perhaps (he had talked about it with Rutee often), perhaps this was because the Big Ones had used the mind-controller, and so in some way were themselves more vulnerable to such power. But neither of the twins had such a talent. Rutee explained, when Jony had grown older (it was just before she had died, when she had him promise to watch over them), that their father had been wholly mind-controlled. And she thought perhaps that might make them more susceptible to influence.

She had made Jony promise then that he, himself, would never try to control either Maba or Geogee by such a power. To do so was an evil thing. Her distress had been so great when she spoke of this that Jony had promised at once. Though many times his exasperation with the twins' reckless disregard for their own safety —and that of others—made him wish she had not demanded that of him.

So he had to use other methods of persuasion to control them, and, the older they grew, the more they resented his orders. Jony stirred impatiently on the rock, which was now almost too hot to make a comfortable lounging place. He sat up and called down:

"You two—time to come out!"

Maba laughed and jumped back, so the falling curtain of water hid her slim brown body. Geogee bobbed up and down in the stream and made a face.

"Come and make us!" he hooted.

However, if they disregarded Jony's command, they had still to reckon with Huuf and Uga. Huuf moved up behind Geogee, his hands out, to close upon the boy's upper arms. In spite of Geogee's irate yells and kicks, he bore him calmly to the bank, to dump him on the grass not far from where Geogee's kilt lay in a tangle. Uga disappeared under the spray curtain, to return in less than a breath, not carrying the screaming Maba, but leading her by the long streamers of her hair, on which Uga had a good and unshakable grip.

"Jony—" Maba screamed as soon as she was through the water curtain into the open. "Make her stop! She's hurting me!"

"Do as you're told," he replied with satisfaction, "and you won't get hurt. It's time to head back and you know it."

Though perhaps she did not. None of the three had the built-in sense of time which moved the People calmly and serenely through their days, a time to eat, a time to doze, a time to make nettings, to heap up bedding for the night, to look about them.

The People used some tools. They knotted nets which they employed as loose bags to carry fruit and edible roots with them. Also each treasured a staff such as Jony now reached for. These were carefully made from a well-selected thick branch or sapling.

One end curved in a hook for pulling down fruit-laden branches. The other end was sharpened by much patient rubbing between stones to aid in digging up roots and grubs. It could also be a weapon upon occasion. Voak had slain a vor bird with his staff. Though after he had thrown away the staff, since a kill-thing must not be used again.

The People were equipped with their own armament. The tremendous strength of their thickly-muscled arms and their fangs was enough to make them formidable opponents. Only the vor birds, which could attack from aloft, and smaa, a legged reptile with lightning lash speed, were any real danger. Of course there were the Red Heads, too. Jony had only seen them once, and the memory was enough to make him shiver even now. They had looked (to the unknowing) like tall plants, with huge flaming scarlet balls for flowers, one large ball aloft on each stalk. By day they were root-fixed in the ground—growing. At dusk their life changed. Feet, which were also roots, wriggled out of their chosen pits of sod as they set out to catch and devour any life they could meet.

From the lower parts of their ball heads they discharged a light yellowish powder, the brisk waving of which had seemed like leaves wafted out into the air. Whatever breathed that powder became quickly insensate; the Red Heads would gather up the limp body, enfolding it in thorned leaves which aided in sucking the juices from it. Once this grisly meal was concluded, the shrunken remains were hurled into the open root holes, as if the refuse of their horrible meals would nourish them even longer.

The People knew no way of defeating the Red Heads. One merely avoided them as best one could. Luckily their coloring was such that they could be easily sighted. And they were the first enemy to scout for upon coming into any unfamiliar territory.

Jony watched Maba and Geogee dry themselves off

Afterwards the Big Ones had used what Rutee called the controllers on their prisoners. Some—Bron was one of those—fought, and he had been put into the dump

He looked about him. Not too far away was a plant with big leaves, each one the width of Jony's hand or more. He twisted one of them loose, holding it with up-curved edges where a trickle of rain poured off a vine stem. When he had all he could gather without spilling, he edged carefully in and raised Rutee's head a little,

with bunches of grass and belt on their kilts. Rutee had taught them how to weave those, using the same fibers, but thinner and split, which the People processed to construct their nets. In addition all three possessed squares of more closely woven stuff, packed tighter with feathers of vor birds, which they pulled about them in the cold times.

Jony leaped down from his rock perch, crossed the stream with a couple of jumps from rock to rock. The cubs already headed purposefully toward that clump of trees which marked their present campsite. Both had full nets; their morning had been spent to better purpose than just playing in the water.

"You let them pull us out!" Maba's lower lip stuck out as she scowled at Jony. "You think they know more than we do!"

Geogee nodded in agreement, his scowl just as heavy.

The twins resembled each other in that their hair was fair, almost white where the sun had bleached it, and they had the same general contour of feature. Jony had never been able to see anything of Rutee in them. But Rutee had always said that Jony, himself, was like his father. He often wished that Maba, at least, had had Rutee's dark hair, her face. Now it sometimes seemed he could not, in spite of all his concentration, recall Rutee at all. Except as just a shadowy shape whom he continued to miss with a dull ache.

"They do know more than you do," he said shortly. "If you'd copy them a little, it would be better—"

"Why?" Geogee asked. "We aren't them. Why do we have to act like them at all?"

Jony frowned in return. He had been through this many times during the past seasons. The older the twins grew, the more they wanted to question and argue. At times he had even had to cuff them, as Voak had cuffed him once or twice in the past when he had been foolish and thoughtless.

"We act like them because they have learned to live here. This is their world; they know best how to use it."

"Then where's our world? And why can't we go there?" Maba asked a question he had also answered many times over.

"I don't know where our world is. You know how we came here—the Big Ones had Rutee and me in their sky ship. We got away from them. Rutee saw their ship go back into the sky. We were left here. Which is much better than being in the cages of the Big Ones. Now get going; Yaa is waiting."

"Yaa is always waiting." Maba refused to let his warning silence her. "She wants me to make some more netting. I don't see why I have to. While you get to go off out there." She made a wide circle with her arm to include the hills ahead of them. "I want to go too."

"Yes," Geogee nodded. "Huuf goes, so we can . . ."

"Huuf," Jony tried to put full emphasis on what he said now, "watches all the time. He does not run off and hide, or pretend he is lost in order to have the whole clan out hunting for him."

Maba laughed. "That was fun," she broke out. "Even if Yaa did slap us when we got back. We want to go and see things, Jony, just not always stay around where the People are. They really don't *like* anything different to do."

She was right, of course. But both the twins must learn caution, and they seemed unable to understand, or want to understand, that danger walked with the unknown. For Jony the situation was different. He was much older, bigger, and he had his warning sense to call upon. If the twins only had that, he would not have worried so about their taking off into the unknown. But they had not the least trace of his talent.

"Wait until you're older—" he began when Geogee interrupted.

"You say that every time. We do get older, and still you keep on saying it. You're just never going to let us go. But you wait, Jony, I'm 'most as tall as you now. Someday I'm just going to walk away to go and see things for myself. And Voak and Yaa, they aren't going to stop me, even, any more than you can then, Jony. You'll see!"

Maba was smiling, and Jony distrusted that smile. He had seen that expression before and it generally meant trouble to come. But he could rely upon Yaa; she would not let either twin out of her sight once they were back in camp.

Oddly enough both Maba and Geogee went the rest of the way uncomplainingly and with no more questions. Jony saw them back under Yaa's kind, all-seeing eyes, then went to the opposite side of the campsite where the unmated males had their own small inner circle. The clan was a small one, closely related by blood ties. If any of these younger males wished a mate, he must wait until one of the clan assemblies, which occurred before the coming of the cold, and try then to urge a female away from another family group to join with him. Three of the older ones were already impatient to reach that satisfactory situation in life. But there were four younger, who with Jony, were not yet interested in such complications.

Jony munched a crumbling cake of ground nuts mixed with sap which was their principal noon eating. The food was flavorsome enough, but he looked forward with more anticipation to the evening meal when the results of the morning's fishing would be shared out as additional tasty tidbits.

Trush had had the misfortune to break his staff two days earlier, and had spent the morning largely in careful search for raw material for its replacement. He had been lucky enough to discover a sapling hooked in just the right proportions, and was now engaged in the patient rubbing of its thicker end into the proper point.

Otik had brought back a collection of stones which he was picking over carefully, trying one and then another for abrasive uses. Gylfi worked on the shell of a giant crawler; he had scooped out all the meat (a delicacy greatly appreciated by all the clan), and set the shell with the body side down over a zat nest last night. By morning these obliging insects had divested the interior of the very last vestige of organic material.

Gylfi now had a rock-hard bowl over which he stretched a section of carefully dried and smoked vor bird skin which he had treasured with just this purpose in mind.

He smeared the sap of a vine (a nuisance because of its strong adhesive qualities) around the edge of his bowl and pulled the skin taut across, binding a twist of grass cord about it to make sure of no slippage until the vine sap was thoroughly dry. His work was patient and thorough, and Jony knew what pride he took in it. Once the sap dried, Gylfi would have a handsome drum to thump.

The People did not sing—unless their series of ululating, throaty calls was singing. But they had a strange love of dance. Each full moon overhead brought them to stamp and leap, stamp and leap for hours. Jony usually found such gatherings dull. He would watch for a while and then seek out his sleeping nest. Or else offer, as was more often the case, to go on guard duty so that some clan member could fully enjoy the entertainment.

With all three of his usual companions enwrapped in their own affairs he felt safe, though a little guilty in seeking out what he wanted to do. Finishing his handful of crumbs, he signaled to Trush that he was on scout. Plainly preoccupied with his own affairs, Trush only hunched a shoulder.

A glance across the campsite assured Jony that Maba and Geogee were both netting, one on either side of Yaa. So he slipped away hurriedly hoping that neither saw him go.

There were times when Jony found a certain pleasure in being alone. Though he lacked the homing ability of the People, he could mark his trail when he reached unfamiliar territory and never feared being lost. The world about him was a constant source of wonder and interest. There was always some life-form to hold one's attention, from a strange insect on the wing or underfoot, to a plant with flowers or leaves which were either odd enough to catch the eye, or beautiful and pleasing. On impulse he plucked now a cluster of orange-red blossoms, none larger than his little fingernail, but with gleaming petals and a heady, sweet scent, and tucked the spray into the hair above his ear, just because the color excited his eyes and pleased him for the moment.

The People did not seem to have much interest in any vegetation, unless it offered them food, or some tool, or was an annoyance and an obstruction. But Jony and the twins often picked flowers and wore them. The colors and the scents satisfied some longing in them which they did not understand.

Now Jony turned, started an upward climb, still angling south. If he could find his stone river, perhaps someday he might even trace it to its source. Nowhere else had he seen stones so smoothed, set in straight lines on the ground. It was as if they did not lie there naturally at all, but rather had been placed so for some purpose. By whom—for what?

He reached the top of the ridge. From here he would mark his trail and—But, even as he raised the sharpened end of his staff to scrape across a tree trunk, he looked down slope—and what he saw held him quiet in sheer amazement.

There were . . . what? Jony had no name for those towering things beyond. For one startled moment a thrill of fear ran through him, the dim memory of the ship of the Big Ones. But a second later he knew that what he saw was not the Big Ones, standing silently as a part of the land on which they were based. Yet neither were they piles of rock raised in pinnacles by some chance. The towering fingers of stone were too perfect, too patterned in their arrangement. No, some-one—something—had put rocks to use and built, one atop another, straight-edged mounds and heights.

To the edge of that building ran the river of stone, straight and even, only a little covered by the creeping earth in shallow drifts. It was plain, Jony decided, that this was truly the source of that river. So that, too, must have been made. But how—and again why?

He kept under cover, using each bit of brush, each stand of trees, as he advanced. At the same time he alerted that other sense of his, probing, seeking for some trace of thought—thought which was akin to that of the Big Ones. For only some people with the same powers and needs as his ancient enemies would or could devise what lay ahead. It was not in the nature of the People to work so with stone.

But all his mind-search brought not the least sug-gestion of such life. He could detect only those faint sources which were always about: the native insects, a flying thing. Not even the in-and-out wavering pattern of the People, or the cold menace of smaa, could he pick up. No, there was no life in the pile ahead, Jony began to be certain of that. So he moved on more confidently with greater excitement and an awakened curiosity he would have to satisfy.

BOLDLY AT LAST, JONY STEPPED OUT ON THE STONE river, to walk confidently toward those piles ahead. They varied in size, some merely his height plus that of his staff, if he held it straight upright. However, there were others so tall he had to tilt back his head to see where their tips touched the sky. Now the stone river led him on between the outermost piles.

Jony hesitated. He wanted so much to explore. Yet he was still cautious. Once more he quested intently for any emanation ahead signaling danger. Did the People know of this place? Trush's odd reaction when they had first come upon the stone river remained vivid in Jony's memory. He had not warned Jony off; he had simply pointedly ignored the strange find. Why?

There were many holes in the stone heaps ahead, some small, some large. Again each was regular, as if it had been formed for a purpose, not just because some stone fell out of place during the course of time. Holding his staff at ready, as if he crept up on a smaa's hunting territory, Jony advanced step by wary step, his glance shooting ever from side to side, his extra sense at full alert.

Those larger holes were on the level where he walked now. They reminded him a little of the entrances to caves, but were still too regular and repeated in pattern to be like those dens where the People sheltered during the time of cold. On impulse Jony entered the nearest, peering at what lay on the inner side of that opening.

A limited amount of light came from the other, smaller holes; enough to see an open space, more door holes. Jony's sense picked up a feeling of emptiness. He grew greatly daring, went farther. Unidentifiable masses lay on the floor. He poked at one gingerly with the sharp end of his staff. The whole mound collapsed in an out-puffing of dust.

Jony sneezed, retreated quickly. He did not care for the faintly sourish odor, unlike any he had sniffed before. But his curiosity still held. Those much larger heaps farther along the stone river, were they all alike?

He sighted some straggles of vine, a few clumps of tough grass which had managed to root in cracks of the stone. There was a cawing. A flight of six foraws took off from an upper ledge, as if propelled by some vast need for instant escape. But that was the way foraws were. Jony, ashamed of his own start at their sudden clamor, pushed on at a bolder pace.

Here were other rivers of stone, smaller ones, which branched away from the one he followed. All of those were also walled with the piles which had openings, but lay silent and deserted. Not all, perhaps; Jony sighted the spoor of several small creatures in the drifted earth. Apparently this was a safe shelter they claimed as their own.

At last the river came into an open space ending at the foot of the largest heap of all. Here the blocks of smoothed stone had been set up like the ledges along the falls, but far more evenly, so that a man might climb them with ease. Jony did that, heading for an opening at the top which was four—five times as wide as any he had seen elsewhere. However, as he neared that, he stopped short. For within the shadowed overhead of that opening someone stood waiting.

Jony crouched, his staff swung up, point ready, as he stared at the other. He was taller than Jony—but—he was not a Big One as Jony's old memories first suggested. No, his face . . .

Her face! Jony made a quick adjustment in terms as he saw the waiting one in greater detail. She was like Rutee, a little, big though she was. But she was—stone!

Jony guessed at the truth. Somehow those who had piled up this place had made one of themselves into stone. Or else had been able to fashion stone as the People working a sapling into a shape they desired. And the marvel of such skill made him gasp.

He had to go directly to the figure, venture to touch its cold surface, before he was assured this explanation was the truth. The stone was not rough, but smooth under his fingertips. Somehow he liked the feel of it as he rubbed along, following one curve and then another as high as he could reach. But he could not, even standing on tiptoe, touch more than the chin of the face above him.

Standing so close he could see that once there had

been other colors laid on it beside the gray-white stuff of which it was made. In the folds of the clothing the figure wore, were dim traces of blue. And about her neck was a massive carving of many links which was still yellow.

Her hair did not hang loose as Rutee's and Maba's, but was gathered up into a massing which added to her height. One of her hands was held at a stiff odd angle at the wrist, the tips of her fingers pointing skyward, the palm flattened out toward him. On impulse Jony fitted his hand to that one, palm to palm—

No!

He stumbled back, away from the woman of stone. His mind was confused. What had happened? He had expected to meet cold stone as his touch had already found. But when he had laid his hand right there—the result had been a shock of feeling he could neither understand nor explain.

Warily now, Jony surveyed the figure for every small detail. The other hand lay on the breast, palm inward. The calm, still face in his mind confused with Rutee's, was posed that the eyes might look ever down the river of stone which had led him here. As if they sought someone who had not yet come.

There was certainly nothing alive about the thing. Jony went so far now as to gingerly touch the upheld hand with the very tip of his staff. Nothing happened. He must have been dreaming in some manner. But he decided he had no desire to try the experiment again.

Instead he made as wide a detour as the doorway

would allow around the woman, heading on into whatever might lie behind her in this largest stone heap of all.

At first he went very slowly, for the dim light inside seemed almost nonexistent to his unadjusted eyes. Then he began to see that he was edging into a very wide space down which ran rows of tall, round stones set up to resemble the trunks of forest trees. The upper parts of these vanished somewhere in the high dusk over his head.

Jony shivered. This place brought back old memories of fear. By its size it seemed to have been fashioned for Big Ones, not for creatures of his own height. Yet the stone woman, tall as she was, had looked like Rutee, and had not had the horrifying alienness of his old enemy. It was that thought, as well as his ever ready curiosity, which encouraged him on.

Just as the river of stone had led directly to this heap, so did the lines of pillars produce a guide. Now he could see, too, that there was more light ahead. Jony quickened pace, his bare feet shuffling through a soft carpet of dust as he went.

Here, far above, there was another kind of hole, much larger, giving onto the sky. Directly under that another series of ledges supported a single wide block of stone which was not gray-white as all the rest. Instead, it was made up of many colors laid upon a dark, almost black, background.

Jony, studying it as he drew closer, could not make out any pattern, any more than one could see a pattern to the fur coloring of the People. Yet, these vivid colors (not in the least faded as those on the woman) must have some meaning. They were small dots of brilliance, some widely scattered, others loosely clustered here and there. Many shone as if the sunlight were truly caught within them, although no beam reached through that hole so far above.

Such were pictured on all four sides of the stone, Jony saw, as he moved around it. Yet never once was the positioning, the number of dots, or their seemingly random settings repeated. He could not see the top of the stone as the ledges raised that well above his eye level. Was it the same on top? And what was its meaning?

Jony was at last emboldened to climb. The last ledge, on which the stone rested, was wide enough that there was good room to circle about the block without touching. Jony was wary of any close contact since his queer experience with the stone woman. But he was well able to see that there were no patterns of brilliant dots here. There was—

He jerked back, astonished, nearly losing his footing and tumbling back down the ledges. Had he seen, very dimly—a face?

If he had, it must be that of another stone person, he reassured himself. And what harm could such do him unless he touched it? Resolutely he thrust aside uneasiness, to again approach the stone.

Dust lay thick upon the surface; a dust which had not obscured the dotted sides. Jony swept it off with his staff as best he could. The wood slid over so smoothly there could not be a figure there.

He neared the block within hand's distance, to look again. There it was! But *inside* the stone, in some queer, unnatural way. As if the whole block were hollow as a dead tree trunk, and with a top as clear as stream water, so that one could look down into what lay within.

Greatly daring, Jony reached out his fingers, gave a swift tap to that covering, jerked away. He had had no strange reaction this time, but that touch had assured him that there *was* a solid, if transparent, covering.

His wariness so eased, he pressed close enough to view what did lie within. There was a figure in the interior of the stone right enough. Jony leaned as closely above the lid as he dared to study it. The body was wrapped—except for the hands and face—around and around with strips of material which gave off a very faint luminescence, a little as did the eyes of the People in the dark.

Save this was not one of the People. The hands were much like his own in shape, though larger, as the whole figure was larger. They rested on the body at breast height, the fingers loosely locked over a staff which was not unlike the one in his own hand, except that it did not possess a crook at one end. And it was a dull red in color. Jony could not make out the features of the sleeper (if sleeper this was), for there was a mask of the same red covering the face smoothly, bearing no hint of eyes, nose, or mouth.

Was this a dead man—left so by his people? Jony glanced around him at the great dusty hall. If so, the stranger must have lain here for a long, long time. The People walled their dead in caves, leaving with them food for the Night Journey and a stout staff made new just for their going. Rutee had been left so.

Jony did not know what waited beyond death. Rutee had always said to die would be like waking in another place, a better place. There one would meet with those one loved. Even as she had died, she called out once:

"Bron!" And her voice had been one of welcome.

He did not know if the People believed the same, but they were careful in their burials. Thus he thought they, too, might judge death a gateway to another place and time. Someone had taken great care to put this stranger in this place. He should not be disturbed.

Jony descended to the floor of the great space. How long had he slept here, that masked man (or perhaps it was even a masked woman, he could not be sure)? Standing there, watching those points of light on the stone, Jony shrank a little. It suddenly seemed to him than many long, long seasons were crowding in upon him all at once, that he could not breathe because they hung about so thick.

He gave a gasp, ran for the door, skimming past the woman of stone without giving her another look. It was better outside. But that feeling of being entrapped in time was still with him. Now he wanted out of this place entirely, back to the open world of the People.

Down the river of stone he pounded as if pursued

by one of the Big Ones in person. His side ached as he reached the open, away from all those dead heaps of piled up stone; he skidded off the river, to the familiar, welcoming ground.

He did not halt in his flight until he reached the top of the ridge from which he had first viewed the stone place. Then, gasping, he did turn to look over his shoulder. The time was close to sundown. Shadows had crept out, as if during the light hours they had hiding places within the piles of stone. Jony shivered. He was not sure what had happened to him, only back there a burden had rested and had almost fastened on him. Perhaps Trush had been entirely right: the river, the heaps—they were to be avoided.

Still, as his breathing slowed and he made his way back to the campsite, Jony kept seeing somehow the red-masked sleeper caught in the stone. Curiosity still nagged him. Who *was* that one? Why did he lie there? As if waiting . . .

Waiting for what?

Jony shook his head vigorously, as if he would shake those disturbing thoughts well out of his mind. He saw ahead a vine heavy with pale green fruit, prepared to jerk it down to hand level with the crook of his staff. At least he would not return empty-handed. He decided not to let anyone know his adventure of the afternoon.

Whether he would ever return to the stone place, he did not know. Perhaps it was enough that he had seen it this one time. Better that way—or was it? But at least he had no intention of making this journey again soon.

He was just reaching for the vine when his extra sense broke through his preoccupation with what he had seen that afternoon. Something was the matter—he was needed urgently!

Jony began to run at the best pace the rough ground allowed, all his speculations and discoveries lost in the rising knowledge that trouble lay somewhere ahead, and that it very definitely involved him. An attack by a smaa on the campsite? He thought of the worst danger he knew. But those enemies were seldom found in this part of the country. There was the possibility, in its way even worse, that the Big Ones' space ships had returned!

Old fears closed in about him. Neither he nor Rutee had ever known what had led to the swift departure of the alien ship after their own escape. It could be that the ship had returned to hunt them down. And no weapon which the People had could successfully stand between them and swift capture if the Big Ones willed it. He had heard too many times over Rutee's description of how the aliens had so easily taken the colony which had been her home.

Jony had not yet reached the camp when Trush materialized in that odd way the People could from their shape-hiding coloring of the vegetation. The clansman had his staff, only half prepared for real action, in his paw-hand. His other hand signed a message Jony was not expecting.

"Little—light fur—gone!"

Geogee, Maba, or both! Jony had been too ready to

believe Yaa could control them. He held up two fingers to signify both twins. To that Trush assented with a quick dip of his muzzle in the affirmative gesture of the People.

Jony, breathing hard, plowed to a stop opposite Trush. The first thought which had flashed into his mind was that in some manner the children must have sneaked away to follow him, perhaps become lost in the territory around the ridges. While the People had excellent night sight, his own was far inferior.

"Which way?" he asked in sign language.

With the end of his unfinished staff Trush pointed over Jony's own shoulder, toward the ridge from which the boy had just come. So the twins *had* followed him! But had they gone all the way—into the place of piled stones? Jony thought of the many hiding sites there and also of what else might lurk in the darkness which was fast falling. Remembering Trush's attitude toward the river of stone, Jony feared that the People would be reluctant, might even completely refuse, to help him search there if he must.

Trush, shouldering his staff, moved ahead, his eyes bent down as if he could read plainly some track. Jony, well realizing how inferior his own ability to trail was when compared to that of his companion, fell in behind. He longed to know how long the twins had been gone, but the People never measured time.

Behind Trush's more massive person Jony once more ascended the ridge. When he gained the crest Trush was standing very still indeed.

"Where . . . ?" Jony signed.

That round head turned a little, and the large eyes regarded him unblinkingly. Jony, not for the first time, wished desperately that he could read the mind behind those eyes, know just a little of the other's thoughts. But all he could sense was a strong disturbance, as if Trush were being forced to face some danger much against his will, struggling to find a way out of such an entrapment.

Very slowly the clansman raised his staff, though he half-averted his face as it pointed with its tip straight at the distant stone piles. Trush did not even make a hand gesture to underline his answer.

Jony drew a deep breath. In the fading light the stone piles had an odd repellent look which he had not seen earlier as the sun had brightened them. As if, with the coming of dark, an old evil awoke. Jony closed his mind resolutely against such fancies, centered his questing thoughts rather on what lay at the end of the stone river.

Yes! He touched one mind—that was Geogee somewhere ahead. Jony leaned upon his staff. If only he had not promised Rutee, sworn to her never to mind compel either of the twins, he could bring them out! A little alarmed now, Jony quested farther—where was Maba? Her pattern of thought was usually as clear to him as her face was in his sight, but now he could not locate it at all!

Fear came fully alive. Only unconsciousness could prevent mind-touch. Was Maba hurt—or perhaps even dead?

Jony found himself frantically descending before he realized he had even moved. He did not expect Trush to follow. If the twins were in the stone piles he, himself, must find them and bring them back to safety.

His feet thuded dully on the river of stone, and he carried his staff before him at the ready. Though this afternoon curiosity had drawn him to this place, now he was angry and ashamed. The twins must have seen him go, followed in their usual reckless, unthinking fashion. Who could guess what they might meet within those dens now so shadow filled? His own experience with the stone woman—he had no explanation for that. And there could be other traps, or dangers, which were totally foreign to everything they knew.

Jony's rush took him past the first of the dens, those which were smaller. He made himself slow down. This was a time to use questing thought, not to rush blindly about accomplishing nothing in the dusk.

At once he was able to pick up Geogee again. With that touch came fear, naked and sharp—Geogee was afraid. If he, Jony, could not compel, surely he could call the other; use mind-linkage as a guide through this place of unknown dangers.

"Geogee!" He built in his mind as strong a picture of the boy as he could hold. "Geogee, where are you?"

Fear built a barrier. Geogee was so torn by terror he was not thinking in any clear pattern Jony could pick up and analyze. Communication came as distorted jolts like blows, aimed out wildly in every direction.

Jony could not maintain rational contact, but he

could use that center of disturbance itself as a guide. This Jony probed grimly, held to what he could discover. The way took him, not back to the vast pile where the stone woman and the sleeper in the rock waited, but down one of the smaller side streams of stone which was much narrower. Here the piles on either side appeared to lean out above him, as if at any moment they might free themselves into individual blocks and crash down to blot him out.

Jony had to conquer his own growing uneasiness in order to hold to that center of mental disturbance which marked Geogee. He drew closer with every stride, at least he was sure of that much. Then—his head turned, as if jerked, to the right. In there!

As all the other holes, the one beside him had no barrier, nor did any stone figure stand there in welcome or dismissal. Within it was quite dark. For the first time Jony raised his voice:

"Geogee!"

The boy's name echoed hollowly, until Jony was almost sorry he had called. However, in answer, something scuttled from an inner section of the pile, threw itself frantically at Jony, head burrowing against him, thin arms in an imprisoning grip about his middle.

Geogee was shaking so much that his sudden onslaught nearly upset Jony in return. Though the older boy still held tightly to his staff, he dropped his other arm about Geogee's shoulders, holding him in a tight answering grasp. When that shivering seemed to lessen a little, Jony spoke again:

"Geogee," he repeated the name quietly and firmly, hoping to break through that terror which manifestly filled the other, get from him a necessary answer. "Geogee, where is Maba?"

Geogee gave a little cry. Nor would he even look up at Jony. Rather he rubbed his face more strongly against Jony's breast.

Jony held onto his calm as best he could. He must break through, learn what had happened so he could find the girl.

"Where . . . is . . . Maba?" He spoke very slowly and evenly, spacing his words with all the impact he could summon.

Geogee gave a kind of wail, but he did answer.

"The wall took her. It swallowed her up!"

WHATEVER HAD HAPPENED, JONY REALIZED, GEOGEE believed what he had just said was true. But—a wall which swallowed?

Jony himself gulped down his fear as best he could. He wanted nothing so much as to run with Geogee, get free of this place which, taking on the evil memories of the cages in the dusk, was far more alarming than any trap. Only—there was Maba. He could not leave her here. Instead he must get Geogee quieted enough to make better sense.

He caught the braid of the boy's hair in a firm hand, exerting enough pull on it to bring Geogee away from him so he could view the twin's convulsed face in what small light was here. Rutee had made him promise—never use the control.

But Rutee could not have foreseen this situation. Jony must free Geogee from the clutch of his wild terror long enough to discover what had happened. Or else . . . or else Maba might be lost.

Conquering, at least for this moment, his own uneasiness, Jony gazed steadily into the boy's eyes. They were fixed, staring, as if Geogee still watched something so utterly horrifying that he was caught within that moment of horror as a prisoner. Jony used his mind-touch, soothing, trying to break through the fear barrier.

The younger blinked; his mouth twitched. Jony concentrated. He was here—Geogee was not alone—they must find Maba! As he had earlier spoken emphatically, he now fed those thoughts.

Geogee's frantic grip on him was relaxing. Jony knew he was getting through. His own impatience warred with the necessary overlay of calm. While they wasted time here—what could be happening to Maba? He firmly shoved aside such thoughts; at present his task was to learn all Geogee knew.

After a time that seemed to stretch endlessly, Jony made a question of her name: "Maba—?"

Geogee loosed his hold, stood away. His face was now calm. Jony remembered the mind-controlled from the cage days, hated what he saw. But otherwise—he did not really have Geogee under full control, he had only managed to reach beyond the boy's fear as he had had to do.

"Back there," Geogee gestured to a darker portion of the den and another opening. "We were back there . . ."

Jony wet dry lips with the tip of his tongue. To go into that darkness . . . But it had to be done. He scooped up his staff. At least he could probe shadows with that, not walk straight into disaster unprepared. His sense told him there was no enemy, no living enemy that he could recognize within these stone heaps. Yet from the heaps themselves came a strange awareness, which to him was a warning such as he had never known before.

"Back here." Geogee was already pattering away into the dark. Jony quickly followed.

They went through two of the open spaces which had wall holes giving a small amount of light. Then Geogee halted in the third, facing what gave every appearance of a completely solid erection of stones. Yet the younger boy advanced toward this as if he saw an opening invisible to Jony.

"Maba—" Geogee reached out his hand. "She put her hand right there." With that he forced his palm flat on the stone.

There was a dull grating sound. Under Geogee's push not only the block he touched, but those above and below moved. The boy, offbalanced, stumbled forward through the black hole now open. Jony aimed his staff. The stones were swinging back again to seal Geogee in, but they were stopped by the stout length between.

Jony heard Geogee cry out. Then he levered frantically with his shaft. The stones opened again more fully, but he could see their strength had nearly bitten through the wood.

There was no help for it, he must follow into whatever secret the wall concealed.

He groped through, heard the stones crunch shut behind him. Panic filled him. This was a cage, worse than those of the Big Ones; it was dark and the wall was solid. And . . . He took a single step away from the edge of this new cage. His foot did not meet a surface; there was nothing there!

With a cry Jony fell into that nothingness.

His fall was not far. Only after he landed heavily, he was on a slope down which he continued to slide, though he struck out with his staff trying to find some hold, some way of staying that slip ever downward. So intent was he on such struggles, that it was a moment or two before he realized that he was not moving over a rough stone surface which would have stripped his skin by the friction. Rather under him was soft stuff which gave at the pressure of his exploring fingers and then rose again. It was as if this strange way of traveling had been devised with maximum safeguards against injury.

Down and down, Jony had no way of judging how far this slippery passage reached.

"Geogee!" he shouted, waited for some answer.

Finally that came—thin, faint, and Jony believed far away, a mere thread of sound reaching him. He sent a mind probe instantly.

Geogee was again in a state of fear and confusion, but he was alive, unharmed. If there ever was an end to this worm hole, Jony would catch up with Geogee, and, doubtless, with Maba.

The purpose of such a passage—Jony did not even try to guess at that. Was it a trap set long ago to catch any invading the stone heaps? Did each stone heap have one? If so, what bitter enemies had the people here faced?

The dark was no longer absolute. Ahead, Jony saw a grayish gleam of light. And that cheered him. To be out of suffocating darkness was enough to raise his spirits.

Also, he was not sliding so fast now. The angle of the way under his body was less acute. The light increased, coming from a round opening ahead. Jony began to hope that he had reached the end of this nightmare passage.

He could see better, use the staff as a brake, so that he did not fall through that hole, but crouched at its mouth, to look out warily.

"Jony!" Geogee, his dirty hands smearing at his cheeks where there were the marks of tears, hunkered on the floor of a vast place filled with the gray light. There was no opening to the outer world. In fact, Jony was sure that they were far beneath the ground in some cave. He could not see nor understand where the light came from. But he accepted thankfully that it was there.

Before him was a very short drop to the floor. Jony jumped, then thought-quested. Something . . . He swung away from Geogee, facing out into the wide open of that space. Maba—that way!

He stooped over Geogee, drew him up onto his feet. "Come!" He must find Maba and then a way out. To climb up the passage he had just descended might be impossible. Jony shrugged away such speculation. Let him find Maba, perhaps then further exploration would show them an escape.

"Jony, I want out of here!" There was a shrill note in Geogee's voice.

Jony could have applied the calming influence again, but his concentration was needed to guide him to Maba.

"We'll get out," he gave assurance which might be a lie, but which must serve him at present as a tool. "But first we find Maba."

"Where is she?" Geogee demanded, his head turning from one side to the other as if he sought her within eyesight.

"This way." At least Jony was confident of that much. He kept hold of Geogee's shoulder, urging the boy on. At least Geogee seemed willing enough to go.

As they struck out straight across the center of the open space Jony noticed the open space itself was much larger than he had first guessed, stretching farther and farther ahead. He caught sight of other holes in the walls, similar to the one through which they had come. It would seem that this was some central meeting place for many such.

There was an utter silence here, a deadness which did not exist in the shadowed heaps above where small life had made hiding places and dens of their own. Jony shook his head impatiently. He had the odd sensation that the deadness also blanketed thought, that it was becoming harder and harder to retain his guiding tie with Maba. How far had she gone? He was startled when Geogee suddenly shouted: "Maba!"

The name echoed, re-echoed, so that it seemed many

Geogees cried that aloud. The boy whimpered and crowded closer to Jony.

"Please," he said, "I don't like this place, Jony. And Maba—where is she?"

Jony was wondering if the girl was on the move, straying farther and farther ahead of them all the time. He knew she was there, but when would they catch up?

The hole openings along the walls were no longer to be seen, while the open space through which they trotted was narrowing. Now they moved between two walls without any breaks in them at all. At the same time the gray light grew stronger, changing hue. It was then Jony saw the barrier ahead.

This was not like the walls on either side, but gleamed a little, while in it was a crack placed vertically. An opening they could force? He hoped so. Maba?—his mind-call went out. To his relief he knew that at last she was close, perhaps only behind that barrier.

When he reached the surface Jony could see that the crack indeed marked an opening. But there was no manner of pulling it open. When he pushed, it closed only more firmly. Again he tried his staff, working the now splintering tip into that crack, exerting all the leverage he could.

Slowly, reluctantly, the crack widened; the door was opening. Jony's hands were slippery with sweat as he worked. Then Geogee joined him, adding a small measure of strength to the effort. Inch by inch they won until they had opened a space wide enough for both to slip through.

Jony stopped short. The contrast between what faced him now and the stark corridor which had led them here was so great it took a moment for his eyes to adjust. Here was color in plenty, so much that it battered against one, dazzling and deluding the sight. Ribbons of brightness were along the walls, and, between the same type of stone tree trunks that Jony had seen in the largest pile, were stacked tightly, from the floor under them to the surface high overhead, blocks of color, no two alike. Some of those blocks were transparent, like the one which held the sleeper, so that he saw many objects piled inside them.

The glitter and brilliance of this place bothered Jony. There was no sign of Maba, yet she was here; his sense told him that. Lost perhaps among the ranges of blocks.

"Maba!" He raised his voice in the loudest shout he could summon.

"Jony . . . ?" Her answer was low-voiced, drawing him to the left, along that painted wall. Now that he could focus on one single part of this cluttered place he could see that those colors made up pictures. Not too far ahead Maba sat, her feet straight out before her, her dirty, dusty face turned up, staring intently at what was just before her.

"Maba!" Geogee broke from Jony's side, ran toward his twin. "What—"

She raised her hand to point, never looking in her brother's direction at all, her voice eager and alive.

"Geogee—Jony—look! People—like us . . . see!"

The paintings on the wall had a strange look about

them. They did not exist on a flat surface, but somehow stood out and away from that, with the semblance of figures only partly caught in the stone, a portion of their forms protruding beyond.

The section Maba had chosen to study showed a number of females who were doing things with their hands which Jony could not understand. Before them were a number of boxes of different sizes and shapes, on which were dots in various colors. The women appeared to rest their hands upon some of these dots. Piled about them at foot level were a number of things, among which all he could recognize with any certainty was a roll of woven substance, very much finer than their own kilts or the knottings of the People. Some objects reminded him unpleasantly of articles which had been in use in the labs of the Big Ones, save that these were of a brighter color and a shape more pleasing to the eye.

He glanced at the next picture. Here were males, and they each had in hand one of those red rods such as he had seen in the hands of the sleeper. One man pointed his rod, and a beam of light was pictured as springing from its tip to strike a rough, unshaped rock. A little farther on was a rock which was its twin, but that had one side smoothed and squared. Jony guessed that those in the picture used their light beams to cut stone, even as the People used sharp stones to hack some length of wood to proper measure.

That such could possibly be done he knew from his memories of the ship's lab. But that was a power of the

Big Ones, and therefore evil. Jony frowned at the picture. The men in it looked not unlike those of the mind-controlled the Big Ones caged.

"Look!" Maba picked up something which had lain on the floor beside her, flaunted it at Jony. "See what I found!"

The substance fell in graceful folds between her hands, and he realized that it was cloth—not coarse and heavy as their own clumsily woven kilts, but smooth, soft, beautiful. The color was a clear green, like the leaves of some plants, and, over that, waved a pattern of clusters of small flowers. Jony's hand went to his head. The sprig he had broken off earlier that day had not survived. He had wanted for a moment to compare that with the pictured ones on the cloth, for by his memory they appeared very similar.

"I shall wear this—so—like that one . . ." Maba stood up. She let fall her kilt, struggled to drape the length of green about her in imitation of the covering on the painted woman she had pointed to. Deep in Jony his extra sense stirred in warning. He did not want to see Maba strutting back and forth before that picture, the cloth clutched about her thin brown body. This was—wrong!

"No!" Jony moved on that instinct, snatching at the material before Maba could hold it more tightly. Becoming aware of what he was doing, she cried out, clinging to it stubbornly. There was a ripping sound. The cloth tore so that the larger part was in Jony's hands; she only held the end.

The stuff was so soft, seeming to cling to his skin. He wadded it together in a fierce gesture, threw it from him.

Maba stared incredulously at the ragged scrap she held. Then she let that fall, to rush at Jony with her hands balled into fists, pummeling him with all her strength.

"You—you spoiled it!" she gasped. "You tore it!"

Jony dropped the staff he had caught up again, took her by the shoulders, held her away, kicking and flailing her fists. The girl screamed in sheer anger, and he shook her sharply until she stopped and began to cry.

But she smeared away her tears, as if angry that she shed them, and continued to glare at Jony.

"You spoiled it!" she repeated, her eyes hot with anger.

"Listen!" Jony shook her again. "Now, you listen to me, Maba. Do you remember what happened to Luho? Do you?"

Her eyes were held by his level stare. "She—she ate the yellow thing that smelled good . . ."

"And after that?"

"She—she hurt bad, real bad. And—and—she died . . ." Maba's voice trailed away. Then some of the fierceness came back into her face. "But I didn't eat any yellow thing, Jony. I had—had something nice."

"Did Luho think she had something nice?" he continued, hoping to drive home his meaning by reason alone.

"Yes. But that was growing, Jony. It was a live thing.

Mine wasn't a live thing. They made it, I think—" she gestured toward the women on the wall. "It wouldn't hurt me."

"You don't know, Maba. Luho didn't listen when she was told strange things must be handled carefully. This place, it does not belong to the People, nor does it belong to those who are like us either—"

"But they are, Jony! Look at them; you can see! Maybe Rutee was wrong, maybe the sky ship brought her back to this, her own world." Maba spoke faster and faster.

Jony shook his head. "No, Rutee would have known. The People never lived on her world. Think about the hoppers, Maba. Remember how they catch the pincher ones?"

"They—they can make themselves small and they hide a part of their bodies—so they look like a pincher—" she replied. "You mean," her head turned away from him now so she could gaze searchingly once more at the wall, "You mean—these people could be like hoppers—make themselves look like us . . . ? But, Jony, how could they know about *us?* This place is old. It must have been here before Rutee and you came out of that ship, before we were born."

"Not to catch us. But I mean that, though they look more like us than the Big Ones, they could be as different really as the hoppers are from the clawed ones. Do you understand?"

She looked back at him and then once again at the pictured wall.

"Yes. Only what if you're wrong, Jony? What if they

are really our kind? Jony"—she pulled away from his loosened hold—"those things over there." She pointed eagerly now to the ranks of colored squares and ob-longs. "Those can be opened up and they're full of things. Things like what you tore up. And others—just come and see, Jony!" She caught his hand and pulled him toward the nearest of the squares. Before they reached that, Geogee came running.

"Look what I found!" he shouted. He waved over his head a red rod, swinging it around so that light flashed from its surface.

Jony, again with only instinct to guide him, made a grab. Their hands met on the surface of the rod. From its tip shot a beam so brilliant that Jony was temporar-ily blinded. He heard screams from the twins, the clatter of something metallic falling, as he reeled back against the wall, his hands pressed protectingly over his eyes.

"Geogee—" somehow he managed to get out, "leave that thing—leave it alone!"

"I—I can't see, Jony . . ." Geogee's voice approached a scream. "Jony—Maba—"

"It's all right." Maba answered him. "This is me, Geogee. Take my hand. That—that thing. It . . . Jony," her voice trembled. "Where the light went . . . there just isn't anything! Jony, what happened?"

He blinked, his eyes were tearing, but he could see, as if through a watery haze. His first horrible fear was dulled. The red rod lay on the floor. He made a careful detour around it to reach the children. Maba had her arms about her twin, was hugging him close, but she was looking beyond him and Jony followed her line of sight.

Where the top row of squares had been piled upon a firm base of their fellows there was—as Maba had reported—nothing. The power of that lancing light certainly was a threat which seemed now to him worse than the devices the Big Ones had used.

Had the twins learned their lesson? Nothing here must be touched again. They had no idea what a careless mistake might loose. What if Maba had been in the line of that beam? Jony shuddered, feeling more than a little sick at the answer his imagination offered. He picked up his staff. Now he moved in on the twins.

"We must get out of here," he said tersely.

As he did not see any way of going back up that sliding hole, they would have to explore this storage place further. But there would be no more opening of boxes, no more touching anything which belonged to the people of the stone heaps. No wonder Trush had shown such a marked dislike for the traces these people had left behind!

The twins, now very subdued, joined him readily. They walked together down between those rows of containers, past the clear-sided ones in which strange objects tried to ensnare their curiosity.

The pictures on the wall beside them changed continually. While the first had shown the people of this place in semi-incomprehensible action, these were scenes from outside the city showing reaches of land such as the three knew from their own wandering across it. Then Jony was halted by a vivid scene.

A sky ship! The Big Ones *had* been here before! Yet, as he peered more closely, he was not quite sure . . . This ship seemed different in outline, though he would not swear to that. His own glimpse of the outside of the alien ship had been limited. It was enough that these people used sky ships. In his mind that linked them with the Big Ones, and he no longer wondered at the strange weapon or tool Geogee had found.

"Jony!" Maba had not done more than glance at the picture which had so excited him. She was ahead again, pointing at another. "Look—there are the People!"

There they were indeed, seeming alive, ready to walk away from the wall and join them, Trush, or Voak, or Yaa. But they . . . Jony's lips thinned and his hand tightened on his staff— These People went on fours, which the People did not, unless the footing was very bad and they had need for extra bursts of speed. And around their bodies were straps from which hung cords. The People here were prisoners; some—some were pictured in cages!

Jony snarled. Just as he thought, those who had lived here had the same evil nature as the Big Ones even though they looked like himself! The People in their time had escaped, just as Rutee and he had gained freedom. Evil—he felt now he could sniff the evil in this as if as rank and air-filling as the stench of the Red Heads!

"What were they doing?" Maba asked still intent on

the picture. "Why do the People have those things on them?"

"Because," Jony said between his teeth, "they were prisoners—prisoners of evil ones. As we were once. Oh, let us get out of here!"

He pulled her on. There must be some way out; he had to find it!

THEY FINALLY REACHED THE END OF THAT HUGE space. Jony was unable to judge just how large it was because of all that was crowded into it. Here stood another gleaming door, twin to the one he had forced open at the other end. To his surprise, just as he was wondering how effective his mistreated staff might prove for another such assault. Maba moved confidently forward. Standing on tiptoe, she put her two hands as far up as she could reach so that they met in a slight depression.

"Maba!" Jony was reaching to snatch her back when he saw that the door line was enlarging, reluctantly. They could catch a faint grating sound from within the wall, the first sound save those they themselves had made to be heard here at all.

The crack was wide enough open now for Maba and Geogee. But Jony did not trust it in the least. He turned about, grabbed at the stacked colored boxes, catching one which yielded to his tugging. With this he wedged the door panel, holding it open.

They passed into another gray-lit, plain-walled passage. However, this slanted upward, and Jony hoped that that meant they would eventually reach the surface and freedom. He had no idea of what this place was, save that the ones who had built the walls with their rods had apparently gathered therein things which they had made and perhaps treasured.

There was a crackling from behind; Jony whirled, shaft ready. All he saw was that the brace he had put in the doorway was being crushed by the weight of the closing panel, though the debris kept it from closing completely.

Maba—how had Maba learned the secret of the doors? He was more than a little puzzled by that. Now he asked her directly.

"I could see there was a line," she answered promptly. "And I kept feeling along up and down. 'Cause that's the way the wall opened before—when I put my hands on it." She smiled with that particular smile she used at times when she believed that she had been clever. Maba was only too ready to believe in her own powers, and lacked the wariness which Jony had learned in the cages when he was far younger than she was.

"Jony," Geogee had been scuffling along, frowning a little, as if some thought was troubling. "Those People on the wall—you said they were prisoners—like you and Rutee. But the others, the new ones, they looked like us, not as you said the Big Ones do. If they were like us—why would they shut up the People, make them wear those straps around their necks, stay in cages?"

"You heard what I said to Maba," Jony gave the best answer he could summom. "Just because those in the pictures look like us, that doesn't mean they were like us *inside*. We know the Big Ones are bad, and they look different, so we learned from the beginning to be afraid of them. But the mind-controlled—they were like us. Yet they did just what the Big Ones told them. So unless we were sure, we could not trust them, ever."

"Then those in the pictures were mind-controlled?" Geogee demanded.

"I don't know." Jony could not somehow believe that the very alien Big Ones were responsible for the building of this place. The sky ship picture had alarmed him at first glance. But then, Rutee had told him his own people had such ships. That was how she and Bron had come to the world where the Big Ones had caught them. There might be different kinds of sky ships. In the wall pictures there was no hint of Big Ones.

All he was certain of at that moment was that this was a place which threatened them. The sooner they were out of it and back in the open country they knew, the better.

"I'm tired," Maba said suddenly. "And I can't go fast any more, Jony. I'm hungry—"

"I'm hungry, too!" Geogee reinforced that promptly. "I want to get out of here, Jony. We keep going up and up but we don't see outside."

He was right. The slope they followed kept them going up and up, but Jony had no way of measuring how far down the tube descent had taken them in the first place.

"We'll get out—soon—" he tried to make his assurance sound convincing. The trouble was he had no idea whether he spoke the truth or not. And he was hungry and thirsty too. He wanted to run, but both children were lagging, and he knew that he could do no more than keep them encouraged and moving forward, even though their pace slowed.

"I'm tired," Maba repeated again with more emphasis. "I don't think I can keep on walking up and up, Jony."

"Sure you can," he rallied her. "You're so clever about doors, Maba. We'll need your help if we find another one up ahead."

She continued to look doubtful, and she was climbing very slowly indeed. Geogee bettered her, was farther ahead, so that Jony had to call him back. What worried the older boy was that the strange light filling these under-surface passages was distinctly fading the farther they climbed. Jony had no wish to lose contact with either child in that complete dark which he had met before.

"Listen," Jony spoke sharply. "You, Maba, take hold of this!"

He held out the half-splintered shaft, thinking when they at last got out of here he would need to make another. As the girl closed her hands on the butt end, Jony called ahead:

"Geogee, wait right where you are." When they caught up to the impatient boy, Jony pulled him into line with his twin. "Take hold—right here, and don't either of you let go. I want to know where you are in the dark."

He held the crook part in his own hands as he

walked in the lead. This last part of the climb was at an even greater angle, and Jony made it slowly, fearing that either twin might lose its link. At last before him was an opening (without any of those sliding panels, Jony was thankful to see), and they came out onto a level space. Here was a freshness of air, yet walls arose about them. It was dark enough so that Jony moved very slowly.

Finally he caught sight of small, sharp sparks of light ahead. Whether those meant more danger or not he could not tell. But he had to have some guide to center on, and those were the only such he could find. Linked by their hold on Jony's staff, the three came at last to a place the older had been before, in that great heap which was the heart of the forbidden place. There on its dais, glittering with living fire, was the block of stone which held the sleeper.

Those dots of color had been bright in the daylight, but in the dark they were even *more* alive, some sparkling, some burning with a steady glow. Jony wanted no part of this place, but at least he now knew where they were.

"What's that?" Geogee asked.

"I don't know," Jony answered shortly. "But I do know where we are *now*. And we can get out of here easily— Come on!"

They skirted the stepped blocks which supported the container of the sleeper, and continued on down the dark way, moving around the stone woman. In this manner they found again the river of stone which would lead them out of this danger zone.

Danger zone it was. Jony's skin prickled with more than just the chill of the night air. He felt as if an emanation rayed out from all these piled blocks, alerting his warning sense, although he received nothing specific, just a general feeling of uneasiness and the need to get as far away as possible.

Maba stumbled and fell. She sat on the ground. "I— I can't get up, Jony. My feet hurt. I'm so tired."

There was only one thing to be done. Jony thrust his staff at Geogee. "Carry that and stay close," he ordered. He stooped and picked up the girl.

Though she looked so small and thin, Maba was a heavy enough burden, and Jony was tired also. But he knew that he could not manage to keep her going on her own now.

They stayed strictly in the middle of the stone path on their way between the piles of stone. Though the night was dark, it was a straight enough guide to get them out and away. Geogee trailed the shaft, the butt bumping against the pavement. However, he did remain close to Jony. Perhaps he, too, felt that undefinable menace which Jony was sure was a part of this place.

They wavered on, passing one side way after another. Twice Jony had to put Maba down and rest a few moments before gathering her up again. She lay a limp weight in his hold and never spoke. She might have been asleep, but, if so, this was no natural rest. Jony's uneasiness grew.

Maba had handled the cloth, wrapped the length around her. She had been longer than he or Geogee in that storehouse of the alien things. Could it be that because of her curious prying, she now lay under some influence from that place resulting in a weakening of her body? Jony wanted to get out—and yet their way seemed longer and longer.

He was breathing in gasps as they passed between the last of the heaps to reach the outer world. There was no moon tonight, and Jony's night sight was not good enough to do more than show the ridge up which he must go to find the clan camp. He was well aware that he could blunder about in the dark and be lost.

Putting Maba down on the ground, well away from the river of stone, he caught at his staff, drawing Geogee to him. The boy immediately crouched down beside his twin. Jony stood surveying the dark bulk of the ridge. Though he could not communicate by mind-call with the People, he knew that such an effort—if concentrated enough—did in some manner summon them. Just as his plea had brought Yaa when he had called for help for Rutee.

Now he put his full concentration into such a summons. The People did not travel much by night, though their sight was far better than his. But they had already been out seeking the twins and might still be somewhere about. Trush had known Jony had come in this direction in his own search.

Yes! Jony gave a great sigh of relief. Trush, or at least one of the People, was not too far away. He had touched that alien thought pattern which he could not read. Again he concentrated on trying to relay his need.

But, to his surprise and disappointment, as the time passed, no furred form shuffled down out of the brush to answer him. Was that because he and the twins had been in the place of stone? Did the People hold the site in such a degree of either fear or dislike they would now treat Jony and the twins with the same refusal to admit their existence as Trush had turned on the river of stone at their first sight of it?

Jony thought of that picture on the wall, the People in bondage and in cages. Somehow they had won their freedom from that state. However, Jony and the twins physically resembled their one-time captors, and the three had returned to the place of captivity. Could the People now believe that Jony and the twins were indeed to be identified with their ancient enemies?

The thought of that hurt as much as a sudden blow. Since the first moment when Yaa had come out of the storm to aid Rutee, Jony had accepted the People as wiser, stronger, and better than any other life-form he had known, save Rutee herself. They were not the empty shells of the mind-controlled. In fact, as far as Jony knew, they could *not* be mind-controlled. Neither did they hold him captive with the callous disregard of him as a thinking being the way the Big Ones had.

No, in their way the People were the whole world Jony knew and accepted as right and good. They were not the caged one he had seen, any more than he was of the same breed who had caged them.

"I am here," he thought with all the force he could summon now, "I am me, Jony, the one you have known . . . I am *ME!*"

He had never known how much of his thought-send the People could pick up, whether it was as difficult for them to "touch" him as it was for any message to be sent in the opposite direction. At the moment he could only continue to hope that he and the twins had not been disowned by the clan, that he could influence the watcher up there.

As the moments continued to pass that hope was blunted. The twins could not remain in the open in the night cold. Jony must find them some kind of shelter. Only *not* in the place they had just fled.

"Jony, I'm hungry," Geogee said plaintively. "And Maba—she's sleeping. But she's breathing funny, Jony. I want to go to Yaa. Please, Jony, let's go!"

Jony knelt to gather Maba once more in his arms. Her skin was chill against his, and her head rolled loosely against his shoulder. She was breathing in shallow gasps. Jony shivered. Like Rutee—the coughing sickness? But that illness struck in the cold time. He wanted Yaa as much as Geogee did, but dared he take the children up into the brush?

They simply could not stay in the open any longer. Somehow he got to his feet, Maba once more in his hold. Geogee had the staff.

"Up—there—" Jony got out these words.

Geogee did not move. "It's dark," he objected. "And it's a hard climb—"

"Get moving!" Jony made it an order. He could not carry Geogee also. He was not even sure he could top the ridge under the burden of the girl's dead weight.

That silent watcher from the People was still there, though. It could be that the clansman simply would not come this close to the river of stone.

Jony began the climb, Geogee scrambling a little ahead. Over this rough country the older boy had to exert his strength to the uttermost, testing each forward step before he set his full weight upon it.

He looked no higher than that which lay immediately before him, as much as he could see of that in this lack of light. The climb seemed to take a very long time, though he did not stop to rest, feeling that if he dared that he would not be able to get started again.

Thigh-high brush closed about him, and he had to push through it blindly, dodging the larger bushes as best he could. The watcher still waited. Up—one step —another. Somehow, Jony finished the climb, lurching up onto the crest of the ridge. Once there he stood, panting heavily. He raised his head, looked about him for the presence he knew was there.

Hard as the People were to distinguish in the daytime, that sighting was even more difficult at night. At last Jony caught those luminous circles of eyes. He did not try to advance. Any action now must be initiated by the other.

Geogee moved closer. "It's Voak!" he cried aloud.

Jony already had recognized the clansman leader moving farther into the open under the night sky. There Voak stood, staring at the three, making no gesture of aid or even of recognition.

Geogee halted. "Voak—?" he asked, a very uncertain note in his voice. Plainly the attitude of the other had first surprised, and now daunted him.

Voak was no longer alone. Jony sensed others moving up and in. The People gathered behind the clanleader, hard to see, except for their steady eyes. There was a reserve, a wariness about them which alarmed Jony. Since he could not reach them with mind-touch, he must wait now, let their future actions explain what had happened to cut him and the twins off from that warm feeling of the clan closeness. For cut off he was now certain they were.

Voak raised his staff to beckon. Jony stumbled forward obediently. One of the other People advanced to take Maba from him. He and Geogee followed on their own feet, though Jony did not miss the point that Voak himself had caught Jony's own staff, drawing it easily away from Geogee.

They staggered along, the People closing in about Jony and Geogee in a way which was not protective, but rather gave the feeling that they were now prisoners. So they traveled in silence back to the campsite near the stream.

Voak waved his staff in another gesture, sending them to their sleep nests. The one who had carried Maba gave her over to Yaa, who carried her back into the family place. Jony knew a little relief at that. He still trusted Yaa to give the girl care. He did not know what was wrong with Maba. The thought persisted that she might have contracted some illness connected with the place of stones, and he feared how dire that might be.

Geogee came and curled up beside him under their covering.

"Jony," his voice was the thinnest of whispers in the dark as Jony stretched his aching legs and tried to find comfort from the fact that at least they were back in the camp. "Jony, what is the matter? Why do the People hate us?"

Hate them? Jony was not sure that was the emotion which had built the wall so suddenly between them and the only friendly life they had known. Something vital, and perhaps terrible, had happened to their easy relationship with the People. However, he would have to wait for an explanation rather than guess.

"They may not hate us," he tried to find comfort for Geogee. "We could have broken one of their clan rules by going to that place. If that is so, there will be a judging."

Geogee shivered so that Jony could feel the shaking of his body.

"They will beat us with vines!" He was remembering last warm season when there had been a judging against Tigun after he had acted foolishly and been reckless about leading a smaa lizard across their trail, so that the lizard had come hunting them and Hrus had been badly bitten.

"If they do," Jony told him, "or if they try, then they shall beat me only. I was the one who went to the stone place; you only followed."

"No," Geogee sniffled. "We saw you come out. But we wanted to see inside. We knew it was wrong."

"If I had not done it first," Jony continued, "or gone

hunting for the stone river, you would not have followed. If Voak thinks we have done wrong, I shall let
him know that that is the truth. Now—try to sleep,
Geogee."

In spite of his own fatigue Jony did not sleep at once.
He had told Geogee the exact truth. The People were
reasonable and very just. They would understand that
if any punishment was to be meted out, it must be his
rather than the twins'. The children had only followed
because they had been curious concerning his actions.
His own curiosity was what he must answer for.

After a while he dreamed. Again he stood in that
place by the block whereon sparkled those dots of
colored fire, which could almost be the stars a-glitter
in the sky on a cloudless night. From the box slowly
arose the sleeper. He raised one hand to the red mask
to free his face, so that Jony could look directly on his
features.

Jony shrank from seeing; yet a will stronger than his
own held him there to watch. While—the face beneath
the mask—! It was the same as he had seen now and
then dimly reflected from a pool of water—Jony's own!
Then the other had reached forth with the rod and
tried to make Jony grasp it.

In his mind he knew that, if he did so, power would
fill him. He would be so great that his will would be all
that mattered. The People, even Maba and Geogee,
would be to him as the mind-controlled were to the
Big Ones.

One part of him wanted fiercely, so fiercely that it
was a pain through his body, to seize that rod. Within

his mind, very far away, as if long buried, arose a voice saying that such power was his by right, that he alone was fit to take and wield it. However, another part of him remembered the lab and Big Ones. Jony shook with the force of the battle within him—for he was like two who warred within one body. Now his hand stretched to take the rod, now he snatched it back!

"Jony! Jony!"

He roused dazedly to the sound of his name. There was the gray of early morning around him. But he was not in that place of stones. Over him was the good, familiar arch of tree branches. Then he saw Geogee. The boy's dirty face was a mask of fright.

"Jony!" He had his hands on Jony's shoulders, was shaking him.

"It's all right—" Jony's own mind was coming back, so slowly, from that struggle. His skin was rank with sweat in spite of the chill. He felt weak, as if he had just performed some task which had strained his body strength to the uttermost.

"You were saying, 'No—no'!" Geogee told him.

"It was a bad dream," Jony answered quickly. "Just a bad dream."

However, he could not dismiss memory so easily for himself. Something of that two-partedness remained in his mind. He had wanted the power of the rod; he had hated and feared it. Now, suddenly, he did want to view that sleeper again, to make sure that the mask still lay over the face, that it was not, as in his dream, he who slept.

The People, early as it was, were moving about the

camp. No one looked at Jony or Geogee, or made finger-talk. Laid out on the ground not too far away was a portion of nut cake. Jony gave Geogee a share and wolfed the rest, suddenly realizing how hungry he was.

He had just wiped the crumbs from his fingers when he looked up to see that the males of the clan were gathering in around him. Geogee moved back a little, apprehension plain to read on his face. Jony put his arm protectively about the younger boy's shoulders for a moment, gave him a reassuring squeeze. Then he used both his hands for finger-talk.

"Young ones not to blame. They followed me."

Impassively those ranged about him made no sign in return. Voak reached out and closed a hand-paw on Geogee's arm, drawing the boy away from Jony, pushing him outside their circle, giving him a shove in the direction of the females.

He signed an answer: "Young follow always. Best older do not give them bad trail."

Jony relaxed a little for Geogee's sake. Anything which happened now would rest on him alone. He hoped that Geogee had had enough of a scare so that this lesson would stick with him. Voak was right, he was the one to blame if some law of the clan had been broken.

"Truth spoken," he signed. Then he waited. What would come now—a judging with some punishment to follow?

"You—come—" Voak replied.

He turned purposefully and Jony fell in behind him. Nor were they two alone. Otik of the younger males and Kapoor of the older joined them. No one returned Jony's staff; he drew an ominous conclusion from that omission. Wherever they might be going it was not near the camp, for each of his companions was equipped with a net of journey food.

All the more apprehensive because he had no idea what was intended, Jony went, a well-guarded prisoner, into the beginning of the morning.

THEY HEADED TOWARD THE HIGHER RIDGES AGAIN—
not in the direction of the stone place, but more to the
northeast. Voak led purposefully, as if he knew
exactly where they were bound. The familiar sights of
the open country warred with the shadows in Jony's
mind. Now it was easy for him to accept that what had
frightened him *was* only a dream, born out of yesterday's strange adventure. Somehow he felt a relief from
oppression, even though he did not know what the
People planned for him.

He would *not* go back to the stone place, to face the
masked one and make a choice between the rod and
this freedom. Drawing a deep breath of pure relief, he
luxuriated in the feel of dew-wet leaves brushing
against his legs and the clean, clear air he drew into
his lungs.

Though the People's rather clumsy walk might seem
less effective than his own loose stride, Jony was forced
to quicken that to keep up with his guards. This pushing pace was quite unlike that generally kept when the
clan was on the move. For then they were apt to seek
edible roots, berries, scraper stones, over a wide area,
each some distance from another as they traveled.

The day was clear, with a bright, warm sun. In fact,

Jony was almost too warm as they emerged from under the trees to cross a stretch of open land where grass grew nearly waist high. Those creatures who lived in that miniature turf jungle fled from them, their flight marked only as a quick weaving. Here and there stood some tall spikes of stem, wreathed with blue flowers around which insects buzzed.

On the opposite side of that open land, brush began again. Jony had expected Voak to thrust his way in through it. Instead, the clan leader turned sharply left, following the base of the rise. Jony was thirsty, but he had no intention of allowing any discomfort to make him appeal to Voak now. His pride stiffened his resolve to ask nothing of his companions.

They had gone some little distance before Jony noted ends of stones protruding here and there from the soil of the ridge. These had been squared, though exposure to the weather had pitted their surfaces, rounded the edges. In spite of Trush's reaction to the stone path, the strangeness of the clan since Jony had confessed his visit to the place which had been made by the aliens of the pictures, Voak appeared to be heading on into a section where similar remains appeared.

Nor did the clansmen pause, when, before them arose series of those same ledges Jony had climbed to the place where the sleeper lay in his box. Earth masked these in part, and several small saplings were rooted along them. Yet it was very plain that once they had been used to ascend the slopes behind the first ridge.

Voak brought the butt of his staff down on each ledge with a thud as he mounted it, as if that gesture was some necessary announcement of their coming.

Kapoor and Otik echoed Voak's movements, their staffs rising and falling in company with his. The three also began to utter sounds, not unlike those they used when they were moon dancing, the notes rising and falling as they went. Jony sensed that both gestures and sounds were meant to protect against some menace which the clansmen thought lay ahead. Moreover, their present attitude was so unlike the sensible dispatch they used when actually attacked that his wonderment grew.

For any meeting with vor birds, or the smaa, there was no pounding of spear butts or calling of voices. The People fought in silence or uttered only a few hoarse grunts now and then. Jony used his own protective sense, sending it questing ahead. He felt naked without a staff in his own hand, and the attitude of his guards aroused his apprehension.

Still, he could pick up nothing. As the situation had been among the heaps of stone, so was it here. The life forces he touched were all that could be found anywhere else in the open. Then Jony tried to fasten on a very elusive emanation of . . . What? He found a disturbing hint of alien energy (though what he picked up was not born of any spark of life). Whatever waited ahead was not alive as he had always known life. No, it was . . .

A fleeting scrap of memory halted Jony. This outflow of energy was very near to what he had felt when he had dared touch palms with the woman of stone!

The clansmen had been so enrapt in their rhythmic thudding of staffs, their united sounds, that Otik and Kapoor gained a step ahead of Jony before they noted that he had stopped. They turned only a little, each reached out a hand-paw, clamping on his shoulders, drawing him up between them again.

There was no escaping their united wills. He must face whatever lay ahead. Realizing that, Jony tried to explore with his sense for what did wait there. It was not true life, of that he was sure. For he could not even pick up a hint of communication as he could with the People, unable as he was to ever reach them completely. However, there did exist somewhere ahead a force of some kind, a power to which his extra sense responded.

During those moments of the climb, Jony felt the odd and disturbing wash of that power. His body might have been plunged into a substance less tangible than water, but which had as strong a current as any good sized river might produce. Did the People also feel this, or was the thumping of staffs and the ululating sounds they voiced in some manner a shield against it?

Voak topped the long line of steps. He paused there, though he did not turn his head to see how far the others trailed him. Instead he quickened the beat of his staff against the bare rock on which he now stood. His voice was louder; the sounds he made faster as if he needed to build up his defense.

The smooth space on which the clan leader stood was large, as Jony saw when they joined the older male.

Like the river of stone, the platform extended, a tongue out-thrust from the last of the ledges. Above, the heights had been broken or dug away to give room to that path, and the sides were walled up with stones to retain the earth.

A short distance ahead loomed a tall opening into the core of the hill. That, also, was rimmed with blocks of stone. This must have been the handiwork of the pictured men, Jony was sure. Yet the People appeared to be able and willing to enter here.

Otik and Kapoor echoed Voak's faster beat of staff, his louder voice. They did not glance in Jony's direction, but rather kept their gaze fastened on the opening ahead. They might be waiting here for someone, or something, to issue forth. But there was no hidden life, Jony would swear to that, just a stronger sense of that power he could not understand.

Once more Voak began his march toward the opening, the others falling in behind in the same pattern they had followed since leaving camp. Jony felt a litttle dizzy. Perhaps his giddiness was caused by the thumping, the cries—or the *thing* ahead. He could not seem to think clearly anymore.

Over their heads arched the edge of the opening. What light shone in from behind showed only a pavement of stone, the walls about. The way narrowed abruptly just within the doorless opening.

On they went, the duskiness increasing as they left the day behind. This absence of light made no difference to the three clansmen, but it added to Jony's feeling of disorientation. Was there never any end to the sounds, to this way?

Then, as if struck dumb in an instant, paralyzed by a stroke out of nowhere, the clansmen were quiet. There was no more thumping, no cries. Jony's hands went to his ears. He could still hear—something, a pulsing like the beat of a giant staff unable to rest. Now he swayed, his body seeming to bend in time to that beat, and he heard a mighty cry out of Voak's thick throat. The sound scaled up and up, until Jony's ears could no longer distinguish it, only he could still feel the vibration of that ululation through him.

What happened was as startling as the moving wall in the city. Dark and shadows split apart. Light shone from beyond: a ruddy light, not gray like that which Jony had faced in the storage places. This radiance pulsed also, as if it were a part of the power which now enveloped him, made his flesh tingle, his mind spin.

Their way being open, Voak continued, still silent. In the red glow of the light the clansmen's fur took on odd new tints. An aura surrounded them, made up of many colors which spun, faded, mingled in a glow until one could not be clearly defined from another, while the tingling of Jony's exposed skin neared real pain.

They had entered a place not unlike those underground ways which he had followed with the twins. But this was not so large. And in the center was—

Jony shrank back. He could not help that momentary reaction. All he had escaped when he and Rutee won free of the ship came flaring back into his mind.

For the center of the rounded inner space or cave in which they stood was occupied by a cage!

They were not going to shut him up! Jony's second reaction was as quick and even more fierce than the first. Never would he be in a cage again! The clan could kill him first!

"No!" he shouted his protest, not caring if the People understood or not. But Otik's and Kapoor's combined strength were greater than his. They held him by the arms again, forced him forward, though Jony fought frenziedly for his freedom. He could see no sign of any open door in that barred enclosure ahead. Voak did no more than move a little to one side, watching the boy's ineffectual struggles.

The clan chief dropped his staff to the floor, his hands engaged in an imperative talk sign.

"Look!"

Jony followed the pointing of that dark hand-paw. Now that he was closer he could see that the cage was already occupied—by bones! And below those empty-eyed skulls rested wide collars.

Only the skulls—the bodies—they were not of the People. They were too slender, too small. Who had been imprisoned to their deaths in this place where the dancing light carried the tinge of blood? Also, that light itself—what was it, flashing from a hole in the floor beyond the cage?

Voak squatted heavily and worked one thick arm between the bars of the sealed cage. His fingers closed on the nearest of the wide collars. Bones tumbled as he drew it toward him. He rose, the collar looped over his arm like a massive, ill-fitting bracelet.

The clan chief began to sign slowly, with exaggerated movements of his hands. As if what he must communicate was of the utmost importance and he wished Jony to clearly understand what he would say.

"People," his thumb indicated his own barrel body, "this—" He twirled the collar around, his gesture one of loathing and hatred as he raised it to his neck as if about to fit the band around his own throat. "We do—collar—says—or die. They—" now his pointing was to the bones within the cage, "make collars, use People. They—" he hesitated as if at a loss, feeling the need to improvise for Jony's better understanding, "find bad things—bad for them. They die fast—only few left. People not die, People break out. Put collars on those, then *they* do what People say. But they already bad sick—die. People no wear collars again—never!" His final gesture of negation resembled a forceful threat.

"Look!" Now Voak held the collar only inches away from Jony's face, as if to make very sure the boy would understand perfectly. With the band so gripped between the clansman's fingers, there sprang out of its edge a row of stiff points. Eyeing those Jony believed they were set so that, once about a throat, those points would cut into the flesh were the head moved out of a single, stiffly upright position.

Voak flipped the end of a finger against the nearest point. "Fang—" he signed. "Hurt from collar—hurt People if *they* wanted . . . Bad. You—" Now he gave

Jony an intent, searching stare which traveled from the other's head to his feet and back again. "You cub— People take, help—give food—give nest. But you are like *them* . . . you go to find collar—make People do what you say . . ."

"No!" Jony protested aloud, trying to move his hands in the strongest of the negative signals, but the two who held him did not release him enough for him to complete that denial.

Voak did not seem to hear him. Instead the clansman turned the collar around in his fingers, examining it carefully. Now he pressed again and the band opened. While Otik and Kapoor held Jony immobile, Voak stepped forward and fitted the collar about the boy's throat, snapped the band shut. The circlet was loose, lying down on his shoulders as Jony bent his head to stare at it in horror.

"You wear—you remember," Voak signed. "You go to *them* again—you shall feel fangs also. The People do not forget. You shall not forget!"

The others had loosed him. Jony reached up to jerk the band around his neck. Loose as it was, its very weight made him sick and somehow ashamed. Voak, the others, turned away as if Jony was no longer any concern of theirs. He followed them, suddenly struck by a second and worse fear: that he would be left here forever in a place where that cage of bones stood as a dire warning against enslavement of the People.

He ran his fingertips around and around that ring, seeking whatever catch Voak had found to open it.

But the secret eluded him. Now Jony realized that the clansman meant exactly what he had signed: the boy was to wear this symbol of servitude as a warning. If he tried to return to the place of stones, even worse would follow.

Having set their shaming bondage on him, all three of the People appeared to lose interest in Jony. They did not look back as once more they crossed to the top of the steps and started down. Jony had a feeling that to Voak and the others he was no longer of the clan; he had ceased to exist as an equal.

His numb surprise gave way to a beginning flash of anger. The judgment of Voak and the rest had been given without a chance for Jony to defend himself. What had he done? Entered the stone place, come out again with the twins—that was all!

If, perhaps, he had brought with him the red rod Geogee had found . . . Then—

Jony stopped. His dream! In his dream this had been the way he had felt. With the rod in his hand he could have given orders and have them obeyed—or else. He felt his fingers curl now and glanced down to the hand held out before him. In his mind there for a moment he did not imagine himself holding a staff, but the rod. *Had* that been so, in his hot anger for the burden Voak had laid upon him, he might have raised the alien weapon and used it.

No! Jony shook his head vigorously, as if by strong denial he could drive out that momentary wish.

What would he have done to the Big Ones in the

past had he had the power to be stronger and greater than they? In his fear for the return of the bondage of his people was Voak any different?

Yes, but Jony in the ship had faced those very ones who had caged Voak and his people, and had set upon most of them the terrible fate of the mind-controlled. While now Jony had not threatened Voak and the rest . . .

Their feeling for him must have begun because he physically resembled those others: the ones painted on the walls and the stone woman. Yet how did Voak *know* that? Unless for all their aversion, the People *had* explored the stone place, had seen those pictures, the waiting woman. Still Jony was almost convinced that the clansmen had not. This whole country was new to the clan. Then—how did Voak and the rest know that Jony resembled those ancient enemies? Memory, relayed through folktales and myths, could be passed down through generations. But if Voak and the others remembered their former masters with hatred, then why had Yaa ever come to Rutee's aid? If there were an ancient hatred of Jony's own species dictated by form alone, Yaa would have ignored the fugitives, even as Voak, Otik, and Kapoor now did him, leaving woman and child alone to die on a strange and hostile world.

Yet, until he and the twins had ventured into the place of stones, the People had accepted them placidly, without question—or seemingly so—as living creatures not unlike themselves. Did Voak believe that going into the stone place awakened in Jony a desire for that power which the ancients had commanded?

As Jony thought of one possibility after another, trying to explain actions he could not understand, his flare of anger died. Voak was wrong to fear him, but he, Jony, could not tell what long-dreaded terror ruled the People. To Voak and the rest he might now seem to be the enemy, or at least one who must be watched.

If Jony trailed back with them to the clan camp, what would follow? He did not believe they would launch any attack against him. But, with a growing desolation of spirit, Jony began to guess what might happen. As they had last night, the clansmen would treat him as one who was not. He had never known such a punishment before. Usually their justice was swift, then forgotten. But to be with the clan and yet not *of* it . . . And what of Maba and Geogee? If they showed sympathy toward him, might not the same blighting non-existence be laid on them?

Jony dropped on the top ledge. Already the clansmen had reached the bottom of that descent. Not once had they turned to look back or showed any interest in him. He felt more alone even than he had on the night he crouched beside Rutee, unable to ease her pain. His hand rose to that shameful ring about his neck. He *was* in a cage again. As long as he wore that he was caged within himself, even if he had the whole country free before him.

Voak and the others vanished, treading purposefully back the way they had come. Jony made no move to descend and follow. Putting his elbows on his knees, he rested his head in his hands and closed his eyes. He had to think!

There was no purpose to be gained by his being angry. Voak, the others, they must have acted as they thought best for the clan. Jony could not judge their actions, not when he knew so little of what lay behind all this. He tried now to recall, in what detail he could, that picture on the wall, the one in which the People had been shown tied and led about, or caged.

But he had hurried past it so fast he had now only a jumbled impression. The one fact being that the People, as pictured there, were slightly different in form from the clan. None of them had been depicted as walking erect, rather all had been using both hand-paws and feet against the ground. That was the main difference he could now recall.

Had the People changed after they won their freedom? Or had they been forced by their captors to remain animal-like? Jony shuddered. The Big Ones had done such things with the mind-controlled at times. Rutee had told him that the Big Ones had not considered humans as more than animals; animals to be broken, controlled, used for their own purposes. The horror which this had meant for her had been passed on to him, young as he was. Even if he could not know how life had been before the Big Ones had taken over the colony, he realized he was an intelligent being.

Had the People been mind-controlled also? Or did they remember, with all of Rutee's horror, being "animals" to contemptuous aliens? Were the people of the stone place from off this world?

They must have lived here a long time to build that place. And where did the river of stone run? From this stone place to another such, standing at a more distant site? They had had sky ships—those had appeared in the pictures.

Jony's head ached; he was both hungry and thirsty. But he could not shift off the feeling of burdensome weight on his shoulders. In these moments of confusion and despair, he knew that he was not going back to the campsite, at least not now. Voak had set on him the badge of the owned. Somehow he must be free before he returned; free of the collar in such a manner that Voak and the rest could not place it upon him again.

He sat up straight. The world spread out below him seemed very wide, wide and empty! Since the night Yaa had found them, he had never been aloof from the People. Before that, even though their cages had been separated, there was always Rutee. To think of himself as utterly alone was a realization which brought fear— not of anything he could sense or touch, but, in a strange way, of the land, the sky, the whole world about him.

To sit here was no answer to his problem. And to return to the place of cage—if he could return now— was none either. He must find food, water, a—a staff. His hands seemed so empty and useless without a staff.

Unbidden, unwished, once more the thought of the

red rod flashed across his mind. Power greater than any staff . . . *NO!* Jony's lips moved to shape that word. He must prove to Voak that he was not one with the stone people—he had to prove that!

Food, water, a weapon-tool, they came first and foremost. With those he was himself again. Once given those he could think—plan—find some way to free himself of the metal band so cold and heavy about his throat. In time he might be able to discover the secret of its lock and so get rid of it. But he needed, most of all, to return the collar to the clan with their clear understanding that this was not his to wear.

He descended the steps carefully to the way by the ridge. The campsite lay to his left. Jony turned sharply right.

PERHAPS THIS STREAM HE HAD CHANCED ON WAS THE same one that farther back fed the falls where Maba and Geogee had splashed and played. Only now matters were different. As he went slowly, Jony hunted under upturned, water-washed stones for enough of the small, shelled things to satisfy his hunger. He drank his fill from his cupped hands. At length, with hunger and thirst in abeyance, he looked about him for his third need: a staff.

Traveling along the sand of the stream's lip, he chewed at a handful of tart leaves from one of the plants he knew well as a part of the clan diet. For the moment he had pushed all questions far to the back of his mind, determined to be occupied only by the here and now, though he was unable to forget the weight about his throat, or what it meant.

Foraging proved so good along the stream that Jony disliked leaving the water's edge. But, though he had found pieces of drift caught among the rocks which might have possibilities for a staff, he vaguely mistrusted their smooth, bleached lengths. No, he would have to head outward toward a real stand of trees to locate what he wanted.

Even as Jony made to turn away from the bank, he

caught sight of a bright glint from among the rocks just ahead. Curious, he went to see what had been caught there. Another bit of drift? No, for along the side of this piece a length of caked coating had flaked away, to release that gleam which the sun had betrayed to him. He knew of no wood resembling this.

In fact the shaft could not be wood at all. For, when Jony drew it out of the crevice into which it had fallen or been jammed by flood water, the straight length was heavier than any staff he had ever lifted. That coating around the bright slash appeared to be hardened clay, combined with a red substance which powdered off on his hands. Squatting down, Jony chose a stone and began to scrape at his find, his persistence revealing more and more of what he was now sure was metal. This was longer than the deadly red rods of the stone place, and not the same color at all. A little of his old curiosity kept him to the cleaning, first with stone rubbing, and then with handfuls of sand. At last he held something which was not unlike the staffs of the clansmen, though shorter. It even possessed a curve at one end, though that did not altogether resemble those crooks which were such useful tools. This curve (Jony held a cut finger in the flow of the stream) had a sharpened edge which was far more dangerous than any point a clansman could put on his weapon-tool.

The metal sides were pitted with small holes. However, when Jony lifted the rod high, to bring it crashing down on the nearest large rock with all his strength, the length did not snap or bend. Instead, the rock itself was scarred by that stroke. He rubbed it again, this time with leaves, cleaning off the sand and the last of the red powder. What he had was, he was sure, a tool which had been purposefully made, probably by those people of the stone place. However, the thing carried no taint of power as the red rods did. In form it was plainly such a staff as he could never hope to make for himself.

Jony sat fingering the pole resting across his knees. The feel was good, fitting to his hand smoothly in spite of the pitting. He liked the weight of it. And that cutting, edged part at the top—there were many uses to which that could be put. He had not taken this from the storehouse of the stone place, so it did not seem forbidden. Long ago it must have been lost, or discarded as useless. Therefore, Jony made his decision.

Right or wrong, this was his. He had found and cleaned it. If he must go a lone way through this world for now, then he would have the best protection he could lay hand upon. He—

Only that shadow across the sand came as a warning! Jony had been so absorbed in his find that he had not posted the sentry of his mind which was his most important defense. He did not even have time to get to his feet to meet an attack launched from the sky.

There sounded a scream, so high and shrill, as to hurt his ears. The vor screeched aloud its triumph as it dropped, talons spread, its head weaving back and forth. Jony swept the staff upward with a frenzied hope of beating off that plunge. He could see above the first attacker, two others of that noisome species sailing about, perhaps the half-grown young of the first.

His wild sweep of the staff connected with the plunging predator. Only by chance, and no real thought, had Jony used the end with the curved blade. The jar of his blow landing sent him sprawling back, while fear closed in. For he was now totally defenseless before the death strike of the vor.

However the bird had been beaten out of line when his blow fell. It screeched again, not in triumph, but in rage and agony. One of the great taloned legs flopped loosely. Blood spurted from a deep wound opened by the sharp edge.

Up the vor soared with a strong beat of wings. Jony scrambled to his feet, set his back to the nearest rock. The other two birds were plunging down to meet their fellow. He had not escaped, he had only earned a breathing space.

Blood trickled down the length of the staff, was sticky on his fingers. He momentarily transferred hold of the staff, wiped his hand on the side of his kilt. Three vor, and, once they went into combat, they would not sheer off. He had no chance at all.

The wounded one screamed in on a second dive. But this time Jony was ready. He thought now he knew a little of what the staff could do. Only it would be very good fortune if he were able to land another telling blow. He forced himself to wait until the last moment of that strike, then brought the staff around in a sweep into which he put all his strength, aiming to connect it with the long, twisting neck of the raging creature.

He missed that mark. But the curved blade hit hard on the near wing about where it met the vor's body. The force of that blow hurled the flying thing away. Now the attacker could only use one wing, beat that frantically, its screams making a din in the air. Unable to continue air-borne, the creature fell among the rocks on the other side of the stream, where it flopped and cried, blood spattering far from its two wounds. Jony, hardly able to believe in his escape, had no eyes for it. He strained upward to watch the two above. At that moment he also unleashed his concentrated sense of command. As with the People, he could not enforce his will on the brain of any creatures of this world. But he might be able to confuse them—a little.

The pair continued to circle over his head. So far he could detect no signs that either was preparing to strike. Perhaps because they were young, they were more puzzled, wary, than an adult vor would be. Jony edged back between two rocks. In the open he felt naked. Though these stones rose to only about his shoulder height, he gained a small sense of security when standing between them. Staff in hand he waited.

Then he tensed. One of the vors had made up its mind. Jony caught the slight change in flight pattern which meant attack. Though smaller than the wounded one yet flopping and shrieking across the water, the creature was still a very dangerous opponent. Jony gripped his staff, knowing that again he must wait. Only his superior weapon had saved him so far, of that

he was convinced. But he could not rely on that good
fortune to continue. He must be ready to—

The vor dropped, this time silently, without warning.
Jony readied himself for a swing. He thought he had
little chance of striking the neck, but his success in
catching the wing of the other had given him a lead as
to the best way to meet any attack. He swung again
vigorously.

Once more the blow hit home. The vor squalled. The
creature seemed unable to halt its downward swoop,
and hit the sand beyond the rocks, flopping. Jony took
a chance. He burst from his rock defense and lashed
down with several blows. One hit the darting head,
smashing it.

Breathing hard, Jony backed into his poor refuge,
looked up for the third and last vor. Unlike its fellows,
it was not of a mind to carry on the battle. Instead,
after circling twice and hooting mournfully, it flapped
away. Jony stared at the still twitching vor near him,
that other which tried to deny death on the other side of
the water. Two *vors!* He was dazed at the fact of his
escape. His staff was sticky with blood, more was
splashed on him, on the rocks about. But he was *safe!*
Weakly he leaned back on the stones which half-supported him.

Clansmen killed attacking vors, yes. But only when
working as a team with a thought-out defense plan.
Jony had never known one of the People alone who
had finished off two of the great predators.

Near his feet the second one had gone limp at last.

While that on the far side of the water was moving only weakly, loss of blood bringing death. Jony forced himself a stride or two forward, used the blade end of his staff to prod the near body. There was no sign of life.

The fetid stench of the creature, together with the blood about, made Jony queasy. He moved further upstream. There he not only scrubbed his new weapon with sand and water, but washed his own sweated body and stained kilt, so that no possible taint of his kill remained.

There was movement downstream. He saw some of the scavengers that were always quick to find any kill dart out of the rock's shade and scuttle toward the body. By tomorrow there would only be well-cleaned bones left. Jony eyed the vicious talons of the dread creatures. Those had uses. He might stay near enough to claim them as trophies when the feasters were done.

Suddenly he smiled grimly. Though the People did not adorn themselves with anything but their food gathering nets, he had a sudden idea. Those talons he might hang from the collar. If he ever returned to the clan and was able to loosen that yoke they had laid upon him, it would please him greatly to have added this proof of his own ability to survive the burden they had put on him as a punishment and warning.

This staff—never had there been one like this! His hands slipped back and forth along the surface, avoiding the sharp hook at the end, caressingly. Jony took time now to study that edged hook with great care. It was shaped not unlike a fang, a giant fang. He had no such natural fighting equipment of his own, as the People carried in their jaws. But now he could boast of a fang in his hand, use it well . . .

Prudence dictated a withdrawal upstream. Those dead vors would draw more than these small scavengers already busy. Also Jony wanted to get away from the stench of death and blood. He would find someplace near where he could make a night nest. Only, never again must he relax to the point he was unaware of life about him. His own foolish mistake had nearly provided him as fodder for the flying death. He must learn how to use his sense wisely. However, not with such a power of induced concentration that he would not also be conscious of what lay immediately about him. For here there was no one of the clan to give him the illusion of safety while he freed his mind for questing ahead.

He found a good space among rocks and made several trips into a stretch of grassland to pull up that wiry growth in armloads and bring his harvest back to his nest site. As he moved now, Jony kept instantly alert for any return of the vor, any suggestion that there was other danger abroad in this land. The time was still well before the coming of dusk when he harvested fruit from a couple of high growing bushes, returned with it back to his camp. The land here was rich in provender, but there was no sign that any clan had wandered into it. Perhaps there was a roost of vor too near to make the country safely open for the People's accustomed daylight roaming by twos or threes.

As Jony settled into his retreat, he thought once more of Maba and Geogee. Voak had stated the twins would not be held responsible for their visit to the stone place, so he believed that they would not have to fear an exile like his. And Yaa could control Maba; Voak would probably have Geogee under close watch. Neither would be allowed to return to the stone place.

All those questions which had filled Jony's mind in the morning were still to be answered, if he could ever find answers for any of them. The main one which troubled him now was: would his collar shut him off from the People forever? He did not want to consider what that might mean, yet he could not push the thought aside.

To be always and ever alone! There might be other clans near. There were such, he had contact with them during those meetings which were held from time to time. But he guessed that as long as he wore this collar he would not be accepted among any of the People.

Within his heaped nest Jony moved uneasily. It was one thing to spend the night thus, knowing that within arm's reach were curled companions. But he had never been alone. He lay back now, his eyes closed, though he did not sleep. Instead, Jony journeyed back and back, as far as his memory would take him. To escape the present, he thought of the past.

At first he tried to envision details of the lab in the sky ship. He had always been able to recall as mental pictures small scenes when he had wished. What had been the very first memory of all?

He had been with Rutee in her cage. She had patiently told him over and over who he was, how they had come there. They had once been as free as the People. Then the Big Ones had come, and they were caged. Some of their kind the Big Ones killed slowly, studying them as they died. Rutee had looked sick when she had told Jony that, but she had made him listen. Others they made into the mind-controlled. But a few could not be so trained, Rutee was one, he even more so.

The Big Ones had traveled through the sky away from Rutee's world. There had been other worlds visited, too. Other captives, though none resembling Rutee's own people. At last they had reached here. Though Rutee had never known where "here" was.

She had shown Jony the stars at night, pointed to this one and that. But she said that they were set "wrong," that none of them seemed the stars she had known when she had lived outside before. Therefore the sky ship had taken them very far from her colony world. There was no chance of their ever getting back to their own kind again.

Her people had also had sky ships. They had flown out from a world which was their own, settled on other worlds. For a long time they had been doing that. Rutee was not even sure just where their first home world was. It had not been the world on which she and Bron were born, before they joined to help make up another colony. Long and far . . .

Could it have been this world? Was that why he,

Maba, and Geogee looked so like the stone people? But
Rutee had not known the People, nor heard of them
before. However it might still be a world her people
had found once and lived upon.

Jony remembered now, with a fierce desire to hold
to every fraction of the pictures in his mind, the seasons they had wandered with the clan. From helpless
babies Maba and Geogee had grown to bigger, more
thinking creatures. Rutee had talked always with Jony
about his own kind. She hoped some day that chance
might bring one of their scout ships here. So she taught
him the speech of her people, even how to trace marks
in the sand or on pieces of bark, signs which carried
and held the meaning of those words after one had
forgotten them.

Then Rutee had died. He missed her very much. Still
there were the twins, the clan. He had not been alone.
Jony sat up suddenly, his eyes open, fighting fear and
loneliness. His hands clenched on his wonder staff. He
was fed, he had fought such a battle as few of the People had faced, all by himself. He had a safe camp. But
—he wore the collar.

If he only knew more! Could he, dared he, return
to the place of stones to learn?

Perhaps those other people, if they were of his kind,
even so far divided, had made signs for their words.
The dead cannot speak, but signs could speak for them.
Would Voak, the clan, know if he attempted such a
mission?

Voak's warning was still clear in his memory. How-

ever, if he were exiled, what would it mean to Voak
that he went back? Jony would never turn against the
clan, he could not.

Maba—Geogee? What if Voak used them to punish
Jony for breaking the command he had laid upon the
boy? No return then—at least not yet. Jony must do
nothing which the clan leader could use as an excuse to
make trouble for the twins.

Then—where would he go now? He could trail behind the clan on its wanderings. But he did not want
to, not on their terms. Either he would return wholly,
one of them as he had been before, or he would keep
away.

Jony nodded his head vigorously, though there was
no one there to witness this affirmation of his decision.
So—in the morning he would follow this stream as a
guide. It led on up into the higher hills beyond these
beginning ridges, toward those mountains where the
earth seemed to challenge the sky and the night stars.
Perhaps he would find another stone place, one which
Voak's people did not watch. There . . . Jony did
not know what he could do there, what he honestly
wanted to do. But to move on was better by far than
to sit here waiting, or to trail behind the clan as if they
had a leash fastened to his shame collar, and so led him
along at their will.

How he wished now that he had paid more attention
to the pictures on the wall of the storage place. He
scowled over that loss of opportunity. Odd—though
there had been power there—the sensation had not

been as strong as it had when they had gone to the place of the cage.

Was that feeling really the power of hate held within the cage itself: hate of the People, hate of those who had died there? Jony had always been able to sense emotions, even physical pain that had troubled Rutee or the twins. To a much less extent he could also sense pain and trouble with the clan. But could such feelings continue to exist after death?

The stone woman—had the shock from her hand been a remembered emotion passing from that cold, impassive palm into his live one—or something else? He knew so little. Impatience burned high in Jony, just as momentary anger had flared after Voak's sentencing. There was so much he did not understand, and he needed to! The desire for knowledge was now like real pain in him.

How had those captives in the cage died? Quickly, or slowly? Had they been left to perish from hunger and thirst? Or fed and prisoned until their spirits died first, and they had no will left in them to live on?

His collar— Jony put both hands to the band at his throat. Did that loose hoop of metal hold the power of past emotion? He could sense nothing directly from it. Any more than he could from the shaft with the mounted fang of death.

Slowly he turned the collar around, taking care lest some touch of his release those tormenting fangs Voak had demonstrated. Under his fingers the surface was smooth. Unlike the shaft, here was no pitting. The thing could be fresh made, though he believed it was of an age he could not begin to reckon.

No power in it. Then where had the power lain in the cage place? Had it been summoned by the sounds the clansmen had made with their thumping and their cries?

Jony tried an experiment of his own. With the butt end of the shaft he began tapping gently on one of the rocks which guarded his nest, trying to keep to the same speed Voak and the others had used. Vibration did run up the shaft into his arm. But he experienced none of that tingling sensation.

Perhaps the sensation came then from the red light. Could one draw upon such power, feed it into one's own concentrated energy? What was the use of thinking that? Jony had no intention of trying to find the place of the cage again. Contrarily, he preferred to travel as far away from its site as he could.

Within the past few days his mind had become crowded with questions, enough to make his head ache. During all the seasons he had roamed with the People, Jony had never speculated so much about matters which were not concerned with the daily round of existence. He felt, oddly enough, as if he had just now wakened from a kind of lulling sleep. After Rutee died, he had not tried to share any of his thoughts with the twins. To him they were responsibilities, not real persons. He was to watch over them, not communicate to them his own doubts and uncertainties. His limited contact with the People themselves had been confined to the level of what was only necessary for the continued well-being of life.

So Jony had ceased much to question where there could be no answering. His discovery of the river of stone had first shaken him out of the dull shell that lack of real companionship had built about him. Jony had always been different, but he had ruthlessly tried to suppress that difference, to be as like the People as he could. Now he was exiled into difference. So his imagination awoke, pricked at him with new questions upon questions.

Nor could he sleep as this new wakefulness possessed him and made him restless. He would have liked to have strode back and forth out in the moonlight, under those stars Rutee did not know, attempting to dull his thoughts again.

For Jony was no longer complacent. He was uneasy, on edge. Somewhere he must find answers—somewhere . . .

He had been facing downstream. But also he had been looking skyward. The vor did not attack by night, his sense found no menace there.

Then—

Across the sky a burst of vivid fire.

What—?

Jony's hands gripped the staff so tightly his knuckles stood out in hard knobs. He trembled as if reeling under some strong blow.

Perhaps because his awareness had been so aroused that he knew—somehow he *knew!*

Had Rutee ever told him? Now he was not sure. But he was as certain as if he had witnessed the planeting. That had been a sky ship! And it was going to land!

The Big Ones!

Hate drew Jony's mouth tight, brought him to his feet, his wonder staff up and ready. No!

The flashing sweep was gone. He strained to hear any sound. And thought he caught a hint of a far-off roar. Yes, the ship was down. Now the Big Ones would come hunting. The People—the twins—they had no idea of what hellish things the Big Ones could and would do. He must return to the clan, make them listen! Collar or no collar, he had to make them listen.

Jony was already running lightly along the sand on his back trail. All that lay in his mind now was how much time he might have before the Big Ones came hunting for their prey.

A BAD FALL BROUGHT JONY BACK TO HIS SENSES. TO go charging along without caution at night through this unknown country was stupid. He sat on the sandy ground nursing a skinned shin, eyeing the dark as the enemy it now was.

There was no way of judging how far away that landing of the sky ship had been. Perhaps it had planeted so distantly from the clan campsite that all his fears were unfounded. But, from Rutee's tales, he knew that the Big Ones possessed other means of travel besides the sky ships themselves. They carried within the larger vessels small craft made to grind steadily ahead over any kind of ground, or take into the air for a distance, if there was need.

How soon would those craft be out searching?

Jony beat one balled fist against the ground in frustration. He must get to the campsite, make Voak and the others listen!

Would the stone place draw the Big Ones? He knew from his life among them that they had explored such sites on other worlds, bringing back objects they had stored with care.

Jony got to his feet and, leaning on the sturdy support of his new staff, limped stubbornly on. He would follow this stream which ran in the general direction southward. If it *was* the same as the one that ran near the camp, he had now a sure guide. And, if he took more care, he could travel even in the darkness.

But even the stream side was none too easy a trail. Twice he came upon piled rock barriers through which he had to find a way, prodding ahead with the butt of his staff to make sure each stone was secure before he put his full weight on it. Once he had to make a detour around a pile of drift embedded in the sand, a menace he dared not cross in the dark.

His leg ached and there was more pain if he put too much weight on that foot. However, slowly as he must go, he would certainly reach camp by morning. He could not have traveled too far north after Voak and the others had left him.

The graying of pre-dawn filled the sky as Jony reached the lip of the falls. There was no sign of the People below. The boy half fell on an outcrop of stone, the throbbing of his leg matched by a weariness throughout his body. Yet he had still to descend the drop beside that veil of water.

Maba? Geogee? For a long moment he played with the thought of using the mind touch to draw the children to him, to relay the message he had come to deliver, the warning. Then he knew he dared not. Neither of the twins was receptive enough to pick up his clear thoughts, though they might be moved to come hunting him. And, if they did that, their own safety with the clan could be endangered. He dared not work through the twins, but must meet Voak face to face.

However, when he concentrated on the camp, he met only a blank nothingness. Not even the flickering in and out of his usual touch with the People answered his probe.

Jony knew panic then, which, if he had not instantly controlled it might have sent him ahead with a recklessness leading to disaster. Nothing—there was nothing there!

The Big Ones! A raid on the campsite already?

Jony crawled to the drop and began to scramble from rock to rock. He had earlier tied his staff to his back with a twist of fibre so that he would have both hands free. Twice his weapon clattered against stones with a sound loud enough to rise above even the rumble of the falls.

Down, down. Now he was near that very place where Maba had been dragged unwillingly ashore, her hair fast in Uga's grip. Jony limped on, leaving his hands free. To enter the campsite with his shaft on his back would surely be a gesture of peaceful intent. As he breathed heavily his mind-sense ranged ahead, intent on picking up the least hint of where the People might be camped.

There was nothing. Just as he found nothing in sight when he came into the glade within the brush screen where there should have been the night nests, the stir of awakening People.

Nests were there, but they were empty. Jony went to

that one to which Yaa had taken Maba the last time he had seen her. Under his fingers the withered grass and leaves were cold. By the appearance no fresh foliage had been added, as was usual, the night before.

Therefore the clan had not slept here. They must have moved on!

Taking Maba and Geogee where?

Jony slowly circled the edge of the site. He was not really surprised to find the traces of that withdrawal as he reached the south side. The People must have decided they were too near to the stone place, that they were going to change their direction of slow drift.

But it was also to the south that the sky ship had planeted. Was the clan now walking straight into a danger they could not understand?

He made a careful search of the campsite. His gleanings were a food net with a hole in the side, a castoff, and some of the rubbing stones Otik had been putting to use. There was nothing else.

Nor could he throw off the knowledge that he must now do what he swore only yesterday that he would never do, trail behind the clan until he found them. He could only hope that their pace would continue to be normally leisurely, that they followed their usual occupations of food gathering to slow them as they went.

A day—or at least a part of a day ahead. That should not delay too much his catching up. Heartened by that belief, Jony ate the last of the bruised fruit he carried from last night's meal and returned to that southward direction.

This was a trail easy enough to follow. He could readily pick up the broad paw prints of the People here and there where there was a bare stretch of soil, and twice smaller tracks left by the twins. However, their going was different this time, not spread out in a loose numbering of one, two or three, but rather remaining in a close group, all together.

Jony climbed the next ridge, favoring his leg. From here he could look down once more to where the river of stone cut across the open country. He was too far west to see the place where it ended, ridges to the east masking the walls. But any Big One exploring would be able to detect such a site immediately.

The trail of the clan led straight, still compact, down ridge, on to the river of stone. Had they gone up to the heaps? Jony could hardly believe they would. Yet their tracks ended at the edge of that pavement.

He ventured out again on the smooth surface, only to strike directly across. His guess was right, the People had dared make contact with the evidence of all they hated only because there was no other way to reach the ground beyond. There once more he could sight their tracks, still close together.

This very unusual method of travel was a warning in itself that all was not well. He had never known the People to bunch as they traveled, unless they were skirting some ground in which a smaa had hunting trails of its own. There had been no move either, Jony noted, to harvest the heavy seed heads of a growth of vegetation only a short distance away.

South—and straight across the open where the Big Ones (if any of them prowled afar from their ship) could easily sight them.

Jony made the fastest time he could himself crossing that same stretch. Tall as the grass was, the growth could not hide even Maba. And the clan still marched together in an almost straight line. There was a promising darker rise of trees and brush before him, but that was some distance away.

He ate as he went, snatching handfuls of the seed, chewing them vigorously to get what nourishment each contained before he spat out mouthfuls of husks. Dry eating indeed, and he began to long to see the stream again. However, below the falls, the river had taken a curve to head farther west.

As he went, Jony kept his search sense alert. There was, as yet, no contact with the party he sought. Which meant that they had out-distanced him more than he had first guessed. He tried to quicken pace, eager to be under the safe roofing of the trees ahead, since the sky could now be a roadway for the enemy.

The heat of the sun was shut off abruptly as he stumbled under the taller growth he had sought. Here was still an open trail, no wandering from it. Jony could not guess what moved Voak and the others to set aside all their ordinary ways of travel. Or—was it because of him?

Did they wish so much to lose all contact with Jony that they had moved the clan out immediately upon their return, pushing on so he could not easily catch up?

Slow moving as the People generally were, they had great endurance, much more than his own. For some time he had not sighted those smaller prints marking Maba and Geogee's presence. It could be that the twins were now riding on big shoulders, as they had when they were much smaller and tired quickly during a journey.

When he had started out on this trail, Jony had been sure he would catch up with the clan fast enough. His concern had been all for their acceptance or denial of his warning. But, as the day wore steadily on and his own endurance flagged (not only from the ache in his leg, but from sheer weariness), he began to wonder if he were ever going to find them at all.

This wooded country proved to be only a small tongue thrust out from greater thickets to the west. However, evidence of their passing gave him a thin hope the clan had not turned in that direction (where, indeed, they might well have lost him completely), but held to their southward trek as steadily as if they traveled with a definite purpose in mind.

Jony noted now, however, that at last their foragers were out seeking foodstuffs, although none strayed very far from the line of march. Jony himself snatched fruit from the same places in turn. He came at last to a spring and threw himself down in deeply dented, moist, clay to drink. It was plain the clan had found this water earlier. The sight of those tracks renewed his spirit and determination, for they had not been made too long before.

He settled there knowing that he must rest. His

weariness wore on him as if the collar was a mighty burden sinking him, under its pressure, to the earth. It was as he lay thus that he heard the new sound.

A humming, buzzing, a little of both, yet not entirely either. But a noise he had never listened to before. He mind searched . . .

Jony sat up.

"No!" He even cried the word aloud. Then once more he made contact.

Not Maba, no, not Geogee. Patterns of thought reached his mind, as individual as faces were in his sight. He had, in that moment, contacted neither of the twins. But the mind he had touched so briefly, it *was* one of his own kind.

The scattered bits of thought which were his only answer when he tried to communicate so with the People—he was well versed to recognize those. And he believed he could never forget the way the Big Ones thought, though those were as strange to follow, if much clearer.

This—this was like touching Rutee! Not mind-controlled, a free mind—one with the same pattern as his own.

Meanwhile the sound grew louder, more persistent. Jony hunkered back under the largest bush near enough for him to reach. Then he raised his staff and cautiously pushed aside some branches to bare a piece of sky hardly larger than his two hands laid together. In his shock at what his alerting sense had told him, he dared not use his talent again—not yet.

Through his hole he caught only a glimpse of what hovered overhead: not a sky ship, but a vehicle much, much smaller, possessing the appearance of several trees, denuded of both branches and roots and fastened tightly together to form an object curved at either end. Sunlight glinted as the craft swooped over his sky hole and was gone, the ship's brilliance having some of the same quality as the light from his sand-polished staff.

The Big Ones? No, that had been no enemy mind he had touched in that startling moment of contact. Rather some life-form akin to his own rode in the sky on that flying thing!

People from another stone place? One which had not died long years ago? Jony thought not. The People would have known of their continued existence, he was sure. Then—could this be a ship of his *own* people— such as Rutee had sworn had carried her in the long ago to the colony world?

Jony's excitement flared. Still, caution, taught by the past, kept him where he was, quiet and attentive. Warily once more he tried mind contact. He was sure he could recognize the mind-controlled. If this was some trick of the Big Ones to entice their prey out of hiding . . .

Jony found the right level of contact, held it. Again only for an instant. For that other had reacted, had felt Jony's invasion, and had met his quest with a sudden alert.

Surely *not* mind-controlled! One of *them* would never have known, or cared. They were too used to being directed by the Big Ones. Jony tried to sort out the jumbled impressions he had gained in what was less than a second of direct touch.

The being above was on scout and he was not used to direct mind contact. But his pattern was Jony's own. And . . . Jony thought furiously . . . maybe, just maybe, he could control this stranger for a space. That would be a way to gain knowledge.

But that would be using mind-control! Just what Rutee had feared he might someday try with Maba and Geogee, and had made him promise that he would never do. Still the flying invader was not kin, and Jony desperately needed to learn all he could. He stirred uneasily. Rutee had said: What the Big Ones did to their kind had been wholly evil. And if he did the same, now, how different was he from a Big One?

The flying thing flashed back into view, steadied almost directly above. Jony stiffened. Could the being on board trace Jony through his attempt at contact? The Big Ones had machines which achieved that very thing, which also made the mind-controlled what they were.

Stealthily Jony dropped his staff, allowing the branches to swing back to their proper places. He had no idea how much the hunter up there could see, or guess. But he had no intention of lingering for a meeting that might end up in capture.

Jony crawled on hands and knees. The buzz of the flyer remained steady; it neither grew louder nor faded. Which meant that the craft must have the ability to hover directly above Jony, something no live-winged thing he knew was able to do.

He was afraid to try contact again. Now he must depend upon his hearing more than any other sense. Belly-flat, he found a way which gave him complete sky cover and wriggled along very slowly indeed.

Could he depend on his hearing now? Dared he really believe that the sound was a little fainter, as if he were drawing away from it? He could not count on that; he might only do the best he could to escape.

His treetop cover thickened until Jony dared to get to his feet, though he had to weave in and out here to make any progress at all. Also he had lost the trail of the People as he crept away from the spring. There was only one way left to go unless he wanted to be under observation from the flyer—straight ahead—which meant south and toward the direction in which the sky ship must have planeted.

The sound receded, as if the flyer still hovered near the spring waiting for Jony to betray himself. About him the wood lay unnaturally quiet. All life there might be cowering to listen even as he did. Jony held his own passage to a minimum of noise.

His problem now was the lack of any trail as a guide; and his sense of direction was confused. He tried to fix on some particular tree ahead, reach that, then select another, always dreading to find himself caught in an endless circling. A broken branch, Jony fairly leaped for that. Work of one of the People! Yes, he could distinguish the stripping of leaves and twigs as the limb had been pulled down into the reach of someone taller than himself. Perhaps even Voak. Though Jony searched the ground here, he could find no prints. But there were other fruit vines and branches torn and mishandled. This had to have happened only a short time ago, since sap still oozed stickily from some.

Once more the growth thinned. Jony crouched behind a screen of leaves and branches. Immediately ahead was another open space. And, not too far away, the grass was beaten flat or torn up by the roots. He stared at that evidence of a struggle and was bitterly afraid. This could only mark a site where the People, or some of them, had been attacked without warning. Jony detected no signs of blood. But he did sight a staff, unbroken, and beyond that a net of fruit, half the contents squashed and now attracting insects.

The flyer!

He dared not venture into the open, even enough to examine more closely what evidence lay out there. Working a way about the fringe of the woodland would double both time and distance, but provided the cover he must have. Grimly, Jony began to move to the right along the line of detour. A moment later he dropped, freezing into instant immobility.

The buzz of the flyer was louder. He peered up as best he could without raising his head. Over the trees the alien craft swept, circling once about the place which marked what Jony was sure had been a struggle.

Then, to his unbelievable surprise, a voice sounded out of the sky:

"Joneeeeeeeee . . ." His own name, only distorted, sounding like a wail.

How did they not only know where he was, but who? This was more frightening than the red-lit chamber of the cage—all he had seen in the stone place—because it was personal, threatened *him* directly.

"Joneeeeeee . . ." again that cry.

Was this some new type of mind-control, reaching one's prey by the use of his closest possession: his own name? If they expected him to be lured so, then they must think him mind-controlled himself. And *who* were those prepared to play the Big Ones' old game?

Three times the flyer called him. Jony's anger changed to a sullen determination to track them down, though he could not follow through the air. The idea had now come to him that they must have captured Maba, Geogee, or both, and so knew of him. Safety was gone from this world; he had nothing to depend upon now but his mind, his two hands, and this weapon he had discovered from the past.

He was not fool enough to believe that the metal staff could threaten the sky craft, good as it had proved against the vor birds.

However, now the flyer seemed to be giving up the quest. No longer circling, the craft flew straight. Not to the southwest as Jony had confidently expected, but back north. Still hunting him?

He remained in hiding until the faintest of the buzzing stilled. If these others did have Maba or Geogee, if something dire had happened to the clan, he must know. So he believed his way now led south, toward where he had seen the ship planet. He no longer had any hope of finding the clan. And, undoubtedly, any warning he might have given was already far too late; useless.

Jony was driven to rest at last, simply because he was staggering and had fallen twice, in spite of the support of his staff. He made no nest, merely pushed back under a bush and pulled branches down as well as he could to hide his body. Once more he was thirsty, the fruit had only partly allayed his need. However, there had been times in the cold season among the folk when one learned to go hungry and even thirsty. Jony's plight was not a new one, save it came at the wrong season.

Weariness hit him so that he slept. Though even in that sleep he kept his hand on the shaft of his staff. Once more he slid into a dream . . .

He again visited the place of stones, climbing the ledges to face the woman. There was that which he alone could do, must do. Still he dreaded what would follow, not knowing what the result could be.

Reaching the figure he put out his hand as he had before, laid it palm to palm against her larger one. His body quivered. From that touch there flooded a fire, not to burn his flesh but rather to fill him with a power which he understood dimly he was to hold, contained, until the moment came for its full release.

Filled with that power, still obeying an order he did not understand, Jony went then on into the long space of stone trees, seeking the sleeper. As he looked down, that covered form moved; a hand arose to twitch aside the concealing mask. This time it was not his own features that were revealed. This was Maba. Not as he knew her now, but as she would be seasons ahead when she was as old as Rutee. Nor did she offer him the rod. Instead she signaled for him to come and aid her out of the box, bring her to her feet. This also he had to do.

She threw aside her clinging covering to step outside—and she smiled. But never as he had seen Maba smile. There was in her expression a hint of that look she assumed when she planned a bit of mischief or was stubbornly set on forbidden action—yes, that remained. But over all lay a cold knowledge of power and the will to use it.

That compulsion which had led Jony here and had made him free the one wearing Maba's face, broke. He struck out, not to grasp her rod for himself, but rather to capture the alien weapon, fling that dangerous thing as far from them both as his strength of arm could hurl it. Maba must not do what lay in her mind! That he understood.

Easily she avoided his grasp. Her smile deepened, she laughed. With the end of the rod she pointed to him and her words held a jeering note:

"Animal! Who are you who dares to rise?"

There was a tight strangling constriction in an instant about Jony's throat. He cried out, caught at the collar to tear himself free. Where that had once hung loose on him, now it was tight. From the band dangled a cord. Also, his back—he was being pressed down on all fours in spite of his frantic struggles.

The woman who was Maba caught the point of her rod through the looped cord, drew it to her. She laughed a second time, stepped away from the box which had held her for so long.

"You see," she said lightly, "you cannot be both—man and animal. Animals are ruled, men rule." Her twitch on the cord appeared light but drew Jony after her. She began to descend the ledges, never looking at him now as he followed on all fours at her heels, the animal so easily tamed.

THE GROWTH ABOUT JONY WAS SODDEN WITH A RAIN which fell with a steady persistence. That same rain erased any tracks of the People which might otherwise have been traced from that place of disaster in the open. Had all the clan been captured?

Jony roused from a night of unquiet rest, still ridden by that singularly forceful dream. It was seldom possible, beyond a few moments when one first awakes, to remember such details. But he continued to be haunted by vivid memory, just as he had by that earlier vision, when the sleeper, awaking in his box of stone, had worn Jony's own face, not Maba's. The feel of the constricting collar remained with him also. So that, now and then, his hand went half-consciously to his throat to see if the hoop still hung loose.

He caught no sound of any flyer. Perhaps the bad weather had driven it from a stormy sky. However, the same rain and wind did not keep Jony from his steady course south. And, after a climb up another line of ridge land, he came upon what he had sought ever since that flash of evil-to-come had swept across the night sky.

Below was a valley cut by a sizable stream, angling south and west. Not too far from that placidly flowing water stood a sky ship erect on its fins. About those supports the ground was charred, blackened, fused by the force of the beams down which it had ridden to this landing.

Jony concentrated on the ship. He was quite sure this one was not as large as that of the Big Ones, though it was of the same general shape. Perhaps most sky ships, no matter who piloted them, followed a like pattern. He had expected a ramp out from an open hatch, but the body remained sleekly closed, no manner of opening to be seen at all.

Nearby, however, there rested on the ground the flyer which had sent him into cover the day before. Now that Jony could view it from above instead of below he could pick out the features which made it readily recognizable as an intricate machine. There was an over-curved hood covering the top, under which, he supposed, the pilot and any passengers could shelter while the thing was aloft.

On the side of the standing ship there was a marking also, though it was dim, as if old.

Jony stirred unhappily. Here his shelter from the storm was poor, and there seemed to be no way of finding out what was going on below within the sealed ship. He wondered if he dared to try a thought-send—but hesitated. Somehow he was sure it was by that means he had attracted the attention of the flyer before. But—

He stiffened, instantly alert. At last something was happening. A roll-back opening appeared in the side of the ship; a ramp for landing curved out as might a questing tongue. That struck the ground, anchored firmly. Now, down that incline walked a man.

Not a Big One. Jony knew relief, then immediately regained his wary distrust. What kind of men rode the sky? They might be mind-controlled. If the kinfolk of Rutee had at last made their way here . . . But then why had they attacked the People?

Maba—Geogee—and how many of the clan were now down there, imprisoned?

The spaceman's whole body was covered with clothing fastened about his arms, his legs, up to his throat. The material was a green-brown in color, making his face seem very dark. His hair had been trimmed into a short stiff brush. Now the invader descended to the end of the ramp, to just stand there, holding something before his eyes, turning the upper part of his body very slowly. As if, through that object Jony could not distinguish very clearly, the stranger was making a careful survey of the very slope upon which the boy crouched.

Did they somehow know he was here? Were they now seeking him again? Jony had dabbed his body with sticky mud and leaves before he had settled here, making the best attempt he could to copy the ability of the People to be one with their background when they chose. Now, with a fast-beating heart, he waited any moment for the stranger below to center directly on him.

What would happen then? Could the invaders loose some vapor into the air as did the Big Ones, leaving him unable to defend himself as they came to collect another prisoner?

However, the other swung past, no longer centering on Jony's perch. Instead he was continuing his examination of the terrain. At last the spaceman dropped his hands, though he still held the object through which he had studied the countryside.

Just then the rain hit with a heavier gust. Apparently the stranger did not care for that. He turned and ran back up the ramp into the open hatch. A moment or so later, the ramp itself was lifted and drawn in. Jony, however, did not relax. The ship was now a cage, the most secure cage he had ever faced.

Should he have tried to fasten on the mind of that watcher, perhaps control him? Had he lost his best opportunity of rescuing those inside? If he only knew a little more! He had been able to work on the Big One because he had watched them, studied them with all the concentration Rutee had taught him to use. But Jony knew very well that an approach which might work with one life-form would not serve as well for another. Also, his own advice to Maba held true. This stranger might seem to be kin physically, but that did not mean that he really was.

Jony edged backward from his spy post. Mistrust still held—suppose that watcher *had* detected him, but had been cleverly concealing the fact by his actions? Better be gone from here and find another place from which he could still spy on the ship.

Crawling backward he again came to a complete halt. One of the People—and not too distant! Jony sat up, sure that he was far enough into the brush not to reveal himself to any ship lookout, and stared straight in the direction from which that shadowy touch of mind had come. A space of time as long as several breaths passed before Jony's eyes detected the lurker apart from his brush cover. Otik!

Jony's first impulse was to join the clansman—try to discover what had happened to the rest of the People and the twins. Then he remembered only too well how they had parted. His hand went to the collar. The first gesture must come from Otik; he was very sure of that.

The clansman knew Jony was there; had probably had him under observation all the time Jony himself was spying on the ship. Now Otik's head was turned so his eyes watched the boy. Well as he knew the People, Jony had never learned to read any emotion by the expression of their faces. He could not tell now whether Otik would allow contact at all.

Patience was one of the first lessons to be learned when dealing with the People. They lived by deliberation for the most part, and Jony had seldom seen them hurried. He waited, trying to match Otik's impassive stare with an answering one of his own.

Then the clansman hunkered forward, not rising to his feet, but using his hands against the ground as had his ancestors in those pictures. He came forward deliberately and slowly. There was a food net slung about one of his thick shoulders, but he had no staff.

Reaching a position several arms distance away from Jony, he sat back on his heels, his paw-hands dangling loosely between his knees. Otik was young; he had been Yaa's first cub some seasons before she had come to aid Rutee. As yet he had neither the bulk nor the

strength of Voak or Kapoor, though he could best
Trush in friendly wrestling. Had the clan done as always this year and met with other families, Otik might
well have gone hunting a mate.

The clansman continued to sit and stare. Inwardly
Jony fought his own impatience. He longed to sign a
question, a demand, for all the information Otik could
supply. Had others escaped? What had happened back
at that trampled space of grass in the open? Only now
he must wait until Otik accepted or rejected him.

The paw-hands moved. Otik gestured, grunted also,
as if to emphasize the importance of what he would
say.

"You go flying thing?" He gave that the quality of a
question, not a statement.

Jony had planted his staff close to hand to have his
fingers free to answer. Now he tried to keep his gestures as unhurried as he could.

"No go—yet."

"Your clan—they be so." Otik continued.

Jony found it disturbing that the other's face remained without expression, that he could learn so little
from Otik's attitude as to what thoughts moved behind
those large eyes. He had not really realized until this
moment how frustrating it could be when their powers
of communication remained so meager. Probably because, his mind now suggested, the daily life of the
clan had been so based on the essentials of food, familiar action, and the routine of ways Jony had known
for years, that he had not had to improvise any means

of conveying messages outside the bounds of those basic elements.

"Not *my* clan," he chose the best answer and the simplest he could think of. "Where Maba—Geogee?" He spoke their names aloud, aware that Otik would recognize those sounds, just as he could recognize and attempt to imitate the sounds which identified each of the clan by name.

"With your clan." Otik signed uncompromisingly. "Those came from sky." He stopped word signs and was acting out with his two paws what must have happened. One set of fingers pattered along the ground, plainly the clan traveling. The other hand flattened, swooped down upon that small band from the air and held in position over it for an instant or two. Then the fingers against the ground went limp, sprawling out flat. The hand representing the flyer scooped them up —made to carry them away.

Both hands returned to signs. "So Otik see."

Jony moistened his lips with the tip of his tongue. He must ask the next question but he feared what the reply might be.

"Dead?" he signed.

Otik made the sign for "not sure," and then, hesitatingly, the one for "sleep."

Perhaps the space people had a stunning device such as the Big Ones used. Jony hoped with all his heart that was so.

"Who?" he signed now. If Otik had escaped—had others also?

"Voak, Yaa," Otik barked the sounds Jony knew, added two more names.

Four of them in all then, as well as the twins. And the rest . . . ?

He did not need to ask, Otik was already signing that those were in hiding, watching. Though what hope they had of getting their people out of the sealed ship, Jony thought, was very small indeed.

"You go—your clan—" Otik repeated his earlier accusation, or was it simply a statement of fact as the clansman saw it?

"Not mine!" Jony made the gesture for firm repudiation.

Otik's hands were still. Did the clansman believe that? Jony knew of no proof he could offer to back up what he had said. Though he was certain at that moment he did speak the truth.

For a very long instant Otik simply sat and looked at him. Then the clansman made one of those lightning swift moves which could startle even one who knew them well but had become lulled by their usual placid, slow-moving attitude. Before Jony was aware, Otik had Jony's new staff in his hands.

Jony's reaction to grab for it, was, he knew at once, useless. That Otik had taken it at all was ominous. For a staff was its maker's and should not be handled by anyone else.

"You get—where?" Otik signed with one hand, keeping the staff closely gripped with his other.

"Found—by running water. Long time hidden in sand," Jony returned.

Otik inspected the find carefully, running fingertips along the pitted metal of the shaft, even bringing it to his nose for an investigative sniffing down the whole length.

"Thing—of old ones—" he declared.

"I found it—in sand, by running water," Jony returned with all the force of gesture he could muster. He must not let Otik get the idea that he had returned to loot the place of stones.

The place of stones! An idea which was wild, which he was sure no clansman would agree to, flashed into his mind. Against the weapons those of the ship must be able to muster what chance had the clan with their wooden staffs or their strength of body? But, suppose they possessed rods such as the sleeper held, with which Geogee had experimented so disastrously? A beam from one could bring down that flyer; might even eat a doorway into the ship for attackers.

One idea joined another in his mind. Jony breathed faster, unconsciously his fingers flexed in and out as if he were already to grasp one of those terrifying weapons right now.

There was a honk from Otik which startled Jony out of his own thoughts, back into the present and the realization that there was little hope of doing what he had dreamed in those moments of anticipated triumph.

The clansman had laid down the metal shaft. Once more he regarded Jony with that searching look. Then his paw-hands moved.

"You know a thing to help." Again no question, but a statement.

Jony's amazement was complete. How had Oti guessed that? Could it be that, athough he was unabl to tap minds with the People, the same difficulty di not exist on their side? Such a thought was more tha a little frightening.

"You know," Otik repeated. "I smell you know What this thing?"

Smell? Jony was bewildered. How could one sme. thoughts? The idea was dizzying, but he had no tim now to explore it.

"Things—in place of stones—" he took the plung. Otik could only say yes or no to that. "They better tha staff—like things from ship."

Otik made no answer at all. Instead, once more o hands and feet, he backed into the brush, leaving Jon alone. That was probably the end of any contact wit the remnants of the clan, Jony decided bleakly. Hi first move was to secure the metal staff. His second wa to think again of his wild idea of turning the finds i the storage place to use.

But the stone dens lay to the north. And suppos. Maba or Geogee had already told their captors abou the things found there? If so, the spacemen could easil fly that distance, take what they needed, and be awa before the People—or Jony—could cover half tha journey back on foot.

Maba had been so excited about the finds. Jony coul well imagine her telling these strangers about them. O was Maba a prisoner?

Jony tensed. Movement about him. Not Otik alone

there were others of the People ringing him nearly around, advancing toward him. There was only one opening in their circle, down-slope. To take that way of escape would bring him into view from the ship. He could only wait . . .

His suggestion to Otik might have touched off a reaction which—Jony's hand went to the loose collar. He remembered only too well those concealed fangs within it which Voak had displayed as a warning. On the other hand, he knew he had no chance of escaping from the clan's steady advance, nor could he use the staff—not against them!

Otik, then Trush, Huff, two of the younger females —Itak, Wugi—none of the older members of the clan. Jony could do little against even Itak and Wugi; he could not choose to fight.

The newcomers squatted down as Otik had done, their staffs beside them where a paw-hand could drop easily to a familiar hold. Otik had something else in his grasp—a coil of the cord they used to weave their nets.

"Talk—" Otik signed.

About his wild plan for looting the storage place among the stone walls? Jony could only guess. He signed slowly, trying to make sure he chose each time the most effective gesture to clarify his meaning. Though, with the limits imposed upon him, he despaired of making them understand or believe what he had to tell.

He told of his own journey underground to a great

cave—of the many strange things there. Finally of the
rod Geogee had found, and what happened when, in
the struggle to get it away from the boy, the alien
power had been inadvertently fired. That they would
believe in the instant disappearance of what it had
been pointed at, Jony was doubtful.

They listened, but did they understand?

No one signed a message for him to read as he finished. Instead they spoke among themselves, leaving
Jony baffled as always by the succession of sounds
which had no meaning for the ears of his species. Each
made some comment in turn. Then, though Jony was
not sure of what had been said, he sensed that the ver-
dict was against him.

He reached for his staff, though he was sure he could
never turn its terrible might against any of the People.
But Otik had again gotten paw on that, and it was
gone! At length Otik rose to his feet and loomed over
Jony.

When Jony tried rising to face the young clansman,
the weight of Trush's paw-hands on his shoulders held
him where he was. Otik uncoiled his cord, hooked an
end through the collar, and made one of the deftly tied
knots the People used.

He gave a jerk, bringing the edge of the collar tight
against Jony's throat as if he meant that as a warning.
Then he turned away, and Jony, now released, had to
follow. It was plain that he had worsened his cause
with these clansmen, instead of bettering it. He was
angry now with his own stupidity at voicing a sugges-

tion which must have aroused their deep-set rage against their one-time captors, turning it toward himself.

The clan had no campsite, but they had taken up station within a thick covering of brush which would give them cover overhead if the flyer came cruising. There were four more awaiting the return of Otik's squad with their prisoner—three were females, the fourth old Gorni, who had once been chief, but who had yielded to Voak as his strength had lessened.

It was to him that Otik went, reaching down to put the end of Jony's leash in the paw-hand of the old one. One of Gorni's eyes was covered with a white film so that he had to always turn his head slightly to view anything directly before him, as he did now.

But he did not use sign language; instead he gave the leash a tug which again brought the collar painfully against Jony's flesh. At that rude demand that he sit, Jony dropped down. Otik also laid the metal staff before the elder, as if to clinch some argument. But Gorni only glanced at that briefly.

With his free hand, the other never losing that tight hold on the leash, the clansman began to sign very slowly:

"You are now walker on fours. You do what People say. You are People's *thing*." He touched the fruit net looped about him. "This People's thing. You like this —not People—just *thing!*"

Jony wanted to loop both hands in the leash, tear it loose from the oldster's hold. He knew better than to make any such move. He was now a "thing," perhaps having some use for the clan, but without any freedom to be Jony.

The anger which he had known, young as he was, when in the cages of the Big Ones, burned in him once more. Only he could see the side of the People, too. They did not trust him. What of those the flyer had taken—the spacemen who looked like Jony, who resembled the pictures in the storage place and the stone woman? Perhaps the People had always feared that Jony himself might revert, to become one with their enemies. Only when he was small had they tolerated him, as they did the twins, as a weak, helpless thing not to be feared. Then he had directly sought out the place of stones, aroused in them the fear that the old days might so return. After that, to add to their fear, had come the arrival of the sky ship and the capture of the clansmen. The People were only doing what they could for their own protection.

What was the worst was that he must have, by his suggestion of raiding the storage place, aroused in them a belief that he was intending to take over once again. They had undoubtedly dismissed his talk of their finding and using the weapons as being deliberate falsification on his part, or as an indication that he held them in contempt.

Looking at Gorni's impassive face, then glancing from one to another of those ringing him around, Jony could see no way of impressing them with the fact of his own innocence of any desire to harm them. Yet he had to do just that.

The ship might lift now, taking with it, into the unknown of the far skies, their own people and the twins! Above all else the People must somehow find a way to prevent that—though Jony could not see now any hope of rescue.

JONY'S LEASH WAS RELEASED BY GORNI, ONLY TO BE fastened by another of those tough knots to a sapling strong enough to resist any attempt of his to break loose. For the moment the boy had to accept the knowledge that he could do nothing. But neither could he believe that this was the end, that the clan would continue to consider him a "thing," and that he might not be able to find some way to rescue those on the ship.

If he could reach Maba or Geogee . . . Just as Rutee had once instructed and trained for the day when he could get to freedom, perhaps he could work through concentration to make the twins aid him now in the same fashion.

Wugi came near enough to place on the ground two fruits and a leaf twisted around about a handful of grass seeds. Even a "thing" was to be fed. And Jony ate the portion hungrily.

His metal staff remained lying on the ground near Gorni. Nor did the elder make the slightest move to examine it as Otik had. Jony eyed the sharp edge of the hook longingly. By the use of that the leash could be easily severed; he freed. But to go where, do what?

Impatience ate at him until he wanted to pound the wet ground with both hands and howl aloud his misery. If he could only make them understand! Concentrate on the ship? Or would such mental touch guide the spacemen here? He wanted . . .

Otik returned. The young clansman had been away in the brush, perhaps once more spying on the invaders. Going directly to Gorni he conveyed some report. Jony watched, longing to be able to understand. If he could only share such open communication perhaps he might make the People understand the folly of not listening to him. They had, he was sure, little idea of the weapons and instruments which the ship people might use. Jony's own knowledge was only the bits and pieces relayed to him by Rutee, who had, in turn, a very limited grasp of the subject. That, and what he had learned in the lab of the Big Ones. But those scraps of information were certainly infinitely more than the People possessed.

Both Gorni and Otik eyed Jony now. He could guess that what they said had to do with him. At last Otik came to the sapling, loosed that knot and gave a jerk, to signal Jony to follow. A call from behind made Otik turn his head.

Wugi, leaves wrapped about her fingers so she did not touch the bare metal of the staff, had taken up Jony's find. She carried the weapon with the attitude of one disposing of a loathsome thing and held it out to Otik. Plainly this was not to be left behind.

If Wugi did not care to touch the weapon-tool, Otik had no such scruples. He lacked a staff. Perhaps, in spite of clan opinion, he had a lurking desire to keep this one. At any length he readily took it into his hand. Then, with another jerk, but no signed command (as if Jony now lacked the intelligence to understand such a thing), the clansman pushed out of their small brush camp, heading back up-slope of the ridge.

The rain was slacking, though periodic gusts struck them in the open, driven by a new wind. At least the sky was lighter. Jony could see the position of the ship and the flyer nearby in clearer detail than he had earlier. Also the ramp was run out once more, and there was a cluster of figures gathered on the lower edge of it. The spacemen now wore coverings over their heads which made them look unnatural, as if they were in truth a race as alien as the Big Ones. But the smaller figure with them—even at this distance Jony recognized Maba!

As far as he could determine she was under no restraint, but mingled freely with the off-worlders. As he caught plain sight of her, she flung out one arm in a typical exaggerated Maba gesture, the fingers of that hand pointing north. Telling them of the stone place?

But why was Maba free? Mind-controlled? Memory supplied that as a very probable answer. Jony's anger against circumstances, and now against these intruders, flared higher. Maba, to be so controlled! What Rutee had always feared for any of her children had happened.

Because of that anger Jony sent a sudden probe, striving to find out just how much they had taken over the girl. Was her normal mind totally blank so that she was only animated by the wishes of the space people, after the fashion of those blank-eyed captives of the Big Ones who walked blindly through what life their owners allowed them to retain?

His probe met no barrier, no hint of mind-control! Jony's shaft of Esper power had sharpened to meet the resistance he expected, but instead went straight into Maba's own thought-stream.

"Maba!" Aware that the worst had not happened, Jony was excited. Could he plant a thought of escape —of aid—now?

He watched that small figure eagerly. Her arm had dropped limply to her side, she swayed, and perhaps would have fallen to the ground, had not one of the spacemen caught and steadied her. Jony had put too much force in that contact. He retreated at once, aware of the danger of his move as caution returned too late.

The invader who supported Maba gathered the girl up in one swift movement, turned and ran back up the ramp into the ship. However, his two companions did not follow. Instead they headed for the flyer, throwing themselves through an opening which appeared in its bubble top, as if they sought safety from attack.

Jony guessed that they were aware of his attempt to contact Maba, that now they would again be on search for him. He turned to Otik. Let the clansman understand that Jony's presence was what would draw trouble straight to the People. He signed with all the authority he could bring to the matter:

"Those know I am here—they will hunt—they can track—"

Otik gave that small turn of the head which signified indifference.

"No one can find when People are warned," he returned.

"They can," Jony had kept part attention on the flyer. The bubble was closed, the machine rising steadily into the air. "They have a way—"

Was he getting Otik to really listen? If the clansman would not, the People were probably doomed to the same fate as had already swallowed Voak, Yaa and the rest.

"Show— You go—that way—"

To Jony's momentary relief, Otik dropped the leash before he pointed with the metal staff along the ridge, away from that section where the clan had gone to cover.

Jony began to run, scrambling down under the roofing of the brush, indeed leading any chase away from the others. He had not the slightest hope that the People could match the weapons of the strangers. But he had once mind-befuddled a Big One, and he might just have a chance to do the same with these new invaders. If he could escape detection, and was sure he had, he would head back to the stone place, arm himself with the most potent weapon he could find there. Unless, with Maba's help, the strangers got there first.

Why was Maba helping these invaders if she was not mind-controlled? The question haunted him, but Jony could give no real time to such a problem now. He must use all his wits to try and escape that flyer whose buzzing grew ever louder.

The leash dangling behind him caught once on a bush with a backward jerk which nearly swept him off his feet and brought the collar constrictingly tight against his throat. Jony tore the cord loose and then made a tight roll of the end about his waist, unable to take the time to pick the knot on the collar. Here ground was rough and the rain had slicked clay into greasy slides, so that twice he lost his footing and tumbled down.

He kept to cover with all the skill he had learned when in vor bird country. Only that buzz overhead was continuous; they were apparently able to follow him with the same ease as if they saw with their own eyes every movement he made, every dodge and evasion he tried.

Then—

Jony stumbled forward on feet which suddenly refused to support him. A sense of weakness, of floating, made him feel as if he were no longer trying to run, but rather rested on air which was moving . . . He made one last desperate attempt to hold on to his consciousness—and lost.

His head hurt. That was the next thing of which he was truly aware: a headache so strong, so vast, that it filled not only his skull but his whole body. At the same time a sour nausea moved him into retching. When that shaking passed, he endeavored to lie very quiet. For a little then the pain seemed to lessen.

He opened his eyes. Then shut them quickly as light (a glaring light which had nothing of the sun's glow in it) stabbed deeply, adding to the pain in his skull. Sounds—

Jony tried to concentrate on the sounds. Those of wind in the grass and across brush? No. Here was a murmur of a voice, but he could not make the effort to try to understand what words came so faintly.

Scent—smells . . .

Jony's body went rigid with the old fear. Once, long ago, he had been used to such smells. In the lab of the Big Ones. He was back—back there! The horror of it left him trembling.

See—he must see! He forced his eyes open; endured the pain that glaring light caused. There was a smooth expanse over him—not the sky. He must be in the flyer —or even the ship!

His old hatred of the cage came back full force. As he forced his head to turn slowly, his eyes to remain open, he discovered he was lying full length on some support he could not see. Facing him were the furnishings of a lab— NO!

Maybe he uttered some sound aloud, for a body moved into his limited range of vision. Someone stood within touching distance. And that face bending above so that the stranger could observe him was not that of a Big One. Or even of a mind-controlled. There was too much intelligence in those eyes, the expression on the dark face too alert and knowing. That this was one of the spacemen Jony now had no doubt.

"How do you feel?"

Jony blinked. He understood the words, save that

they were accented differently from the speech Rutee had taught him, which he used with the twins. Rutee's people?

Making what seemed to him to be an exhausting effort, Jony asked slowly in return:

"Who . . . are . . . you . . . ?"

The stranger nodded as if the fact that Jony could speak at all was encouraging.

"I am Jarat, the medic."

"I am in the ship—" Jony did not quite make that a question, he was already sure of the answer.

"In sick bay, yes."

"Maba . . . Geogee . . ." he hesitated then and licked his lips unsure whether he dared ask his final question. Would it awaken the suspicion of this —this—medic (whatever that could mean)? "The People . . . ?"

"Maba and Geogee are safe with us," Jarat replied.

But he said nothing about Voak, Yaa, the others. Were they—*dead?*

"How is he?" Another had moved up beside Jarat, to stare down at Jony. "Can he answer any questions yet?"

"Let him get orientated first, Pator. You know what a stunner can do—"

The one Jarat had addressed was plainly impatient, Jony thought. Ask him questions, about what—the People? The place of stones? In that moment he made up his mind, he intended to answer nothing until he knew what had become of the People, if he were now a prisoner in this place which reminded him so much of the old captivity.

He closed his mouth tightly, his return stare nearly a glare of defiance. Whether the spacemen understood his attitude or not, Jony could not guess, but the second did step back out of the range of Jony's sight, leaving Jarat there alone.

The medic held something in his hand which he touched to Jony's upper arm. There was no pain from that contact; instead there followed a soothing of the ache in his head, then throughout his body. Unconsciously he relaxed against the pad on which he lay.

"That better?" Jarat did not wait for any answer. "Take this now—"

He put a tube to Jony's mouth, and, without wanting to in the least, Jony allowed it between his lips.

"Give a good hard suck," Jarat ordered.

Jony obeyed. Warm liquid was the result, and he swallowed. That, too, seemed to have not only a good taste but a pleasant reaction on his body.

"Take a nap," Jarat was smiling. "When you join us again you'll find yourself a lot better."

He was as authoritative as if Jony were mind-controlled after all. The boy's eyes did close, and he was almost instantly asleep. This time sleep without dreams.

When Jony roused, there was no change in the light about him. But the pain in his head was gone, he felt rested, relaxed as he had not in a long time. Levering himself up on his elbows, he looked carefully around.

The place in which he lay had some of the same

equipment he remembered from the lab, but all made to a much smaller scale. And there were no cages. As he made sure of that, Jony gave a gusty sigh of relief. He had half expected to see the People shut up so, awaiting what torments their captors would devise, as his kind had suffered with the Big Ones.

His head felt light and he was a little dizzy, as he might have been had he not eaten for too long a time. But he was able to sit up, swing his scratched and bruised legs over the edge of the narrow shelf-like place on which he had been lying.

They had taken his kilt away and—his hands suddenly went to his throat. The collar! That was gone also. Naked, he stood beside the shelf, steadying himself with one hand as he looked around. There were many boxes, shelves with things on them—all objects he could not name. But as far as he could see there was no one about.

Jony tried a few steps, still holding on to the shelf. He was stronger, able to manage. Letting go his anchorage, he began a tour of the cabin, eager to find the door. He had no idea if he could get out of the ship unnoticed. But no one could be sure of anything until an attempt was made.

Just as he reached the one wall which was bare of shelving, though it had no opening in it that he could mark, there came a small sound. That sought-for door appeared, directly before him, with a suddenness which held him immobile through sheer amazement.

The spaceman who had named himself Jarat stood

there. For a second or two his astonishment seemed equal to Jony's. Then he smiled and stepped in quickly, the open slit closing firmly behind him, though he did nothing to make it do so.

"So—you are not only awake, but ready to begin living again, Jony?"

"How did you know my name?" Somehow Jony resented slightly this greeting. The assurance of it made him feel young, small, on an equality with the twins in an odd way he could not define.

"Maba—Geogee. Did you forget they joined us?"

Jony edged back until he felt the shelf against the small of his spine.

"They did not join you," he said. "You captured them. As the Big Ones used to take their prisoners. What will you do with us?"

"Take you home," Jarat said.

"This is home." For Jony, for the twins it was. He had been so long on the Big Ones' ship he could not remember any other Outside except this one.

"You *are* human, you know," Jarat still had that note of one reassuring a cub as he spoke. "From what the children have told us you escaped from a Zhalan slave ship, you and your mother. They were born here, but it is not your world."

He slid a bundle of cloth off his arm, dropped it on the shelf near Jony.

"Brought you a ship suit. Ought to be close to your size—try it on. Captain Trefrew wants to speak to you as soon as he can."

Jony drew the bundle to him. If he put that on, he would be one with these ship people. And what of Yaa and Voak? Perhaps if he seemed willing to obey orders, he could not only discover what had happened to the clansmen, but also be able to help them.

Jarat had to show him how to seal the front of the one-piece garment which so entirely covered the body that it also included soft-soled pieces for the feet. Jony felt queerly stifled, too well enfolded, when he had it fastened up properly.

The medic looked him over critically. "Not too bad. That mop of hair would never fit inside a helmet. But, for the rest, you'll do."

Do for what, Jony wondered? He asked no questions now, hoping that he could discover what he needed to know about the ship without anyone guessing his purpose. Though this spaceman had claimed him as one of his own kind, Jony felt no kinship with him.

There were men and there were animals. Rutee had told him that her people had once used, almost uncaringly, animals as tools. Then *they* had become in turn the "animals," tools of the Big Ones. The People must have been animals as long as those of the place of stone had ruled, and afterwards . . .

His hand went to his throat again, still feeling that he should encounter the collar there. The clan had made him an "animal" for their purposes as a warning and a punishment.

"Strange to you, eh?" Jarat said. "Ask any questions you want—I know you have a lot to catch up on."

Jony shook his head. What the medic said was true, but not in the way Jarat meant it. He had not tried any mind-contact since he had awakened here, being cautious about that. Could he, if he wished, control Jarat? Make the other lead him to the People, free them all, as he had done with the Big One to arrange Rutee's escape? He did not know and, as yet, he was too wary to try.

But Jony used his eyes as they went; tried memorizing their path through this wilderness of the ship as he woud have searched for landmarks Outside. There was no sign of either Maba or Geogee, nor did Jony ask for them yet. Better simply obey orders and wait until he could learn more by himself.

He was aware, however, that his companion glanced at him intently now and again as if expecting more from him. Not that Jony paid too much notice; the ship itself held most of his full attention.

They went down a short way and came to a center well up which climbed a series of steps. The medic swung onto this; Jony followed. His feet, covered for the first time in his life, felt clumsy, and he went carefully.

Twice they passed other sections of the ship above, coming to a third. This time the medic swung off once more into a second short passage. Before him the wall opened to let Jarat through. Jony followed, hiding, as he hoped, his growing sense of being trapped.

This must be the captain. The man was seated at his ease. When he gestured, the medic went to the wall and snapped down two other seats, one of which he took, motioning Jony to the other.

Jony occupied only the very edge of that. In the first place to be seated so far above the ground felt unnatural to him, secondly he was too tense inside to relax much.

"So you escaped a Zhalar ship," the captain began abruptly. "And that years back. You have no idea of your home world?" His words came impatiently, as if Jony presented a problem he could have done without.

"Rutee said," Jony broke silence for the first time, "that it was a new colony. She and Bron had chosen to go. Then the Big Ones came . . . Bron could not be mind-controlled and he fought in the lab. They killed him." It was a story which had never meant too much to him though Rutee had hurt when she spoke of it. He always sensed that hurt when she told it.

"And you?"

"I was very small. They left me with Rutee in the cage. I don't remember back beyond the cages."

"This Rutee—your mother—she was mind-controlled?"

"No!" Jony scowled at the Captain. "Some of us they could not use so. Most they dumped. Rutee thought they wanted her to find out why. They used their machines on her many times . . ."

He shivered, hating this man for making him remember how Rutee had been dragged from the cage, how they would bring her back later. Sometimes seeming as if she were dead, at others moaning and holding her head, crying out if even he came close to her for a while.

"And you—?"

"They could not control me either. But they did not try much. Rutee thought they were keeping me until they got to their own world—wherever that was. She did not know why."

"And the twins?"

Jony's inner anger grew. Just as he had known and felt all Rutee's pain, so he had known her shame and despair. But this was the truth so he would tell it. Let these spacemen know what the Big Ones could do to the helpless.

"They put me in another cage, then they gave her to a mind-controlled male," he said starkly.

There was silence in the cabin. Jony did not look at either of the spacemen.

He heard the captain say a word he did not understand, sharply and bitterly. But the memory of Rutee had fired Jony into what might be recklessness. He arose abruptly from his seat to face the spaceman. Keeping his voice as even as he could, fighting down impatience and fear, he demanded:

"Where is Yaa?"

"YAA?" REPEATED THE CAPTAIN. HE SPOKE AS IF HE could not identify that name. "You mean little Maba. She is with—"

But Jony interrupted, determined here and now to learn the truth. "Yaa, the female of the People. You took her and Voak, and two others back there in the open."

"The female—" Jarat stirred. "She is—" Then he stopped abruptly, perhaps reading Jony's expression better than Jony could that of the captain. Jony rounded on the medic sharply.

"She is where? Have you killed her?"

Jarat shook his head. "Of course not! Specimens are—" Again he paused, almost in mid-word.

Jony fought to retain his self-control, in order not to show either of these strangers his instant hostile reaction.

"Yaa," he said with a deliberation which he hoped would make an impression on the two, "saved Rutee's life. She took the twins when Rutee died. Now—what have you done with her?"

Jarat's eyes dropped from Jony's compelling stare. So the boy turned again to the captain.

"I ask you—what have you done with the People?"

It would seem that he was not going to get a quick answer from the commander of the spacemen either. So Jony unleashed his search-sense, sending it straight into the captain's thought pattern.

A confused picture, but clear enough to bring to Jony a snarl, similar to the guttural utterances of an angry clansman, as his own answer to what he learned.

Yaa imprisoned among machines not too different from those of the Big Ones. Yaa, perhaps, mind-controlled! Jony's horror and anger fed the power of his concentrated talent.

The captain was shaking his head, his hands moved jerkily toward his belt, toward what Jony knew must be his weapon. The boy hurled at the officer all the force he could muster. Finally the man slumped in his seat and slid limply to the floor.

Jony was already turning toward the medic who had risen abruptly to his feet, openly alarmed. Once more the boy concentrated, thrusting ruthlessly into a mind which was wide open to his probe.

"Yaa," he ordered, "take me to Yaa!"

Jarat fought, attempting to raise barriers which Jony, in his fear and ire, overrode easily. Though for how long he might be able to do so he did not know. Stiffly the medic turned to the door, walking as if he fought with every muscle to regain command of the body Jony was forcing to answer to his own purpose. No promise to Rutee could hold now, not after what Jony had read in the captain's mind when he asked for Yaa.

They left the captain lying on the floor of the cabin. Jony did not know how long the spaceman would remain unconscious, and he was afraid he could not control two at the same time. He must reach Yaa and the others as soon as he could.

"Jony!" Maba's voice from below. But Jony did not allow himself now to think of anything which would break his hold over Jarat.

The medic began a slow descent of the central ladder, Jony impatient to force him ahead. He could feel the struggle of the other against his dominion, and he bore down with all the pressure he could exert.

"Jony!"

They had descended two levels. Maba stood there, beside the ladder, her eyes alight. Jony did not even glance at her. For the moment Maba did not count. She was free among these; Yaa, the others, were not.

"Jony, what is the matter?" She caught at his sleeve as he went past her. He freed himself with a quick jerk, intent upon controlling Jarat, keeping the medic moving.

"Jony . . . !" Now she sounded frightened. That did not matter in the least, though he was aware she had started down after them.

They were past the level from which Jony had first come, down by the next one. So far they had been lucky not to encounter any other of the crew. Jarat stepped away from the ladder on this level, stood swaying.

His face was wet with sweat as he made a maximum

effort to break Jony's control. Jony himself felt the drain of that power which he must use to keep the other both his prisoner and his guide. For Yaa—Voak —the People—he could do it!

"Jony—why—?" Maba's voice.

He shook his head against the irritation of her attempt to gain his attention. Jarat, staggering as he went, still battling control, headed down the passage, a very short one.

The medic raised his hand very slowly, his inner reluctance to do this thing strong even in that curtailed movement. Now Jarat's palm rested against the wall for an instant. Then, as had those in the place of stones, the wall itself parted, and they came through into the very place Jony had feared might exist.

The stench of fear here was as strong as the strange smells of the ship. There was Yaa, braced against the wall, metal bands holding her upright, her head encased in a helmet from which sprouted wires of uneven lengths. The purr of a machine was loud; louder still came a plaint which nearly unnerved Jony.

He looked away from Yaa to the other side of the place of torment. There Voak was fastened the same way. His head had fallen forward; his great eyes were closed. He might be asleep, save that that sound issued from his slack mouth.

Another of the spacemen bent over the purring machine, his eyes intent upon a lighted square at its top.

He gave Jarat a quick glance and went back again to his watching.

"Amazing, simply amazing," he commented. "The reading is unique."

"Yaa!" It was not Jony who cried that. Maba had caught up with them. Now she ran across to reach the furred figure against the wall. But the spaceman at the machine was too quick for her. He threw out one long arm and fended her off, fighting.

Jony had been shaken by the confirmation of his worst fears. His control wavered. Jarat broke free, whirling, his hands flying to his belt and weapon which hung there.

No staff, but— From a table nearby Jony snatched up a length of wire, making it into a lash. The People used braided vines so, and he had learned.

That loop flipped out, catching about Jarat's wrist.

"What's going on?" Maba's struggles still kept the other spaceman fully occupied. "What do you think you're doing?" He gave Maba a shake which did not in the least subdue her.

Jony moved in against the medic. The People wrestled and Jony knew their tricks. Whether they could save him now he had no idea. His body slammed hard against Jarat's, driving the man back against a table, jarring loose things which crashed to the floor. But the spaceman struck back swiftly, body-shaking blows Jony did not know how to counter.

He had only one weapon—and used it. Into the other's mind he sent a blighting concentration of all the force he could summon and aim.

Jarat, his hand raised for another attack, stumbled

forward, and went to his knees among the breakage from the table. Jony used his wire thong, bringing the other's wrists together behind his back, lashing them together.

"Jony!" Maba's cry was one of warning.

He hunched around. The other spaceman held her with one hand. In the other was a belt weapon pointed directly at him. Jony must make a last effort, though he was not sure how much of the force he could still summon. But he once more used his talent for assault.

The face of the spaceman twisted. He cried out with a queer rising scream. Maba, loose, sprang for his weapon hand, using her wiry strength to wrest the arm out of his grip. Before Jony could move, she turned it on its owner, pressed a button on the butt.

Her victim flopped forward, falling face down beside the still writhing Jarat.

"Him—too!" Maba leveled the stunner again.

"Don't kill—" Jony began, but she laughed recklessly.

"These don't kill, they just make people sleep." She pressed the button and Jarat also subsided.

Maba looked down at the spacemen, then she gazed up at Jony.

"I didn't know, Jony, truly I didn't!" she begged him to understand. "I didn't know what they did to Yaa . . ."

"Now you do," he answered shortly. "And I don't know if we can get out of here."

He was already at Yaa's side, working on those bonds which kept her thick-set body immobile. There was some trick to the fastening, as there had been a trick to the collar, and he could not discover it. They must hurry. The captain might already have recovered and alarmed the whole ship.

"Please, Jony," Maba hovered at his side. "I didn't know . . ."

He was fighting those stubborn bonds, pressing here and there, tearing with his fingers. What kept them fastened?

How had the Big Ones operated these things? Jony racked his memory without gaining any coherent answer. He backed away a step or so, and struck against the machine over which the spaceman had been so busy at their entrance. Could the machine control the locks? That was not impossible. But which of the many buttons in rows across it were the right ones? He feared to experiment lest he harm Yaa the more.

"Jony," Maba pushed close to him. "Look here." She held the weapon and was shoving it in his direction. "Could you use this to break . . ."

He did not want to touch the thing. Like the red rod, it represented a force he neither understood nor wanted to use.

"Drop that!" he ordered.

"No! With it we can get out of here, Jony. We can just put to sleep anyone who tries to stop us."

He adjusted his thinking. She was right. With that to defend the door of this place, they might have more time to work on the bonds which held Yaa and Voak.

"Jonnnneeee—"

Startled he looked around. Voak's head was up, his

huge eyes open wide. He had twisted his powers of speech mightily to utter that croak which approximated Jony's name. That he had something of the utmost importance to communicate, the boy knew. But his paw-hands were helpless, he could not sign any message. And Jony's sense could not connect enough to receive any real illumination.

The boy realized that Voak was making as great an effort of will as he himself had done earlier when he had held Jarat in control and forced the medic to lead him here.

Opening his mind as far as he could, Jony stared deep into the clansman's eyes. The—the place of buttons! He laid his hand on the edge of it. Voak's muzzle rose and fell eagerly. If the clansman knew . . .

"Maba," Jony gave the order crisply. "Go to the door. Be ready to use the weapon."

She nodded, detoured around their unconscious captives, stationed herself directly before the portal. The stunner, steadily grasped in both her hands, was raised breast high, held ready.

Jony began to hold his index finger over the buttons in their rows. He knew Voak was watching. But there came no signal. Did the clansman understand? He was sure Voak did; that he was feverishly waiting for Jony to reach the right one.

None of the first row, or the second. But, as Jony's fingertip hovered over the first one of the third row, Voak gave quick, vigorous assent. Jony applied pressure.

There was a click, and the bands holding Yaa snapped loose, as did Voak's also. The clansman lumbered across the cabin, reached his mate's side, to support her body against his while Jony raced to free her head from the network of wires. Voak's tongue caressed the fur of her cheek, and, uttering a weak small sound, she opened her eyes.

"Jony, I hear them coming!" Maba called.

There was a thudding from without, as if many feet pounded down that ladder at a speed which suggested attack was imminent. Jony got to Maba, grabbing the weapon from her.

"You hold it so," she told him, "and press that!"

"Where are the others—Geogee, the People?"

"Geogee went with the ones who wanted to see the stone place," she told him. "I don't know where they put Corr or Uga."

"And maybe we can't wait to find out," Jony returned grimly. He wondered if any one of them would win free of the ship. He might be able to control Jarat or any of the other spacemen one at a time. However, he was sure he could not extend that domination over the entire crew at once. He glanced at the prisoners on the floor. Could they be used as a bargaining point?

A grunt from Voak drew his attention. The clansman was leading Yaa away from the wall. Her eyes were only half-open. It was apparent she moved only because her mate urged her along. With one hand Jony made the sign for "danger," indicating the door.

Voak grunted again and dipped his nose in assent.

With his paw-hands he continued to pet and smooth Yaa gently, giving voice to a series of small rumbles.

Then, out of the air about them, a voice spoke:

"Attention—red alert . . . You in the lab. Jony . . . Maba . . . !"

For a single moment Jony thought that had been spoken by one of their prisoners. Only, when he glanced down, he saw that both men were still under the influence of Maba's weapon. Then who—and how . . . ?

He stared around wildly, searching for the speaker. Maba caught his arm, stood on tiptoe, her lips forming words silently, so he stooped closer and caught her whisper:

"They talk so from cabin to cabin. That is the captain."

Perhaps she could recognize the voice, but to Jony the order had an inhuman tone, cold and distant.

"Are you listening?" the unseen asked. "You cannot get out. Neither can you, Jony, use esper against us again. Try . . ."

Such was the compulsion of that command, Jony did. His thought-probe struck against an unbreakable barrier. The force of the meeting hurled his own power back at him like a blow, so he wavered on his feet.

"Jony!" Maba's anguished cry forced him out of that backlash. So, he thought bleakly, the only weapon he truly knew how to use was lost to him.

"Do you understand?" continued the voice. "We can dampen you as much as we want, knock you completely out, as we did before."

Perhaps they could. He had no measure of what forces they could control in turn.

"Use your intelligence," the words came out of the air to plague him. "You are completely in our hands. There is no escape . . ."

Jony threw back his head. That last had held an arrogant assurance which something in him refused to accept. Now he spoke aloud:

"Use *your* intelligence," he countered. "We have two of your people here."

"Just so. But if you attempt to bargain with them as hostages, we shall not play. You can remain where you are until you are hungry enough to agree to come out peacefully."

Before Jony could frame any answer to that, if the captain were still listening, Maba raised her voice with a tone he knew of old:

"You told me Yaa was all right!" she shouted. "You said you would let her and Voak, and Uga, and Corr go. But you hurt her! You *are* like the Big Ones after all!"

Her face grew flushed as her voice rose higher. Maba had always had a quick temper, now she was fast approaching the peak of one of her tantrums. She spun around, seizing the nearest object from the shelf on her right. Then, with a deliberation which spelled her full intent to do the most harm she could, she advanced on the box which had controlled the bands that had held the People prisoner. Raising a heavy bar in her hands, well over her head, she brought it down with all her might on the machine.

The glass panel on its top splintered. There was a flashing of sparks from the interior below.

"Try it now!" she shouted, "just try to use this to hurt Yaa again—or anyone else!"

Gripped by a frenzy close to hysteria, the girl battered at the machine. Jony made no move to stop her. In fact he was a little envious that he had not seen that obvious form of retaliation himself. Destroy the lab equipment, and the spacemen could not use it to torment any other prisoners they might take.

"Stop her! Stop her, you fool!" The man who had operated that installation at last raised his head from the floor waveringly, watching, with a shadow of horror on his face, Maba's destructive attack.

"Why?" Jony asked. "So you can use it on the People? She's right, you're no better than the Big Ones."

"You don't understand." The man tried to crawl toward the scene of action. Jony stepped swiftly between him and Maba, though the obvious distress of the spaceman had given him the beginnings cf an idea.

"She'll burn out the circuits!" The man's voice was half a howl now. "We'll all be fried in a backlash."

"Better that than end in your cages," Jony held his outer calm. The fear of this stranger was convincing— perhaps they were in danger. If they were, so much the better for his own poor hope of their survival.

"Maba—" Jony stepped behind the girl, catching her arms as she raised them above her head to deliver yet another attack on the very battered machine. There was a strange, unpleasant odor leaking from the box now.

"Let me go!" She thrust against him.

"Not yet," Jony returned. "Perhaps we can exchange something . . ."

Maba wriggled her head about so she could look up into his face.

"How about that?" Jony spoke directly to the space-man who was struggling to move closer. Beyond him the medic lay; his eyes, too, were now open. "Now listen very carefully, both of you. I think Maba has the right idea, I think this whole lab should be smashed. I don't like cages, I don't like people who look like me but act like Big Ones. I don't like my friends being hurt. Do you understand that?"

"We weren't hurting them—we were testing . . ." the spaceman returned.

"I have been tested—so," Jony said. "I have seen what happens to lab 'animals.' You believe these People are animals, don't you?" He bore in fiercely. "You need not make up an answer to please me, I can read what you really think—"

Jarat spoke first. "What do you intend to do now? Captain Trefrew cannot be pushed . . ."

"I can let Maba continue with her work here," returned Jony, "even join her. You see, having been a lab captive once, I have no intention of ever being so again. It is much better to be dead—"

"But," protested the other spaceman, "we have no intention of touching you or the children. Ask her—" he indicated Maba with a lift of his chin, "whether she has not been very well treated."

"I don't doubt it in the least," Jony returned. "You

accepted her as one of your own kind. But you see, we do not accept you as one of us! That is the problem for you to consider. We are of the People—" he motioned towards Yaa and Voak.

Whether the clanspeople had understood any of this exchange, Jony did not know. He was glad to see that Yaa was looking brighter, that she no longer leaned weakly against her mate. Perhaps if, by some uncommon stroke of fortune, they could get out of the ship she would be herself again.

"You are human stock," Jarat said.

"We are of the People," replied Jony with the same firmness.

"What will satisfy you?"

"Free passage out of this ship, with your prisoners."

He waited, his hold dropping away from Maba.

"If you have any way of talking to your captain," he added a moment later, "you had better do it. If not— when Maba gets tired—I shall take over, with a great deal of pleasure."

"YOU HEARD HIM, CAPTAIN," JARAT RAISED HIS VOICE a little. "I can assure you he means what he says."

There was silence except for a very faint buzzing out of the box Maba had assaulted. The spaceman who had tended that watched it now with the same apprehension one would feel on a cliff where vors were known to roost. It was plain that he now feared his own machine; was no longer master of it.

"Captain!" It was his turn to call out. "I-20 is building to critical!"

"Order your men away from our path, the other two of the People set free—" Jony restated his demands. "We have nothing to lose but our lives, and in your hands that is an escape of another kind. I know."

When there was no answer, he turned resolutely to Maba. "Give me that!" He reached for the bar she had used to such purpose.

"No!" the word was like a scream from the spaceman. "You'll—the backlash— You don't understand what you're doing!"

Jony shook his head. "The answer is that I do, very well indeed."

"The girl. You can't let her die."

"I would," Jony said slowly and distinctly, "kill her

with my own two hands rather than let her remain here with you."

Maba laughed. "He would do so," she nodded vigorously. "When Jony promises, he does as he says he will. And if he did not smash your machine, then I shall. You lied to me about Yaa and Voak. Uga is my cub-kin. Do you understand!" She leaned forward, her face only inches away from that of the struggling man. "We are of the same season, Uga and I—and so kin-bound. Jony, do it!" She straightened and shifted her fierce glance from the spaceman to the machine. "He is afraid; they are all afraid! Do it, Jony!"

He raised the bar.

"Captain!" The last appeal from the spaceman was frantic.

Jarat did not add to that protest, he was eyeing Jony narrowly as if trying to assess just how much of this was the truth. What he read in Jony's face must have convinced him.

"Captain," his voice was more controlled than that of his fellow. "He does indeed mean it. After all, we cannot judge these castaways by our own knowledge . . . not yet."

"Your passage out—" the words came gratingly as if the captain was forced against his will to utter each. "But we are not finished—"

"Our passage out," Jony returned.

"They lied before, they can do it again!" Maba flashed, but Jony had already thought of that.

"You will raise the barrier, the mind barrier," he

said. "I shall not try control, but I will know it if your men plan against us."

Again no answer for a long moment. Then: "Very well." He could sense the fury behind that agreement.

Now he used the mind-sense. Yes, the barrier was gone. He motioned Maba to the door, Yaa and Voak were already there. The portal slid open. Outside there was no one. Jony held to his probe, spacemen were above, below . . .

"Down—" he gestured to the ladder. If Yaa could not negotiate that descent, he did not know what they could do.

But her strength seemed to be returning. Maba scrambled down first, then Voak followed, Yaa moving more slowly behind him. Jony came last, concentrating on locating every indication of life ahead and behind as his sense sought them out.

Luckily they were only one level above that from which the ramp stretched open to freedom. And below, awaiting them, huddled the two younger People. Maba threw her arms about Uga's furry shoulders, hugged her.

"Out!" Jony made that order urgent. But the People did not need his command, they were already padding down the ramp, into freedom. He followed. So far, his mind-search told him, no one within the ship had stirred. But once they were outside they would be highly vulnerable. Then would the captain keep his side of the bargain? Jony distrusted that as much he would any bargain with an enemy.

They were crossing the open now, heading to the ridge. Uga and Corr appeared unaffected by their imprisonment, but it was plain that neither Voak nor Yaa had their old strength or were able to move at the best speed the People could keep.

Jony played rear guard. He still had the stunner taken from the spaceman, as well as the second which he had twitched out of Jarat's belt before he had left, and which he now entrusted to Maba.

She raced ahead, to stand halfway up the ridge, facing back toward the ship. Jony had no idea how far the range of those weapons was. He only hoped that Maba might cover their retreat from her position as well as he could from his rear guard station.

Luckily the flyer was gone. With that overhead they would not have any chance at all. Could those within the ship now perhaps strike out at them with some longer range attack? He knew so little . . .

The People has passed Maba's stand. Uga and Corr had already crested the ridge. He knew they would get under cover with all possible speed. Yaa and Voak followed.

At the foot of the rise Jony faced around as Maba had done. His mind-probe was blotted out again. Back in the ship they had once more raised that barrier. Which could mean attack to come!

"Jony." Maba's voice— "Come—"

He went, with a burst of speed. Yaa and Voak were out of sight. Maba had moved to the crest where she stood, still on guard. He was breathing hard as he came level with her.

More than anything now he wanted to set that rise of solid earth and stone between them and the ship. He still could not quite believe that they had gained their freedom.

Jony watched the ship closely, more than half expecting to witness an exit of force to trail them. Or would the spacemen wait for the return of the flyer to start pursuit? Geogee! In the stress of their breakout he had forgotten about the boy. What had they said— Geogee had gone to guide the spacemen to the place of stones. Jony had no doubts that meant the storage place. The power rods . . . !

Glancing around he saw no sign of the People. The fugitives had melted away into the brush cover with their usual skill at concealing themselves. Maba pulled at the sleeve of the garment the ship's people had forced on him.

"They—they'll come after us, Jony?" she asked that as a question.

"Maybe they're waiting for the flyer."

"Geogee—he's with them, Jony."

"I know. We'll have to get him away, too." But at the moment he was more worried about what the boy could have shown the spacemen. The captain, those on board the ship, had displayed no dislike for the children, not until Maba had turned against them. Could he believe Geogee was safe—for now?

"You must tell me," he rounded on Maba, "all you can about them. What are they doing here?"

Maba's expression was one of trouble. "They want to come here—to have a colony, Jony. There was a big fight—somewhere 'way out there—" with the hand not holding the stunner she motioned to the sky. "The Big Ones, they were driven away from this part of space. Now these people hunt new worlds for more colonies."

"This world *has* its People," Jony looked down over her head to the bush into which Yaa, Voak and the others must have gone. "These spacemen cannot just come and take it."

"Jony," she moved closer to him. "Maybe they can. They showed us things. They have a big box and you sit there watching it. Inside the box are pictures and the people in them move and do things. They showed us how they live on other worlds. Jony, there're lots and lots of them. There must be more than all the trees you ever saw," she was plainly reaching for some kind of comparison to make the biggest impression on him. "And they have a lot of sky ships, bigger ones than this one. They say that they need more room for their people, and they were so glad to find this world. Because they can breathe here, and it is like others where they already live."

"But it is not theirs," he repeated. "It belongs to the People!"

"Did it always, Jony? Remember what we saw in the pictures . . ."

He seized the girl fiercely by the shoulders, stared straight down into her astonished face.

"That was wrong, Maba. The People are not animals, *things* to be used—"

He remembered at that moment what Voak had said to him when they had set the collar about his neck

Things to be used—like a staff, or a fruit net—a *thing* not a person. The People had won free from that once, such bondage must never be set on them again.

"But, Jony, what can we do to stop them?" Maba came directly to the point. "The spacemen can make people go to sleep with these things," she waved the stunner. "They can fly right over us and do that. That's the way they caught us. The People won't even be able to get near enough to them to fight back."

This was the unwelcome truth and he had to face it. Added to that was the possibility that Geogee might this very moment be showing the spacemen the weapons of the stone people. Jony had no idea *what* he and the clan could do, but he was also certain that they must not allow these others to take this world without a struggle. It remained to be seen what the People would think or do for their own protection.

"Come!" He started down after the vanished clanspeople. If he could only communicate fully with Voak! At such a time as this sign language fell woefully short.

He half expected to be met by Otik, at least when they got into the bush cover. But there was no sign of any of the People there. Now Jony used his special sense, searching for the faint impressions they had for him. Nothing—near. The People were on the move, which was only what he could expect. They would travel as far from the ship now as they could.

And he could send no message to halt them. That they were angling northward again was the only promising bit of evidence for him.

The brush, through which he had learned long ago

to slip with a minimum of obstruction, caught at his ship garment over and over and over again. His body felt hot and sweaty, his skin was chafed where the material rubbed against neck, armpit, along his thighs. At least Maba was not so encumbered.

She did not have the kilt she had worn, but her new covering was only from neck to knee. Jony guessed it had been improvised, there being no ready garment on the ship small enough for her to wear. She was able to slip and duck, weave in and out far faster than he could.

They had trail enough to follow and the People had certainly learned quickly that one must keep under cover. Jony kept listening for the buzz of the flyer. Did those in the ship have any far ranging means of communication to recall that?

As he went he fired questions at Maba, and she answered as readily and promptly as she could. Her account was of very good treatment, that Jarat and the captain had both questioned her and Geogee as to their past. The twins, not seeing any danger, had poured out in return all they knew. The spacemen had been particularly excited about the stone place.

"They might well be," Jony returned grimly to that, "seeing what could be hidden there—"

"You mean the rod Geogee found—that one that made things go away," Maba agreed. "He told them about that. They wanted to see one."

Jony could well guess that they did. What had he and the twins done to the People who had given them life? Brought the space ship? No, that might have landed if Jony and the twins had not explored the place of stones. But to give the spacemen guidance to the secrets hidden there!

In spite of the steady progress of the clan Jony and Maba caught up with them by nightfall. They were not challenged by Otik who was plainly on sentry, but neither were they welcomed. He only stared at them as they went by into the campsite, where the nests were very small and thin, meaning a short rest only.

Voak squatted by his mate who lay full length on the biggest and best of that bedding. He was flanked on either side by Uga and Corr, and Jony thought it plain that they were sharing with the rest the details of their imprisonment and treatment on board the ship.

The boy held Maba by his side when she would have sped to Yaa. Not until he had some form of acceptance from Voak and the rest would he know whether they could stay, were once more clan-kin in the way which would matter most.

Voak was silent as he surveyed Jony and the girl. It was Yaa who voiced some rumbles in their talk. Her mate glanced down at her, then back at Jony. Getting ponderously to his feet, he crossed to face the boy squarely. His bulk and height made Jony seem small, unimportant, or so he felt. But at least the clan chief was not ignoring him as he half expected he would. The collar was gone, but it had not been loosened by the People. In Jony's mind it still lay about his throat until he won full fellowship with them again.

"Ship thing"—Voak's hand arose to sign—"bad."

Swiftly Jony made answer. "Bad!"

"People—sky thing—like—you."

Jony could not deny that outward appearance. He cast around frantically for some comparison he could use to suggest that outward and inward should not be confused.

"Hoppers, Jony," Maba produced the possible key, "remember hoppers and pinchers!"

The comparison he had once made for her! If Voak would only accept that belief. Jony gestured. His hands moved in the sign for hopper, then for hide and hunt —and then for the pincher—and again hide. The People all knew of that strange method of concealment which the hopper could use and how often it deceived the chosen prey.

Having so outlined something which they already knew Jony launched into his parallel thought.

"Sky ones—hoppers. Jony, Maba, Geogee—pinchers. Look alike—different."

Voak appeared to consider the idea.

Jony plunged on. "Jony captured—find Yaa, find Voak, Corr, Uga—make them come out of bad place."

Now that Voak could not deny.

The boy continued, "Jony not clan-kin to ship bad ones, Jony clan-kin to Voak, Yaa."

He waited tensely. This was his bid for acceptance. If Voak refused to believe, then he and Maba would be no-kin—alone—in spite of what they had done to free the People.

From where she lay Yaa again spoke. Voak moved uneasily, his head turned a little toward her and then back again.

"Geogee—take bad ones—place of stones," Voak signed.

"Geogee not know what happened to Yaa, Voak. Geogee, Maba, not told. Think all well."

Would Voak believe that either?

"Bad ones find power to make People *things*. Place of stones have power to do so."

Jony signed assent and then daringly added, "People must keep bad ones from taking power."

Voak's jaws opened, displaying his most formidable fangs. He scowled as he did when facing a smaa or a vor.

"Voak—People—have no this"—he turned and caught the staff out of Trush's paw-hand, shook it in Jony's face—"like bad ones. Those have sleep sticks. Voak go to sleep before getting near to bad ones."

Jony pulled the stunner from the front of his ship suit.

"Sleep stick for Voak." He held it out.

But the clansman retreated a step. "Bad thing. Not for People."

"Better for People than to be in ship again."

From those massed around behind Yaa old Gorni pushed. He held the metal staff Jony had found. Now he pointed the curved tip of this straight at the boy's breast.

"Give paw!" he signed.

Jony transferred the stunner to his left hand, extended the right. Before he could resist, Gorni had caught his wrist, held on in an unbreakable hold. In spite of the clansman's advanced age his physical strength could not be matched by any off-worlder.

He dropped the sharp point of the staff, piercing the skin on the back of Jony's hand. Then he dipped his muzzle and sniffed long at the bubble of blood forming there. The meaning of his action was lost on Jony. But he believed from the small stirs of the watching People, that to them this act held some vast importance.

Gorni gave a last sniff, raised his head. "Smell right," he signed. "Clan-kin."

Jony gave a great sigh of relief. What the smell of his blood had to do with acceptance, he could not tell. Only it was very apparent from the attitudes of those Gorni had so reassured, that he was again one of them. And, being one of them, he must now try to make them understand the danger from the sky ship. Not only for the present, but in days to come.

If Maba was right—that this one ship was the forerunner of a colony—then they were in desperate straits and must move. In what direction and how, Jony did not know. It might be they were already defeated in that instant when the ship had made a safe landing. But he refused to accept that; he dared not believe such a thing could happen.

With more confidence than he had felt for a long time, Jony signed to Voak:

"People must not let bad ones take any power things from place of stones."

Voak hunched his massive shoulders a little. Almost Jony could believe that the clansman felt the same breath of defeat which had touched his own thoughts.

"How stop?"

How indeed? Jony could give him no answer yet. Perhaps if they returned there he could tell. But would Voak agree to break the rule of the People and enter a place the clan held in such disgust and dread?

"We must find a way. What they take—" In his mind Jony could picture very vividly the use of a red rod with intent, not chance the way Geogee had done. "What they take could be very bad."

Voak made the down and back muzzle assent of his species. "People go far—bad ones not find."

"Bad ones can move through the air faster than People can travel." Jony hoped that Voak would agree that was true. He, himself, was under no illusions as to how successful the flyer and the sky ship were.

Perhaps Voak wanted to deny that, but he could not. Instead he made a dismissing sign which Jony must obey. Taking Maba's hand, the boy crossed to the other side of the campsite, allowing the People to discuss the matter in their own way. Only he was sure of his own plans.

"Jony, what if they won't go to the place of stones?" Maba asked.

"I shall have to go anyway," he told her. Best get that settled now.

"And me," she said promptly.

"No! You will stay with Yaa and the People." He was going to be firm about that.

Some of her old rebellion countered that order instantly. "I won't! I know more about the place of pictures than you do. I found the way in. If you try to go without me, I'll follow."

She would, too, he had no doubts about that. Nor did Jony believe that the People would make any move to prevent her.

"Geogee's there," she was continuing. "And, Jony, Geogee, he likes Volney, he follows him around all the time. Volney has promised him he can learn to fly a sky ship someday. I don't think Geogee would listen if *you* told him they're bad. But he might listen to me."

"Who is Volney?" Jony demanded.

"He's the one of them who knows how to make things go up and travel in the air," Maba explained. "Geogee is all excited about the machines. He told them lots about what he saw in the place of stones. And I heard them talking, they think some of those old people left very important things there. Geogee will want to stay with them, not us, unless we can make him understand."

She was very serious about this, and Jony knew that she was telling the full truth. The tie between the twins was a deep one, it could well be true that Maba could accomplish more in making Geogee understand the danger threatened by these strangers than he ever could. But he hated to take her with him into what might be not only hopeless but a dangerous struggle.

"I will go!" She returned to her own statement of fact.

Before he could find any answer, Voak broke from the cluster of the People, came toward them. Jony could read nothing, of course, in that furred face, but Voak's paw-hands were moving.

"We go—to see . . ."

At least he had won that much, thought Jony, soberly, but not in triumph. He could be entirely wrong, leading them all into danger. There was only that instinct within him saying stubbornly that this was all which was left for them to do.

THEIR PARTY DID NOT APPROACH THE PLACE OF STONES (which Maba said the spacemen referred to as a "city") by the way Jony had done so before, openly down that solid river which flowed directly into its heart. Once Voak had assented to this journey, he had taken command of their small party, leaving behind the females and the young under orders to move off to the west, into a region of deeper and more impenetrable woods which they hoped would be a barrier against any more attacks from the flyer.

Their own return journey north had followed, at the best pace of the People. Even Jony, impatient as he was, realized the wisdom of not becoming too tired before they reached their goal. Such progress demanded the better part of two days of travel, with only a short interval of rest during the dark hours.

Once more they crossed the open fields about the river of stone before working back into those ridges which Jony believed were near the place of the cage. This passage took them almost the whole of another day before they reached a ridge point from which the city could be viewed, not from the front, but directly from the rear.

Jony sighted no sign of the flyer. However, the machine could have set down on the far side of the cluster of rising walls. As he lay near Voak, concealed by the grass and brush on the crest, the boy used his own method of locating who might be below.

Even if those on the flyer had been warned in some way (Maba stated positively the off-worlders were able to communicate even at a distance by using machines) to set up that same mind barrier the ship people had used to repel his control, the very fact they did this would be assurance they were still here.

He sought Geogee, fixing a picture of the boy in his mind, sending out a probe to pick up the familiar pattern of the twin's thought processes. Jony encountered no barrier—and—yes!

So faint was it, that he was not sure he could track the touch with any certainty to where Geogee was. But he *had* caught it. Voak raised himself head and shoulders from the ground. His wide nostrils expanded, to flatten again visibly. Then the clansman ducked his head in the gesture of agreement before Jony had a chance to report his own findings.

Crabwise, Voak retreated from the top of the ridge. Jony slipped after him. When that bulk of earth and stone wall stood between them and the city, the remainder of Voak's people drew in to meet the scouts.

"Scent—strong—they—there." Voak signed.

He looked gravely at Jony who was trying to think of what to do next. Whether the ship had warned the men in the city was unknown. If the off-worlders had been so alerted, then the chance of his own party's success was lessened.

Remembering the stone-walled dens, Jony knew that

there were places in plenty where one could play hide-and-seek. Thus the People, with their natural tendency to take cover efficiently at need, might still well work their way in secretly. Only, the strangers had the superior weapons, that could operate at a distance and far more effectively. Also—would the People even consent to enter the city?

His companions were talking in their own speech. Jony sat quietly, his hands clasped on the metal shaft which had been returned to him, frowning a little as he thought of one ghost of a plan and then another, rejecting each in turn. Then he remembered, with sudden and complete clarity, the cage in the mountains. Why it came to him at that moment he did not know.

There lay the evidence that the People, in the past, had been able to deal with those having superior weapons, and very effectively! He hunched forward and his change in position must have registered on Voak. For the clan chief swung his head a little to again eye Jony with that steady regard.

The next move depended on how much Voak could or would tell Jony, and then on whether the People would trust him fully. He longed bitterly for the power to read their thoughts, more so than he ever had in his life before. But he . . .

Voak signed: "What do?"

Had the clansman guessed that Jony did have, at last, a nebulous idea? One, however, that depended so much on others, having so many flaws even he could see, that it might also fail?

"The People were there," Jony tried to sort out in signs what he must learn, if they would let him. He pointed to the ridge behind which lay the city. "They wore collars, they were things . . ."

Voak made no assenting gesture to that. Jony refused to be daunted.

"How People be freed?" He made his question boldly.

For a long instant he was afraid Voak would refuse to answer. There came a series of sounds from others about, until Voak signed silence with a paw-hand. His muzzle sank forward until it nearly rested against the pied-fur on his chest. Jony waited.

Maba, who had squatted beside the boy, moved. Jony put out his own hand in a signal to be still. This time he could guess that Voak was weighing the idea of telling, by doing so perhaps breaking some old rule of his own kind.

At last the other raised his black-skinned hands, beginning to sign slowly, as if he wanted to make very sure Jony understood.

"Those—were sick. Many died. People did not die. People strong. People break collars—out of cages . . . They make trap. Catch those—take them out—away from place where those had strong things to hurt—to kill. Put in place they could not get strong things— Those die. People free. Not again collars for People."

An illness had weakened the makers of the city and left them open to a rebellion of the People. This trap . . .

"In the place of stones," Jony asked, "there was a trap?"

Voak dipped his head.

"It is still there?"

"Long time—who knows?" came the clansman's answer.

"Could you find it?" Jony persisted.

Again that moment of silence before the People spoke together. Finally Voak replied:

"No know."

"Would you seek for it?" This was one of the first of the most important points he must make. Jony had persuaded the People to approach the city, but would they actually enter it?

"Why?" Voak's counter question was a single gesture.

"If the trap there, perhaps catch these also," Jony answered.

"They no sick, they have bad things. Make People go sleep—wake in sky ship again."

"I go—alone . . . place of stones. I find those, make them think I am clan-kin. They listen, I tell of things to be found. Take them to trap."

There, he had outlined his poor plan, and, even as he had proposed it, Jony knew that there were so many ways it could go wrong. If those on the ship had contacted the party in the city, then they would know Jony for the enemy. And . . .

"I go," Maba said, first aloud, and then in sign for the People to read. "Don't you see, Jony," she added in speech, "I can say you made me believe things were wrong. But I have changed now, and I need to be with Geogee, that I want to be friends with them. They know me, they would believe me sooner than they would you."

"No!" Jony's refusal was sharp. There was logic in what she urged. Only, if any message had come from the ship, those down in the city would be aware of the important part the girl had played in their escape.

"They would believe *me,*" she repeated with much of her usual stubbornness, "before they would you."

Voak could not have understood their exchange. However, he arose ponderously to his feet, the rest moving with him.

"We go—place of stones." He made a statement of that, as forceful as an order.

They did not descend the ridge in plain sight of any who might have been watching, as Jony half feared they might, but turned more to the east. Voak took the lead; Trush and old Gorni fell in behind him. Then came Jony and Maba, the others furnishing a rear guard. Their path led along a narrow valley below the ridge, heading on toward those taller heights behind the city.

And, as the clansmen had earlier done on their visit to the cave of the cage, the People strode along in a matched step, bringing their staffs (those who had them) butt down against the ground with a regular thumping. As yet they had not raised their voices, but Jony was worried. Such a noisy advance could possibly betray them to some machine of the flyer. Only he knew better than to try to urge caution on the People at this point. They knew the danger. Undoubtedly they were moving to counteract it in their own way.

The valley became a very narrow slit. Then, for the first time, Jony saw stones cropping out of the thin soil. The city builders had been here also.

It was against certain of those stones (he could not tell why, for their choices seemed to follow no pattern that Jony could determine) that the clansmen now thudded their staffs. The resulting sound was hollow and echoing. Jony tried to listen beyond that muffled pounding, fearing to hear the buzz of the investigating flyer.

At last the valley came to an abrupt end in a wall which a fall of earth had revealed completely. The stones which formed this obstruction were not all alike. Even with the weathering and discoloring to confuse the eye, Jony could make out the outline of a former opening into which rougher and less finished rocks had been forced as a plug.

Two of the clansmen drew apart, stood thumping the butts of their staffs, not against those stones sealing the old opening, but aiming at the solid wall on either side. Voak, Trush, and Otik padded forward, extending their claws to pry between the plug rocks, digging to free them from their long setting. Jony pushed up to join them. Motioning the clansmen back, he inserted the point of his metal staff into those crevices, digging free soil, levering them apart.

They cleared the way at last, to be faced by a dark

opening from which issued cold, dank air. Jony uneasily surveyed the way ahead. He had no liking for venturing into an unknown dark.

Then Voak signed to him.

"Give staff!"

Amazed, Jony gaped at the other's outstretched paw-hand. For a moment he thought that the clansman again mistrusted him, wanted him unarmed as they advanced. So his grasp on the weapon tightened. He was determined not to yield.

Voak must have read his fears, for once more the clansman's fingers moved.

"Must have staff—need for going."

Well, Jony and Maba still had the two stunners they had brought from the ship. And Voak certainly knew more about this hidden way than he did. Reluctantly the boy passed over his find to the clansman.

Voak raised the metal length, seemed to weigh it in hand for the best grip, before he sent the butt thudding against the wall, his round, furred head unmoving as if he listened for some necessary answering sound. The thump was certainly sharper and clearer than that which came from meeting of the wooden ones with the wall. Voak gave one last mighty swing, to clang against rock, and then advanced, passing into the dark passage, thumping the staff as he went. The others fell into the same line of march they had earlier held. As they went, Maba's hand caught Jony's and her fingers tightened.

"Where are we going?" she asked in a voice hardly above a whisper.

"Into the city—somehow," he answered her, trying

to make his tone casual and reassuring. Though, as the light behind them grew dimmer and dimmer, the way before darker, he found it hard to hold to any high pitch of confidence.

The beat of the staff butts continued regularly. Jony wished he knew the reason for this. Was the gesture one only of ceremony, to be used when approaching a place forbidden now to their kind? Or did that pounding have a more definite and practical purpose? At least this passage remained level; there was no sudden drop to slide down into the unknown as had been part of his earlier adventure.

The air was flat and held strong earthy odors. Jony's head began to ache a little, a condition increased by every thump of staff butt.

The boy tried to guess what lay about them in the dark. It seemed to him this was no longer a narrow passage but a wider space, for he fancied there was a different ring to the faint echoing of their pounding. If he turned his head for a second or two, he could catch the faint gleam of his companions' eyes.

Maba said nothing, but her grip on his hand continued very tight, and he could gauge her tenseness by that. Jony longed to give her some assurance that there would soon be an end. But that he could not know.

Again, as had happened earlier, there grew slowly a show of gray light ahead. Shortly, the light showed that they were indeed in a much vaster open area. Voak kept to a straight course between two rows of the stone pillars. Was this another part of the storehouse? If so they must be doubly on their guard, or they might be betrayed by the noise the People continued to make. But there were no signs of any of those boxed containers, no paintings on the walls. This was only a bare, grim-looking burrow revealed in a limited amount of dusky light. They neared another wall. At last Jony could make out against that a series of ledges which the people of the city had used to gain heights above.

Voak had not thumped for the last two strides, nor had any of the others. His head now stretched to the highest angle he could hold it, so his muzzle pointed up the rise of the ledges. There was light enough for Jony to see that the clansmen were sniffing.

To Jony's less sensitive nose there was nothing to be scented but the musty smell which had hung about them ever since they had entered this way. But he knew that the People were far better endowed than he.

Whatever Voak searched for, he seemed satisfied. Without any signed explanation, he began to climb. Now there was no pounding with their staffs, they moved in that absolute silence their big hind paws could keep when there was need.

Before long they emerged into the full light of sunset. That rich glow lay in a broad path directly to the head of the ascent, as if to welcome them, issuing through a wall slit placed well above Jony's head. He looked around, and, not too far ahead, saw the place of the sleeper. The hidden underground ways had led them straight to the heart of the city.

As the clansmen hesitated for the first time, Jony

pressed past them. Sounds kept him from advancing very far. Voices, surely; only so muffled that he could not make out separate words. The spacemen—down in the passage to the storage room!

Geogee? Once more Jony concentrated on reaching the boy. No barrier here as he had feared. The force of his thought swept swiftly into the boy's mind. Too swiftly, too forcefully perhaps. Jony withdrew. Had Geogee betrayed them to the others with his shock as Jony made contact?

He wriggled the stunner out of the front of his ship garment where he had stowed it for safekeeping. If their party could now only take the spacemen by surprise while the invaders explored below . . .

Voices coming nearer . . . Jony did not really have to make any warning sign. The People had already melted away into the shadows, Maba with them. Jony slipped from one pillar to the next, using those huge rounds of stone for cover just as he would the trees of a wood.

He was nearly opposite the other entrance, and he already had proof that the spacemen were doing more than just exploring below. After all, they had had some time to select from the stores of the city people. So there was a tall stack of the colored boxes built up in a wall-like pile, their brilliant hues all mixed together. In how many were power rods? Jony could not possibly guess, and he had no time to investigate. For two of the suited invaders advanced into the open, another box carried between them.

They were pulled to one side by the weight of what they carried. Jony took a long chance to aim in a way which he hoped would catch them both. He pressed the firing button.

One slumped, the other gave a startled cry, dropped his end of the box, staggered a step or two, until Jony caught him full on with a second beam. The noise of the box hitting the floor—that cry! Had the sounds given the alarm to the party still below?

Voak and his clansmen needed no orders. They flitted silently between the pillars, caught up the two unconscious men, bundling them fast in large nets they had brought with them. How many more of the enemy were here? Maba had thought that four had gone with the flyer from the ship with Geogee; but she was not sure.

Now Jony struck in another fashion. He could not aim at either of Geogee's two other companions with mental compulsion, because he neither had them in view, nor knew them well enough to form a mind-picture. However, through the boy, he ought to be able to deal easily with the opposition, as he had once before.

Rutee—his far off promise! Only Rutee could not have foreseen such a situation as this. She would certainly not hold him to any word, if keeping such meant ill to the People who had saved her and her children.

Geogee! Jony aimed an order with the same precision as he had just used the stunner.

Come!

He had the boy! Geogee was obeying.

Come!

Geogee must have been well up the ascent from the storage room, because their contact was so clear, so immediate. Jony held communication to top pitch, until the smaller form of the boy did appear in the open, his eyes as wide and set as any mind-controlled. Jony winced at the sight. But this must be done.

Now Maba ran lightly forward, caught her twin by a dangling hand, hurried him with her, back into the dusk behind where that single high window laid its path of light.

"What's with the boy!" Spoken words Jony could pick up and understand.

"Maybe he can't take this hole any longer. I'm beat out myself. Let's call this the last—for now."

"The last? It will take us months to clear out that place. What a find! I don't think anything like it—so complete—has ever been uncovered before. Who were these city builders? They look like pure Terran stock in those pictures."

"Could be. There were a lot of colony ships which took off and just went into nowhere as far as the records are concerned. Or colonies of colonies of colonies. What I'd like to know is what happened to . . ."

The speakers had reached the top of the ramp. Again they carried between them a box. However, directly in their path lay the first which the now-prisoners had dropped. Sighting that, the newcomers stopped short.

"Down!" One of them loosed his end of their own

burden, fell to the floor behind it. His fellow was only a fraction late in following him. What had alerted them Jony could not tell. But he heard them slithering along behind the barrier of that loot they had already brought out. He shot the stunner twice. Apparently its power could not penetrate that barrier. And, when he tried mind control, he met with the dampening effect of some safe coverage.

They were heading for the open by the sounds, to get out to their flyer. He could guess that much. And, also, if they reached that and were able to rise he and the People would have lost.

Jony began to run along the other side of the boxes. Would one of the invaders now produce a power rod and use it? He could taste his fear, but that did not slow his desperate chase.

THE OFF-WORLDERS BROKE FROM BEHIND THE END OF the line of boxes. Raising his stunner, and aiming as best as he could, Jony was about to press the firing button when he himself was struck. Not by any blow, but with that same weakening of the muscles, that inability to keep on his feet which had made him easy prey for the spacemen before. Only this time he did not lose consciousness; even though he wilted forward, to lie face down, unable to raise or turn his head.

Geogee! Jony received in his still-alert mind the impact of the twin's anger and fear. He could hear the thud of running feet. The escaping spacemen must be well on their way out of the building. But Geogee did not accompany them.

Once again Jony tried mind-touch, control, if he could force it. Now he met the same barrier which the ship people could raise. He fought with all his will against the inert disobedience of his body, but was unable to break whatever bonds held him.

Jony heard the whisper of footsteps from behind. Geogee? Another spaceman? A clutch on his shoulder rolled him over, to lie limply, staring up at Geogee.

The boy scowled down at him. He wore not only a smaller version of the ship garment, but, now, over his head, a bubble-like covering which was far too large, shifting back and forth on his shoulders, so that he had to raise a hand constantly to steady it in place. However, in his other hand, at the ready, was a stunner.

"Geogee . . ." Though he was not able to move, Jony discovered he could shape that name with his lips, utter it as a low whisper.

If the other heard him, he made no sign. Instead he walked around Jony, picked up the stunner he had dropped when he fell under attack. Geogee thrust that extra weapon into the front of his clothing, as if it were very necessary to make sure of such possession at once.

Then, for the first time, he spoke:

"What did they do with them?"

Jony had no idea what he meant. He struggled to give voice in that whisper.

"Who—do with what?"

"With Volney, Isin. I saw the People take them, back there." Geogee settled his helmet straight, then waved his hand toward the rear of the long hall.

So the People had gone, taking with them their prisoners. Jony accepted that with difficulty, startled at first by the fact that they had deserted him. Geogee leaned closer.

"I said—where are they going to take them?" His eyes blinked nervously, he fidgeted. Though Jony could not now use the mind-touch, he was well aware that Geogee was in a state of great excitement, perhaps even fear.

When Jony did not answer at once, Geogee brought

the stunner around, pointing the rod straight at his victim's head.

"I can give you another shot," he shrilled. "You won't ever know anything after that!"

"And if I don't know anything," Jony returned, "how can you find out what you want? Geogee, this is me, Jony! Why are you doing this—?"

Geogee's eyes flicked from side to side as if he expected at any moment to be attacked from another direction.

"You let *them* take Volney," he burst out. "Those animals—they'll kill him! You—you—" His accusation ended in a sputtering, as if he could not find any name evil enough for Jony.

In turn he was struck silent as another voice called from behind the line of boxes:

"Geogee?"

"Maba! What are you doing here? Let me alone!" For a moment Geogee's concentration on Jony was broken. Had the other been able to move he might have used that instant well. But, in spite of his will, his body remained inert.

"What are *you* doing, Geogee?" the girl countered. She advanced into the line of Jony's sight. Both her hands were empty, the stunner she had carried was gone.

"I want to know where they took Volney!" her twin repeated loudly. "I saw them drag him off; he and Isin! They'll maybe kill him . . ."

The twin was lashing himself into a stronger display of anger and fear than Jony had ever seen him exhibit before. Now he actually swung the stunner around to point at his sister.

Ignoring the menace of that weapon, she walked forward boldly, facing Geogee across Jony's body. Her face was as calm as if they had both awakened in a clan nest that morning and there had been no fatal interruption to the peace of their lives.

"The People won't kill them," she stated firmly.

"How do you know? Animals! They always kill when they're threatened." Geogee spat back. "And how did you get here, away from the ship?"

"I came because he brought me," she indicated Jony. "Don't we always have to do as he wants, if he controls us?"

Geogee laughed, a reckless note high in sound. "Not any more! I've got this." He thumped the helmet, which slipped so that he had to hurriedly right it once more. "Jony didn't know about it—so I could grab it when he let me go—when I got to you, too. They know about what Jony can do. But he can't control me any more. Not now. He can't do anything at all but just lie there. Eh, Jony?"

He stared down at his captive; the grin on his face was not a pleasant one.

"Rutee made you promise," he hissed, "that you would never try to control us. But you did! You learned a lot from the Big Ones. But I've learned more—from Volney. I can control *you*, Jony. See, I'll show you how—"

Turning up the butt of the alien weapon he made some adjustment there, and then, with a flip of the wrist, aimed once more at Jony, sending whatever power that weapon emitted to travel the full length of his victim.

There was a tingling in Jony's flesh. Circulation might be returning to some limb which had gone numb. But, though Jony attempted at once to move, he was still in thrall to that terrible inertia.

"Get up!" commanded Geogee.

To Jony's sudden horror then, his body, if slowly and disjointedly, did move. Fear filled his mind—he was *controlled!* Yet this was not the same way as the Big Ones practiced such captivity. He was sure that the effect was different.

Once on his feet he swayed back and forth, his own mind fighting desperately to take over command of his body. He felt enmeshed in an unseen net of alien strength. Geogee backed away, stunner still aimed at Jony's middle. And Jony was drawn to follow, staggering, wavering, but on his feet and moving in obedience to that pull.

"You see?" Geogee laughed again. "Now Jony can't control us, but we can him! We'll march him right to the flyer. Varcar and Hansa, they're there. We'll take him back to the ship. The captain will know what to do with him."

To Jony's surprise and dismay Maba echoed that laughter. "Clever Geogee," she praised her twin. "How did you know how to do that? When you took my stunner you didn't tell me how you could . . ."

"Volney showed me when I told him about Jony. Volney knows more than Jony could ever hope to. Volney likes me. He says when we go back with them he'll see I'm taught how to be a pilot, learn to run their machines. Volney says I learn things easier than any boy he's seen, that I have a very good brain. Volney . . ." Geogee's face twisted again into that ugly scowl. "Volney! Those animals have Volney! We must get him free. Jony knows where they are; he's going to take us there—right now!"

"Jony doesn't know everything," Maba answered. "He tried to make the People come here, fight the spacemen. They came, but they wouldn't fight. They don't want to fight, but just run away. And now they've run off and left Jony. They won't take Volney and the other far; they're afraid of the space people. If we went after them, left Jony . . . He doesn't go fast when you make him move—we could stop them. You have that," she indicated the stunner. "You can take Volney away from the People easily. But we have to hurry now to catch up."

Geogee came to a halt, his attention once more passing from Jony to the girl. Jony was sick inside. What had happened to Maba? On board the ship she had aided in their escape; he could not have carried that through without her quick wit. And he had allowed her to come here because he knew that she did have influence over Geogee. Only now she was using that influence to set Geogee, armed with his alien weapon, on the trail of Voak and the others. Since she had come out of the shadows, she had not once looked straight at

Jony nor given any indication that she was in opposition to her brother.

"Leave Jony?" Geogee said thoughtfully. "But they want Jony, they want to learn how he can control us. Volney said maybe he is a mutant."

"What's a mutant?" Apparently that was new to Maba.

"Someone who is changed from the rest, I guess. But they want to know about Jony."

"Easy enough," Maba made a slight face. "Leave him here. You can stun him again, or just leave him controlled like this. He won't be able to get away. If we wait, the People may be able to hide Volney before we can catch up."

"They aren't *People!*" Geogee still did not relinquish his wary attitude toward his captive. "Volney said they don't have that high a reading on the scale. They're not like us at all. Jony is stupid, always telling us how great they are. About leaving him here . . . I don't know."

"Oh, come on," Maba was growing impatient. "You know he can't get away, not if you leave him controlled. Anyway, those who went to the ship—they'll be back." She gestured to the heaped boxes. "They're never going to leave all this, or you, or Volney and Isin."

Slowly Geogee nodded. Though he watched Jony measuringly, he lowered the weapon slightly.

Now Jony made the move he had decided upon during that short exchange when both the twins apparently ignored him. He allowed his body to slump once more to the pavement, as if he could no longer obey the controls. Until he fell he was not sure that he *could* do that much of his own will. So at this small assertion of his desires, he regained a little of the confidence Geogee's actions had drained out of him.

"Look at him!" A foot kicked lightly against his shoulder, its movement was all he could see of the twins in his now limited field of vision. "You think he's going to escape?"

"All right," Geogee conceded. "He won't be able to get away. And I'd better not give him another raying. Volney says they want him to be all right when they examine him."

"Geogee!" thought Jony. Who or what was this Volney that the off-worlder had been able, in a period of days, to wipe out all Geogee's ties with those he had known since birth? He himself had hated the spacemen hotly when he had seen Yaa as a focus for their experiments. Now that hatred grew into a cold purpose within him. If they could so persuade Geogee, then they were even more like Big Ones. Geogee might not have the outward appearance of the mind-controlled, but he was thinking along a pattern these others had dictated. And for that also Jony wanted a reckoning. And Maba . . .

He had begun to sense she might be playing some game of her own. But that he dared trust her . . . no, of that he was not sure. If she did guide Geogee after the People, then even a small chance of victory would be lost.

Jony listened to the footfalls pacing away from him.

He was not sure whether he could do anything to break the invisible bonds Geogee had netted around him. While the boy was in sight and could bring his weapon to bear again, he dared not even try.

Only deep silence now. Still Jony made no attempt to struggle. He was gathering all his power. Also what Maba had said: that the two spacemen who had fled might return, haunted him, kept him listening, until he decided he dared not wait any longer.

He concentrated on his right hand where it lay touching his cheek, willing fingers to move. There was a barrier there, yes, but not so great a one that he could not achieve a stirring. So heartened, he poured in all the strength he could summon. His fingers clawed, crawled ahead, as might the legs of a lethargic insect.

Though he had still very little real strength, he could move! How long would it take for the full influence of the weapon to wear off, if that ever would? He might have so very little time left. Palm lay flat now in the thick dust—stiffen wrist, raise arm, other hand the same. Now—heave!

Weakly, Jony brought himself up, though he felt that at any moment his arms might collapse and let him fall forward once again. He must do better! Somehow he fought to his knees. His head ached, waves of dizziness, in which all about him swung back and forth, assailed him.

That he could rise to his feet was clearly impossible. But he could still crawl. Crawl he did, half-choked by the dust his hands stirred up so close to his hanging head.

He was headed, he thought, toward the open front of the building where stood the stone woman. And he hoped that, in the open air, he might regain more of his strength. If he were allowed that long.

To his right were the piled boxes. Then shortly, just before him, the steps which raised the coffer holding the sleeper. How far was that point from the outer door? He could not remember now.

Jony crawled through the silence of the stone place. He believed that he felt a little stronger as he went. The exercise might be breaking some of the hold over him. But he could not yet rise to his feet, and he must reserve all he could of his energy, lest he be called upon to exert himself fully by yet some other trial.

To the next pillar . . . and the next . . . and then a third. His throat was parched by the dust; he sneezed and coughed. But he would not pause, nor dared he even try to see how far away was his goal, for that might dishearten him.

The sound of his own panting, wheezing progress was suddenly overtopped by another noise. He knew that, had feared for a long time to hear it again: the buzz of an air-borne flyer. Would the spacemen swoop overhead, use one of their weapons to stun anyone within the pile whether they could see their prey or not?

Sweat streaked through the dusty mask over Jony's face. He shivered as he crawled, waiting for such a blow to fall. However, the buzzing grew fainter. Were they in retreat toward the ship? Or else winging out to quarter over the ways of the city, hunting signs of any other party?

One pillar, another . . . His hands grew sore and raw as, his palms planted hard on the stones, he writhed and dragged himself forward to win the length of another open space.

Around him it was lighter! He must be nearing the outer door. Now he must think past that simple arrival in the open which had been his first goal. What would he do next? Crawl down into the city, wearily along the stone river? The open country beyond was too far, and he would be instantly sighted from the air were the flyer to return.

No, best seek out one of the other dens, hide until he knew whether time could make him whole again. If the only way one could recover from a stunner attack was through some agency of the spacemen, then he did not know what would become of him. That lurking fear he now resolutely battled into the far depths of his mind.

Jony came at last to the foot of the stone woman. His hands were so painful he could not force them into action again. Helplessly, almost hopelessly, he leaned his head and shoulders against the figure, and thereby was able to look back down the way he had crawled.

His heart labored so that his breath came in short gasps; and there was a mist which came and went before his eyes to cloud the back trail. Jony squinted, trying to center on one shadow among the many. Had there been movement back there?

Geogee, Maba, returning? Had the twins so quickly lost the trail of the People? Jony felt he should care, should try for action. Only he was too tired, too strengthless, to do more than crouch where he was and wait for whatever fate moved there to come upon him.

That shadow which was no shadow advanced so slowly. Jony longed to shout to the lurker, urge a confrontation. He was so worn with effort that he wanted a swift ending, not this eternal wait . . .

It was . . . Otik!

Of all whom he might have expected, the clansman was the last. Nor could Jony tell whether Otik was a fugitive from some lost battle, a scout of the People, or had returned for Jony's own sake. He did not even have strength at this moment to raise his raw, scraped hands to sign out any question.

Straight toward him padded the clansman. Otik was nearly as tall as the stone woman behind which Jony sheltered, and he moved with some of that same ponderous solidity which was Voak's. As he loomed over Jony, the boy saw that he carried two staffs: his own laboriously-made one of wood, and the metal-fanged one from the river bed.

Somehow Jony raised his shaking hands, signed a single name in question:

"Voak?"

Otik gathered both shafts into the crook of his arm, leaving his hands free for reply.

"To the place of the cage."

So the People were taking their new captives to that same safekeeping which their ancestors had used to hold their ancient enemies. That is, unless the twins caught up with them, and Geogee fought for the off-worlder who had come to mean so much to him.

"Geogee—Maba?" Jony uttered the names aloud knowing that Otik would recognize those sounds.

"No see," the clansman replied.

With the dignity of his race he lowered himself, to balance on stooped legs. Even so foreshortened Jony had to look up a little to meet his eyes.

"You hurt." Otik might have been gravely concerned or merely curious. Jony, well shaken out of his old belief that he was an integral part of the clan, could never accept again that unquestioning feeling that he was one with the People, so was now not able to guess what lay behind the other's question.

"Strange weapon"—the sign language lacked so much that he needed when he would talk with his old companions—"make me weak, must crawl not walk."

Otik gave an assent gesture. He must have seen the tracks of Jony's painful progress through the wide hall.

"Geogee do," he made answer. "Geogee go with ship ones."

How much the People had witnessed Jony could not tell. But the certainty with which Otik signed that made him sure the clansman had seen the attack on Jony.

"Geogee"—Jony forced his weary hands through the motions—"hunt People. Want shipmen free."

"Geogee"—Otik remained unruffled—"no go right way. He—Maba go other side. Tracks in dust say so."

Jony drew a long breath of relief. Then he had been right in his second guessing about the girl. She was not leading her brother to cut off the clansmen, but rather in the wrong direction to gain them time. How long she might be able to continue that deception Jony did not know. Neither was he in the least happy about her wandering in this city. And what would happen when Geogee realized he had been tricked?

The younger boy might not turn on Maba; their tie was close. But he would hurry back here to make sure of Jony, try to force from Jony where Volney had been taken. Jony had no doubt of that at all.

"Must get away," he signed.

Otik made no answer. Rising to his big feet again with more agility than his bulk of body would suggest, he reached down, hooked one paw in Jony's armpit and drew the other up with no more difficulty than if Jony had been no larger nor heavier than Maba.

With Otik's support Jony could stand. When the other moved, he was able to stumble along upright. The clansman did not turn back toward the shadowed interior from which he had come, rather edged on for the open.

However, as they rounded the stone woman, Jony dragged back for an instant or two. Otik turned his head, stared. What came suddenly into Jony's mind was so wild a thought that it could well have been born out of some disorder in his thinking processes. It was now, when he half-faced the stone woman, when memory moved sharply in him, that he wanted to try an act which might be the height of folly, or else the wisest action he had ever chosen.

He signed to Otik to wait, pulled a little away from the clansman, steadying himself with a hold on the stone figure. Slowly he brought up his bleeding, dust-engrained hand. It was hard to lift, as if *it* were also a heavy chunk of unfeeling stone.

Jony forced his wrist higher, flattened palm, straightened his fingers. Then, with a purpose he could not have logically explained, he half-stepped, half-fell forward, so that his flesh rested as it had once before against the age-pitted surface of stone.

Only what it met did not feel like stone. This was warm, strange. Jony could find no word to describe the sensation. Not the flash of instant response which had frightened him before. No, this was different. It was as if from the larger, immobile hand there flowed into his, rising, ebbing, rising again, an unknown form of energy. Perhaps a man long athirst and chancing upon a spring and drinking his fill might have so experienced this wondrous expansion of well-being, of restoration.

Through his palm, down his arm, into his body— more and more and more! Though Jony did not realize it, tears spilled from his eyes, tracking through the dust on his face. He wanted to sing, to shout—to let the whole world know this wonder happening to him!

JONY WAS NOT HIMSELF AGAIN——HE WAS MUCH MORE. He stood as tall as a Big One, as strong as Voak! With his hand he could flatten the walls about him, snatch a flyer out of the air, overturn the sky ship, so that it could never fly up and out to betray them! He could . . .

Somewhere deep within Jony's mind fear flared. No—no! He dared not be like this. Yet he could not draw back from that wonderful contact through which flowed the power; his palm of flesh seemed united to the stone by an unbreakable bond.

NO!

As he had exerted his talent in the past for control, now he called upon it to sever this dangerous contact. His determination resulted in a sudden sharp cutoff. The stone hand sent him spinning away, rejected him as harshly as before it welcomed him gladly.

Jony would have fallen down the series of ledges, save that he struck against Otik. The clansman stood rock-still, an anchorage for Jony to cling to momentarily.

Otik neither put out an arm to steady, nor a paw-hand to repulse the other. He merely stood and let Jony hold to him, until the reaction to that break in energy flow subsided. The boy drew several deep breaths. What secret of the city builders he had tapped he had no way of knowing, but he was not reckless nor unthinking enough to try it again.

However, it *had* given him back a body obedient to the orders of his mind. For that he was thankful. Now he signed to his silent companion:

"Find Geogee—Maba—"

Otik surveyed him from head to foot. Then he made answer by holding out the metal staff without further sign. Jony took the weapon eagerly, running his hand along its length. That hand, though still dust-grimed, bore now none of the raw marks left by his long crawl. Nor either did its palm when he turned that to the light. His whole strength of body was renewed, as if he had slept well, eaten heartily, and had borne no burdens of mind for a long time.

Otik moved back into the shadows of the long hall behind the stone woman. Here, as Jony hastened to catch up, he saw those waiting boxes. If there were only some way to prevent their ever being taken from this place! To think of their contents in the hands of the spacemen!

Only there was no time now to deal with these. Even if the two who escaped on the flyer returned with an attack force, they surely would be more intent on discovering the whereabouts of their men than transferring loot. At least for the present.

The clansman never turned his head to look as he padded by; that pile of boxes did not appear to exist for him. They skirted the rise of blocks which held the sleeper's box, kept on. It was when they passed the opening through which they had earlier emerged from the lower ways that Jony grew uneasy.

If Maba had not guided Geogee by that passage, where in this pile had she taken him? How far did this hall extend? Were there more passages, other ways? He saw that the path of sun which had struck across the floor from the wall opening had since vanished. The time must be closer now to nightfall. And if the twins were lost here in the dark . . . !

Jony believed there was more to fear in this ancient place than even a vor or Red Head. Recalling the impulse which had made him unite touch with the stone woman, he was surprised at his recklessness. That that had healed and strengthened him was only good fortune. The same flow of energy directed at one of the twins might even kill!

Otik slowed down. His heavy head swung from side to side, as he turned his gaze directly to the floor, examining its surface. In this more shadowed portion Jony could make out a few traces in the dust; undoubtedly Otik could read them more clearly. As it grew darker he would have to depend more and more on the clansman.

Unless . . . he sent out a questing thought. And touched—very faintly—Maba! Jony's confidence rebounded. As it had happened once before in this pile, he had his own guide to follow.

They had not reached the end of the hall when Otik turned right, Jony only a stride behind him. In the wall on that side there was another opening. Jony tried contact again . . . faint still—and not steady! Her pattern seemed to weave in and out, as did the only touch he could ever have with the People, a sense of presence rather than real contact. It had never been so before with the twins. Perhaps Geogee was using some other covering trick Volney had taught him.

The thought of Volney gave Jony certain grim satisfaction. He could picture the spaceman in the cage of the People. At least there the off-worlder could do no more harm. What was the man's power over Geogee? It appeared to Jony that the stranger had, in a new fashion, used mind-control on the boy, erasing all Geogee's former life and associations, or reducing them to something best forgotten, and implanting new desires to make the twin one of the enemy.

As he thought of Geogee, Jony's confidence in Maba was again a little undermined. She had been with the ship's company long enough to be influenced. It was only the vivid memory of her smashing their cherished machine (an act he was sure had not been arranged for his benefit), which persuaded Jony that the girl had not also been mind-warped by the off-worlders.

The door led, not into another tunnel or place of descent, but into a series of small sections above ground. From the third of those they emerged into the open. They now faced the portion of the city which lay behind the huge central pile, completely unknown to Jony. There was no straight river of stone here to serve as a guide out to the country.

Instead, confronting them was a space of ground on

which no stone had been laid or built. This was covered by a thick tangle of vegetation, presenting as thick a barrier as the stone walls behind. Even Otik gave a surprised grunt when he surveyed it.

Between that impenetrable tangle and the place from which they had just emerged there existed a thin ribbon of clear ground. The trail left on that was plain to read. Those they followed had turned to the left, keeping to that narrow pathway.

Dusk was closing in. Jony's sense picked up several forms of small life living within the safe mat of vegetation. Also he listened for something else: that ominous buzz from the air announcing a return of the flyer with more men; men armed with weapons against which the People had no chance. He longed for the stunner Geogee had taken from him, weighed the metal staff in his hand, and knew how little use that would be in a struggle against the off-worlders.

In the half-light he saw Otik's hand move in the sign for water. The clansman's sense of smell could pick that up where Jony's could not. A moment later Otik's staff whirled up at ready. Jony sensed no danger signal of his own, but it was apparent that the clansman was highly suspicious of something. Jony tried mind-seeking. He caught Maba, to his gratification, closer and clearer. Geogee must still be wearing the too large helmet which cut off such contact. But there was nothing else. Except from the section before them there came a complete absence of the small life signals he caught elsewhere.

Otik halted abruptly. His nostrils were fully extended. Even Jony could now catch a faint, sickening stench, as if ahead some rot lay open under the sky.

Scenting that, the boy needed no other warning from his companion. Here, in the heart of the stone place, was a colony of Red Heads! But the twins had gone this way! Had the children blundered into this worst of dangers without any warning?

Otik still held his head as high as he could, sniffing audibly. That they should venture through any part of country those plant-beasts patrolled was pure folly. Over the Red Heads none of Jony's talent could prevail, any more than he could force the People themselves to his bidding. With growing apprehension, he surveyed their surroundings. That wall to the left had no openings big or little. To their right the thick vegetation was far too entangled to crash a path through. Any attempt to do so would shred his skin, even slash Otik, in spite of the other's thick fur covering.

Where *were* the twins? That Jony could still mind-reach Maba meant she was alive—one small hope granted him.

To his utter surprise Jony saw Otik move again. Not in retreat, as the boy had entirely expected, but on along the same path. Jony trailed behind, for this way was too narrow for them to go abreast. The plant-beasts were the one enemy even the People did not face, yet Otik was proceeding as if he believed they had a chance!

The stench grew stronger, while coming dark added to Jony's wonder at Otik's recklessness. Once night had fallen the Red Heads would be mobile, at their most dangerous. He brought his own staff into a good position for a slashing blow, such as he had used with the vor, but it would offer no defense to the stupefying vapor the things broadcast when in action.

An arch of stone arose before them, and, when they moved just under that, the whole scene ahead changed. The matted growth drew away. Though it still formed a wall of its own, there was a far greater open space here.

In the middle of that open area was a large pool which possessed an edging of vigorous plant life. Yet over its murky waters coasted none of the winged things one would naturally find at such a spot. This scene was silent, devoid of any life save that which was ground-rooted.

Spaced around the turgid and unpleasant looking stretch of water were the Red Heads. In terms of general growth, this collection was stunted, rising hardly higher than Jony's shoulder at their tallest. Their red, bulbous tips were faded-looking, more of a sickly, yellowish shade. And many of them had lower leaves which were only rotting stubs.

Also, the blossom-heads were canted at crooked angles, as if the creatures were too weakened to hold them straight. Yet a stir ran through their company as Otik and Jony drew nearer, such movement as a wind might raise when furrowing the grass on the open plain. This growth might be sickly, even dying, but the things still knew when prey approached.

Jony sprang forward. Aroused by his very loathing

of the creatures, he swung his staff so the sharp fang could bite into the nearest stem. There was a dull thunk of sound as the metal sheared in. A liquid of such putrid smell as to make him gasp sprayed forth as the head of the thing fell to one side, attached now to the plant only by a thin strip of outer bark.

The plant-beasts moved so sluggishly that Jony was encouraged, leaping to attack the next in line. Had Geogee used the stunner on them? Or had some illness of their own species half-crippled the plants so that they could be so easily dealt with? He did not know; he was only thankful that these were not the virile species he had seen elsewhere.

Perhaps Otik had been fired by his example and the results Jony was getting. For the clansman stumped out in turn. His wooden staff could not sever stems as Jony's more efficient tool was doing, but he beat down upon red blossoms, which burst under his attack, stripped away leaves with the vigor of his swings.

The two crossed the plot where the plant-beasts festered, to reach the opposite side beyond the pool. Here was another stretch of stone-paved open, cutting through it a runnel of dark water which either fed or drained the pool. The smell rising from that was noxious in the extreme. Then Jony, fired by his easy victory over the enemy the People feared so, was nearly caught in a trap set by his over-confidence.

The last Red Head had been crouching in the stream, its rooted feet sucking up the moisture. If the fate of its fellows had alerted it, it had not chosen to move, either in defense or flight—then. Now, directly in Jony's path, the plant-beast straightened with a snap to full height. And this one was truly a giant among the poor wizened dwarves of the company. Taller than Jony, its ball head displayed a deeper, glowing red, visible even through the growing dark. The boy could see that expanding bag beneath the blossom, ready to empty its cloud of blinding, stupefying pollen in his direction. Its two long upper leaves, lined with fang thorns, were already reaching confidently in his direction.

With a cry Jony leaped back as one of the leaves lashed viciously, nearly sweeping him from his feet. He crouched low, metal staff in both hands, sharp cutting edge up. If the creature released that pollen, he might have only an instant, perhaps two, before he collapsed. Then Otik would have little defense in turn.

Those leaves were reaching again; while the under, more slender growths gathered around the mouth of the pollen bag, ready to fan the discharge toward Jony. The boy would have no time, no chance to get close enough to slash at the ball head as he had when meeting the weaker growths.

His hand slid along the shaft of the staff; he raised it shoulder high, hurled it, the point of its fang aimed at the red blossom. A leaf whirred out to slap that weapon down, moving with such speed Jony's eye could hardly follow. So it deflected the staff.

But, as the weapon fell, the point ripped across the bag of pollen, cutting those areas of tension which worked to expel the deadly burden. The lower leaves waved wildly. Some of them clutched, pulled at the opening of the bag. But that had shrunk back and was closed so that the beating of the growth about it brought no responsive scattering of lethal pollen.

Jony retreated step by step, still facing the thing. One of the spiked leaves had closed loosely about the staff. The plant-beast might be trying to raise the metal length, thrust it back upon its owner with a deadly purpose. Only the fibers and leaf surface could not contract tightly enough, so that the staff slipped out of its hold, clanged on the stone, and then rolled.

It still lay too close to those raking leaves for him to hope to retrieve it, Jony decided. He dared not risk such a try. So he began to move left. The plant-beast turned to match him as it struggled out of the water runnel. If its roots got a good purchase on the ground, Jony would have had no chance at all. However, those fibers slid over the smoothness of the stone as if unable to find any stable grip. The whole creature rocked unsteadily from side to side like a storm-struck tree, as it strove to rush him.

Awkward or not, the Red Head lost none of its threat that Jony knew. He was forced to slip and dodge, in evasion, never relaxing his watch upon its deceptively clumsy movements. The smaller lower leaves worked vigorously at the limp pollen bag, squeezing around that appendage. Manifestly the thing was still trying to release its deadly cloud by such pressure. The fanged upper leaves darted and lashed, until it required all of Jony's strength and speed to keep beyond its reach.

He retreated while the plant-beast followed, unable to spare a single instant of inattention to locate Otik who might now have a chance to reach the metal staff lying on the pavement. Jony had only one hope, that the clansman could take up that weapon and use it in place of his less efficient one.

Back! That time an edge of leaf raked Jony's arm, slashing the materal of the ship suit as clean as if cut by a blade, leaving a smarting, shallow, blood-drawn line on his skin. Two of the roots writhed, began to uncoil from their normal tangle. Both crept out toward him; he could be tripped . . . Once down, he would be a helpless victim. Even if Otik moved in then, Jony would be already dead, caught between the fanged leaves, his body impaled on their armor to feed the hunger of this night-walking horror.

He dodged, skidded, caught his balance again just in time. As Jony gasped for breath, his whole body chill with fear, he saw a flash, brilliant in what light remained. Otik had the metal staff at last; the clansman swung it with all the force of his huge, strongly-muscled arms.

Its sharp edge bit home just under the ball head, slashed on—not as easily as it had severed the stalk of the smaller creature, but with force enough to cut clean across. The blossom ball tumbled free, to be caught by a wildly flailing toothed leaf, which closed instantly, crushing it completely. Still the creature continued to totter on ahead; but Jony, keeping out of its path, no longer drew it after him. Rather it smashed straight on until its writhing roots tangled with each other and it fell forward.

There prone, it rolled back and forth on the ground.

A paw-hand closed on Jony's arm tearing the ripped sleeve yet farther, jerking him back with a mighty heave as a puff of thick, dusty-looking vapor rose from the struggling creature. At last the pollen was loosed. Only there was no concentrated effort to wave it toward the prey, so the dust settled back quickly over the still heaving body.

They made a wide detour around the thing, allowing all the room they could to the lashing upper leaves, the snapping curl and un-curl of the roots. Otik shambled along at the fastest pace one of the People could achieve. Jony wanted to sprint ahead, but he could not desert the other.

Once across the paved space they came to another opening which gave onto a smaller, stone-laid walk place lined with structures on either side. Otik paused there, once more sniffing. He was again fully intent on their search with the single-minded stolidity of his kind.

Once away from the dying plant-beast, he had handed the metal staff back to Jony, who took opportunity, offered during their pause, to tear loose the rest of the sleeve of his garment, with that wiping all he could of the evil smelling stains from the fang edge. Hurling the rag as far as he could from him, he was ready to go on. He felt almost weak with sheer relief.

It was then that the quiet of the early evening was broken by a cry which brought him out of his concern with the battle.

"Maba!" Though Jony had not tried mind-search

since they had encountered the Red Heads he recognized that voice with his inner sense as well as his ear.

"Maba!" He called once, then knew the folly of that. He must not alert any danger which faced the girl, give knowledge that help was on the way. But he did know she was along this way, within one of the side dens. Jony began to run, not waiting to see if Otik would follow.

Before he reached the right opening Maba cried out again. There was such terror in that scream Jony picked up a stab of her fear. Something—someone—threatened her. But where was Geogee with the stunner? Surely . . .

Here was the hole which led to Maba. Jony slowed his pace sharply, trying to creep in without noise. The alien coverings on his feet prevented such a soundless advance. He wished he had had time to shed this hated garment.

The space within was very dark, with only lighter spots to show the wall openings. Jony must use his eyes as well as he could, but he could employ the talent too.

As he had shared Rutee's pain in the long ago, now he knew the full force of Maba's terror. And he could not get any idea of what menaced her from the disjointed thoughts marred by her strong emotion.

He listened. Though there was no sound in the outer part of this den, from beyond came a broken whimpering. Maba! Only—he could pick up no other life trace, not even that blocked-out deadness which marked

Geogee while wearing the helmet. Maba—alone . . . ?

Jony did not take the straight path from the outer opening to the other large one he could see ahead. Instead he chose to slip along the wall. He dared not give full concentration to touch with Maba, only keep an outer alert to prevent sudden attack.

Now! His hand was on the side of that other opening. The dark inside seemed to whirl about oddly, as if the air therein was full of black particles in constant motion. Jony lifted the staff, thrusting it tentatively through the opening. He waited a long moment, his imagination painting for him an only half-visible lurker, something which could close upon any who entered even as the fanged leaves of the plant-beast had tried to do.

But in his slow sweep the cutting part of the staff moved freely enough. Jony slipped through quickly, got his back to a solid wall, held his weapon at ready. A scream sent him into a half-crouch, so sure of some attacker that he could almost see one existing as part of the dark itself.

"No!" Maba cried out from the other corner of the room. "Please, Geogee, don't leave me. Geogee . . . ?" There was a broken pleading in her voice which tore at Jony.

"Maba . . ." he called softly. Her mind was such a whirlpool of frantic panic he could not get through to her. "Maba!" He dared only try to reach her by voice alone.

She did not call again, but he could hear a harsh breathing which was more like half-strangled sobs.

Jony moved away from the wall. He was sure now that only fear itself filled this darkness. Slowly he approached the corner in which he could very faintly see a huddled body.

She cried out again. "No—go away!"

"Maba," he tried to make a soothing call of her own name. "This is Jony."

Her ragged breathing continued. Then—

"Jony?"

That he had gotten that much of an intelligent response from her was promising. He went to his knees, felt out in the dark, his hand finding and moving along her shuddering body. There was something abnormal about the way she lay. Had she been injured, maybe by one of the plant-beasts? But where was Geogee?

Moving slowly, gently, mainly by touch, Jony gathered her up into his arms. Her skin felt chill and her shivering did not ease. He must get her out of here into some kind of light so he could see her hurts, whatever those might be.

She did not move of her own accord, but her breathing seemed less labored.

"I hoped, Jony. I did hope so you would come," she said brokenly. "I knew that maybe you couldn't. Because Geogee did that to you. But I just kept on hoping that somehow you would."

He cradled her close against him and strode for the door.

"Where is Geogee?" he asked.

Her shivering was worse. And her voice was very low when she answered: "He—he just went away."

OUT IN THE OPEN, EVEN THOUGH THEY WERE STILL surrounded by the stone dens, Jony drew a deep breath of relief. Maba's head rested heavily against his shoulder, as if she had no control over her muscles. In his arms her weight was flaccid. Geogee must have used the stunner on her!

But, as he went, Jony could feel the fear draining from her. That was the poison which had tormented her as she lay in the strange darkness. As he reached the open Otik was waiting, his large eyes surveying the girl. The clansman signed:

"She was struck by the evil . . ."

Jony nodded assent.

Nostrils widened as Otik turned toward the den in which Jony had found her. "There is none else here."

Again Jony agreed. Even in this dim light he could see Maba's eyes were open. She watched him. Now tears gathered to brim over, run down her cheeks.

"Jony," her voice was hardly above a whisper, she might have exhausted all its power during her own ordeal by terror, her screams through the night, "Geogee —he used the stunner, on *me*. Then he went off . . ."

"Why?" Jony made his question blunt, hoping thus to get a sensible answer out of her quickly.

"He said I was helping the People. He—Jony, he's

all changed in his head somehow." Her words were choked now with the same sobs which made her body quiver in his hold. "He—he hates the People because he thinks they have done something to Volney. Volney means more to him than I do . . . and you . . . and Yaa, and Voak, and all of us! Why, Jony?"

For that he had no answer. "Do you know where he went?" he asked what might be now a matter of importance. Geogee lurking in the city, hostile. Suppose the boy was hiding out somewhere among these dens, ready to use a stunner without warning? Jony could not guess what so altered Geogee's thinking. But if he would do this to Maba, then indeed perhaps he was mind-controlled by some subtle method the spacemen practiced.

Jony let his mind search free. He could not contact Geogee directly while the other wore that protective helmet, but perhaps he could pick up the boy nearby by that very blank he touched. Only he met nothing he could so define.

"He is hunting for Volney," Maba continued. "Jony, I feel so queer . . . what if I never am able to move again? Jony!" Once more her hysteria was rising.

Jony drew her closer. "It will pass," he assured her. "With me it did."

Or had that full recovery been because he had taken into his body the strength the stone woman had to give? And—Jony caught at this new idea—could it possibly be that such a strength could be passed in turn from person to person as well as from the stone to him?

He lowered the girl to lie on the pavement in the beginning light of a slowly rising moon.

"Maba, listen to me. I am going to try to break you free. I do not know whether I am able to do this, but I can try."

"Oh, yes, Jony!" Her voice was so eager that he was disturbed. Perhaps he was doing wrong to give her even a fraction of hope that this would work. Bending closer, he took one of her hands in each of his, held them fast. Then he began to concentrate on sending, not the mind-thrust he had always used, but rather a sensation of returning energy into her body. When there followed a slight tingling of his flesh, he had to stifle quickly his own sense of wonder and triumph, keep his mind occupied only by the need to pass to Maba a portion of that strength he had won from the stone woman.

"Jony—Jony, I can feel!" she cried out. "Oh, Jony, it is true you can make me feel!"

He, in turn, was aware of a feeble flexing of her fingers within his hold. Then her limp arms arose a fraction, her head moved from side to side on the stones as if she must learn for herself that this was again possible.

She was sitting up, though still weak enough to need his support, when Otik joined them. Jony had not even noticed the clansman missing. Now as he stood there, he held not only his staff, but Jony's. He must have gone into the blackness of the den to get that.

"I thought maybe you would never find me," Maba

said, the remains of her sobs still making her voice shaky. "I thought I would just lie there . . . maybe forever!"

"But you did not." Jony put what he hoped would be a bracing briskness into his voice. "Now, do you have any idea of where Geogee was heading?"

"It was the helmet, you see," she answered, and then went on to make her explanation clearer. "He believed me at first. I thought I could lead him far enough away from the People so that he could not hurt them. But I didn't know about the helmet, except that you could not mind-control him if he wore it. I didn't know *they* could!"

"How?" Jony's instant distrust of any of the equipment used by those from space gave him a core of belief already.

"There is a way they can talk through the helmets— I didn't know about that, really, Jony. I thought they had to use those boxes they have in the flyer and the ship. But there are talk places in the helmets, too—inside somehow. And Geogee heard Volney calling through his. He knew somehow that the call came from another direction. But he did not tell me at first. We came to the place where the Red Heads were," she shuddered. "Geogee, he used the stunner. They all went stiff and did not move so we could pass them. But, when we got here, he was all of a sudden very mad. He yelled at me about taking him the wrong way. And he said he'd show me what it meant to tell lies! He—he wasn't like Geogee at all! Those space people made him like them. I got afraid, Jony; he was so strange. So I ran, and then I tried to hide. But he found me and used the stunner. He laughed, Jony, he just stood there and laughed. Then he said he'd find Volney all right; Volney would tell him just how to go. Only first he was going back and get one of those rods. And when he had that—he'd know what to do with it, too . . ."

Jony tensed. Geogee running wild with one of the destructive rods! Supposing he did, by some chance, find the People and their prisoners? He believed now that Geogee was as much under the control of this Volney as those poor creatures of his own species had been when in the lab of the Big Ones.

"We have to stop him," Jony said more to himself than to the girl. Nor dared he keep the seriousness of this action from Otik. Still kneeling beside Maba he signed to the clansman what had happened as best he could.

Otik said nothing in return. Rather he turned around, facing the way down which they had come. Once more he was sniffing. Then he made a negative gesture. Whichever way Geogee had gone, he had not doubled back. Now Otik did something that Jony had very seldom witnessed among the People: he went down on all fours, bringing his massive nose close to the pavement about them. Several shambling steps away from the door of the den he stopped short, made a prolonged inspection by smell, and then raised a hand-paw to beckon.

Clearly Otik had found the trail. But, though Jony

knew that they must follow, he did not want to take Maba. She had recovered in part, but that she could keep up, he greatly doubted. Yet he could not leave her here alone in the dark either.

As he hesitated, Otik moved back. His head went down to sniff at Maba. Then, without wasting time on explanations, he stooped ponderously and picked up the girl, setting her on his shoulders, one thin brown leg on either side of his short neck. In this manner the People carried small cubs on a long trail, and Otik moved as if Maba's weight were nothing.

The problem of her transportation was only part of it. If Geogee was waiting in some ambush . . . But perhaps Otik could give warning of such danger also, and they really had no choice. Once more Jony took up his fang staff; Otik already held his. Letting the clansman take the lead, they moved on between the dens.

Jony went uneasily, glancing from one side to the other, trying to see farther into shadowed holes. He feared Geogee, yes. But also, by night, this place of stone had an uncanny kind of life which was beyond his powers to explain. It was as if, just beyond the fringe of his natural range of vision, things moved, so that he was aware of a vague fluttering he could not really see. In addition there was a dampening of spirit; not fear, as Jony had known it so often in this place of many surprises, but rather as if the inner core of his spirit was weighted down with a vast burden he could not understand.

He wanted nothing more than to flee from the

sight of all these dens, get out into the open land which meant freedom. Yet he must follow Otik who now turned left into an even narrower slit running between high walls. They were heading back in the direction of the central building again, for Otik had made a second turn, moving with the certainty of one following a well-marked, open trail.

Before them reared a wall taller than the others, and in it an opening, through which the clansman padded confidently. Here the moonlight was brighter. Jony saw in detail the bulk of the structure ahead. Yes, he was certain now that they had come around, back to the place of storage. At least they were approaching the place from a different direction than that treacherous path of vegetation where the Red Heads rooted.

Otik did not lead them to one of the large ground-based openings, but to a smaller one up in the wall. He halted there, his muzzle just topping the lower edge of it, and sniffed. Jony needed no gesture to understand that this had been Geogee's entrance.

It was easy for Jony to clamber through it and gather Maba as Otik handed her in. But the clansman found entrance more difficult. His thick body was never intended for climbing, and the hole itself was a tight wedge. However, Otik made it.

The darkness within, away from that hole, was almost as thick as that in the den where Jony had found Maba. Now the three linked hands, Maba's in Jony's; his fingers grasped in Otik's strong hold. It was plain that the clansman's night sight would still be their guide.

All Jony could make out were shadows, with here and there one of the tall pillars looming up near them. Maba had uttered no sound since their journey had started. He was glad that she seemed able to make her way on foot here without weakening.

They came to the door they sought by a different angle so that Jony at first did not quite recognize the opening. Then he knew this was the one through which his own party of clansmen had invaded the city. Otik paused there, sniffing deeply. He even took a step or two toward the front of the large space as if to verify his discoveries. Then he resolutely returned to the entrance.

The way was too dark to see any tracks. Otik himself was only a black bulk in this deep dusk. Now the clansman caught Jony's hand again, drawing him toward the opening. If Otik were certain that Geogee did have some way of following Volney . . .

They were almost within the long-walled run when Jony heard a dread sound even through the stones of the great den. The buzz of the flyer! Faint—but growing stronger. Volney had been able to guide Geogee. Was he also in communication with those coming to his rescue? And with the air speed of the flyer . . .

Otik had been listening too. Now he grunted, jerked at Jony's hand. Apparently the need for speed had also impressed him.

They went on at this swift pace, the best the clansman could produce in times of great necessity. Jony feared that Maba could not keep up; but she continued to trot along beside him with the ease she had shown when they had traveled across country, before the evil of the stone place and the sky ship had broken into their safe lives.

Down the passage they went, coming out into the open land among the ridges. Jony believed that he knew their destination now: the place of the cage above in the heights. At least Otik kept on to the northeast. That Geogee must still be ahead, he was not certain. And what of the rest of the clansmen who had retreated with their prisoners?

Jony's throat was dry; he was vaguely aware once more of both hunger and thirst. And what of Maba? She still made no complaint, but she did stumble frequently, and finally fell. Jony dropped back beside her. Then Otik, grunting something in his own tongue, once more scooped her up.

From time to time Jony sent out a questing probe. He had not yet picked up that deadness which he thought might identify Geogee. Instead he touched on an awareness which heralded one of the clansmen. That brief contact heartened him for a second spurt of effort.

The path they followed was so confused, winding from one ridge valley to the next, that Jony worried from time to time if Otik himself knew where they were bound. Yet the clansman never hesitated, turning right or left with the authority of one following a well-marked trail.

Now—yes! In the moonlight Jony saw the ledges rising. This he knew—the way to the cage place. And, at the top of that climb, hunched in the moonlight like a craggy rock, was Voak. Otik set Maba on her feet at the foot of the ascent. He took not only his staff, but Jony's, and began to drum with their butts. Jony threw his arm around Maba's shoulders, aiding her as they climbed.

At the crest Voak stood in the bright moonlight. He made no gesture of welcome; neither did he bar their way, but only turned and walked ahead, his own staff raised to thump in unison with Otik's two. They had slowed their pace to walk with a ponderous dignity. Then Voak raised his deep voice, echoed by the younger clansman.

"Jony—" Maba began.

He tightened his hold on her. "Hush!" he gave a single whispered warning.

Once more he felt that tingling. Only this time it was heightened, striking him as a series of small shocks. He refused to allow himself to think of what that power might do, this must be followed to the end.

The red-lighted cave opened before them. There was the cage. Only this time it held not bones, but living bodies. Here were the two spacemen and Geogee, who crouched near one. The boy's helmet was gone and he looked as if he had been rolled in mud and dust. But as far as Jony could see he was unharmed.

If the clansmen had imprisoned their captives, they had not yet collared them. But their off-world weapons and helmets were laid out in a row on the floor just beyond the bars of their prison. Stunners—and one of the red rods! Jony's fingers curled. He wanted nothing more than to seize upon that, hurl the thing so far away no one could chance on it again.

"You—Jony!" It was the spaceman who had been Geogee's companion. He advanced to the front of the cage, caught the bars with his hands.

Jony dropped Maba's hand. He paid no attention to the hail from the off-worlder. Instead he concentrated on Geogee. He read his thoughts, his memory; he reached as far as he could into the other's head.

Each new discovery he sorted out, filed to incorporate in his own store of knowledge. But what had happened to Geogee? He was—alien! Not mind-controlled as Jony had known that state before, with the boy's personality erased either temporarily or entirely, so that he knew only such thoughts as his captors wished. No, Geogee's mind was as alive as it had ever been; it was simply that he had somehow accepted an entirely different way of thought.

Geogee now held hot resentment against the clansmen. They had trapped him in a net, spoiled his chance to rescue the man beside him, to prove himself worthy of Volney's interest.

Worthy! Jony knew bitterness at that. He could read all Geogee's thoughts concerning himself. And now began to examine his own feelings in relation to the boy. Because Geogee and Maba were Rutee's, he had given them all the protection and care he could. But he never had felt toward them as he had toward Rutee, that he was a part of them, and that they were, in a way, a part of him. No, perhaps he felt revulsion because they had been born to Rutee by will of the Big Ones, the children of a mind-controlled who had taken Rutee by force. Deep down Jony hated the act which had brought them into the world. Only the promises to Rutee and his own control of his emotions had given him a friendly surface relationship with the twins.

Had the children always sensed this reserve in him, even if they could not read his thoughts? Perhaps. Now Geogee had discovered in this spaceman someone to whom he felt truly akin. The boy's mind had opened to this man, had taken in greedily and joyfully all the other had to offer. Geogee was mind-controlled by his own choice. He longed only to be another Volney.

So, having found Volney, he was now prepared to turn fully against Jony, accepting Volney's values without question. Geogee—Geogee was lost.

Was Maba also? But there was no time now to think of Maba. Jony must deal with Geogee, Volney, and the other one. That the three could be kept here as the People had imprisoned the others was impossible; not with their flyer already cruising, hunting . . .

But neither must they be allowed to use their wills on the People, this world!

Jony could see in Geogee's mind the distorted picture of the People as the spacemen judged them: great shambling animals to be dealt with as one deals with a slight obstruction which can be easily swept away. The People would not last against the might the invaders could summon.

Once more Jony searched Geogee's memory, soaking up all he could of Volney's teaching, seeking a way out for his people. He burrowed for all the details concerning the ship-communication. What he found there —but he must have time to think!

Geogee was on his feet in the cage, his face a tight grimace. He had no protection against Jony's invasion, still he was fighting dully. Jony withdrew, and Geogee lunged against the bars, his voice suddenly raised in a scream of defiance.

"You let us go, Jony! You make them let us go!" He was once again a small boy swept by temper tinged with fear.

"He's right, you know." Volney watched Jony narrowly. There was a lazy curl to his lips as if he saw in the other nothing to fear, that he himself, in spite of being a caged prisoner, had full command of the situation. "I don't know how these animals have managed to influence you, but—"

Jony gave him a long, measured look, then tried swiftly to probe. His mind-thrust was met by a locked defense, even though Volney wore no blanketing helmet. The spaceman threw back his head to laugh derisively.

"That you can't do, my friend. We have sensitives among us, too—but trained ones."

At the same time he spoke, he counter-probed. Jony could feel his attack. However, though Jony had not consciously raised any barrier, the other could not penetrate. Volney was putting full force in his desire to reach Jony, perhaps to implant his own ideas as he had with Geogee. But those pulses of power did not reach as he intended.

The easy curve faded from the other's lips. His mouth became a grim line. Those eyes stared straight into Jony's, as if by the power of an unblinking stare alone he could force a way for his power to enter.

"You cannot," Jony said, knowing that he spoke the truth.

The other relaxed. "So it's a standoff," he said. Jony did not recognize the word, but understood its meaning. "We'll get you, Jony, you know that. Sooner or later."

Jony thought of the returning flyer, of those it might have brought with it. He knew Volney was right, yet he had no intention of surrender. Now he spoke aloud.

"You have no right here. This world belongs to the People."

"Did they build that city?" countered Volney. "You, yourself, know of the status they had there. Animals —pets—things to be owned. We tested your People. They are not of a mind pattern to be considered equal with human beings within the range of galactic law. That city is a storehouse. A find such as men make once, perhaps, in a thousand years. This world—our breed need this world."

"You need, so you take," Jony replied. "The Big Ones needed; they took. *We* were then the animals within their labs. I have been caged. I have seen what they did—for sport—to increase their 'knowledge.'

Yes, they considered it gaining of knowledge from our torment, blood, death. You would do the same here, as you tried with Yaa, with Voak. Animals? You and the Big Ones are less than animals. Not even the Red Heads torment before they kill, and they kill only to live. You would take this world and make it yours, but you shall not!"

What Jony had gained from his probe of Geogee, what had lain as vague ideas in the back of his mind, now came together in a grim pattern. He was not quite sure of his counterplan as yet, only in general outlines. But whatever he could do, he must.

A hand slipped into his; Maba had moved forward to stand beside him, just as Geogee stood beside Volney radiating defiance.

"You—" she spoke to Geogee, "what have they done to you, Geogee? Yaa—they hurt Yaa! When you were sick, she carried you, and hunted a long time for the leaves to make you well. Yaa is real; Voak is real. They are not just things to be used. They are our *people*."

"People?" Geogee cried out in a choked voice, his face flushed. "The ship's people are ours, and you know it. They've come to take us home, to live as we should, not wandering around with a pack of animals, with him"—he flung out a hand to point to Jony—"telling us what to do, getting into our minds and making us obey him! He's got you mind-controlled and you don't even know it. But I guess the mind-controlled don't—not when they're caught forever and ever . . ."

Jony had not heard more than a jumble of words. Gently he released Maba's hold. Then he took two steps to where the weapons of the strangers lay on the rock. Geogee's helmet was there, too. That was an added aid in what he must attempt.

He picked that up first, tried to settle it on his head, but the thick club of his hair prevented it. Impatiently he reached for the metal staff Otik held. Using its sharpened edge, he sawed through the hair, dropping that to the ground. Now the helmet would go on. He reached for the nearest stunner and the red rod.

Voak moved to bar his way.

"What you do?" the clan chief signed.

Jony had only one answer. "What I must to make sure the People remain free."

Apparently Voak believed him, for the clansman stepped aside. Jony took up the stunner with one hand, the rod with the other.

"You can't do anything, you fool," Volney's voice reached even inside the helmet. He sounded very confident.

"Do not be sure," Jony answered as he turned toward the entrance of the place of the cage. There were many ways his poor plan could go wrong. He could only hope to try as hard as he could to make it succeed.

ONE CHANCE IN HOW MANY? JONY SHOOK HIS HEAD. If Geogee had been right in what he had learned from Volney, such counting seemed almost like an action of a bad dream, like comparing one blade of grass to all the rest which grew in one of the wide-bottom lands. Could that be true? That the chance against the space-men finding this world had been as small as that? Volney's own reckoning—might that be depended upon?

And if that ship never lifted from this planet, never returned to base with its burden of information concerning this world, then the chances of any such coming again were far reduced. One man—to defeat a ship? That, too, might rank with the impossible. He could only try.

"Calling Spearpoint. Come in Spearpoint! Can you read me!"

Jony's head jerked, one hand flew up to the helmet on his head. Whose voice rang in his ears? The sound had a metallic rasp he could not associate with normal speech.

Then he understood. The communicator in the helmet was working. Those who had come in the flyer must be trying to locate the rest of their party.

The voice had changed now to an annoying buzz which made him want to free his head. Until he discovered that grew louder or lessened as he turned this way or that among the ridges, heading back toward the city through the night.

A possible guide! He could follow the volume of the sound to bring him to the flyer party. But he must not contact them yet. There was a greater need . . .

Jony could picture in his mind that row of looted boxes the spacemen had been bringing from the storage room. Those were bait, and they were also the danger. He swung the rod in his hand. The alien weapon weighed much less than the metal shaft which he had left with Voak, but, as he knew, this was far more deadly. How many of these lay encased there? Only one or two might be needed to win this battle with the off-worlders.

Jony filed that plan in the back of his mind and concentrated on the buzzing guide which he had not expected to bring him so easily to his goal. He traversed the ridge valleys at a steady trot. Hungry, yes, he was hungry, thirsty too. But since he had taken on that flow of energy from the stone woman, neither of those states of body seemed able to slow him. There was no time to answer his own physical needs.

Twist, turn, right and then left, with the sound growing, fading ever in his ears. At last he could see the lump of the city, silver and black in the moonlight. The buzz urged him left toward the far side. However, that was not yet his goal.

"Spearpoint come in!" Again the words, imperative and demanding.

Jony could not have replied, even if he had wanted to. These spacemen spoke to each other in patterns which they had set up before they ventured out of their ship. Even Geogee had not been able to supply him with the key to such.

The buzz dwindled. Entering the city from this angle, Jony was deliberately heading away from the ship. However, he had only to lift his head to see the rise of the pile which was his present goal. Though again he had to work from one of the paved ways to another until he came out on the main river of stone. Shadows afforded him protection. Jony dodged from one pool of them to the next, keeping to the best speed he could.

He had become adjusted to the directorial sound in his helmet. Still, as once again the voice suddenly cut through the steady buzz, he was startled into a quick halt.

"Last broadcast came from that center structure. We can only start a search from there . . ."

Those from the flyer were headed in the same direction! Hearing that, Jony threw away caution and began to run. He must get there before they did. What off-world weapons beside the stunners they might carry he did not know; Geogee's information had only concerned those. But if the spacemen could lay hands on the rods, knew their use . . . !

Gasping a little, Jony reached the ledges, looked up into the dim opening where stood the stone woman.

As he scrambled up that ascent, he kept his eyes on her. Was that power which had flowed into him from her touch also something he must make very sure *they* did not use? He could not tell.

As Jony stood once more before her, gazing into that calm face, into the eyes which stared over his head at the city, he raised the rod. To do this was fighting a part of himself. What was her purpose? Had she been set here to guard in some way what lay in the den behind? Or the sleeper? This was no time for speculation. But he could *not* blast her into nothingness, not yet.

He thudded past her, running down the lines of stone trees toward the block of the sleeper, and beyond him those rows of boxes. The light in the great inner den was scant, yet something in the clear face portion of the helmet gave him power of seeing as well as if he had come here by a mid-day height of sun.

Jony reached the end of that pile of boxes. What did lie within them? Wonders of the vanished people, more than he could guess? For a second or two his curiosity and desire to learn battled with his purpose. Surely not all could contain things deadly to life. Or could they? The People must have known of this wealth, of what would be to them treasures, all these years since they had escaped the city. Yet they had turned their backs on everything to do with their former masters. At this moment it was better to accept the judgment of the clan than his own desire to explore for forbidden knowledge.

Resolutely Jony raised the rod, found that button

near the base, set his thumb firmly over it. He aimed at the pile and pressed. This time the flame of the flash did not blind him—perhaps the helmet eyeplate helped. Instantly those containers at which he aimed simply were not, leaving not even dust to mark where they had once stood. Again, he raised the weapon and pressed. A second pile was gone. However, at his third attempt there was no answering flash, though he thumbed the button furiously with all his strength.

What was wrong! Did the devastating energy within the rods only last for two or three times use? Jony looked about wildly. Where could he find another? In the boxes left before him?

He leaped for the nearest, grabbed at its top and pulled. There was no response. Fastenings like those on the cages in the Big Ones' ship? Holding down his impatience, he examined the upper edges, searching for some indications of locks. With his fingers he alternately pressed and pulled. All at once the lid yielded, and Jony tore it up and back furiously.

The glitter of what lay within was visible even in the dusk. He ran his hand through the contents. Smooth bits of bright metal, sparkling stones . . . but no rod.

"That's the place, right ahead, captain!"

Jony whirled about. Those words resounding within his helmet were a startling warning that he had no more time for searching. Rod? The only one which remained that he knew of was that in the sleeper's hands. He caught up the one he had tossed aside, moving swiftly up to stand beside that stone in which the sleeper was encased. For the first time he dared to run his bare hand across the transparent surface of the block. It felt far smoother than stone to his touch. Could he break through it? Holding the dead rod in both hands, as Maba had fiercely beat upon the machine in the ship, so did Jony bring down the useless weapon upon the smooth lid on the block.

Once, twice. There was no sign of any cracking or breaking. Jony tried to strike in the same place each time, hoping that the concentrated pounding could bring about such results. The surface remained unmarked.

When again he used his fingers over the area where he had been striking there was no promising roughness to his touch. Was this sealed in some way as were the boxes?

Falling to his hands and knees, Jony began a closer inspection of the rim where that clear surface joined the sides. He pressed and pulled, striving to wedge the end of the rod into some invisible joint as a lever. But there was no spot he could find to apply such a pressure.

Getting to his feet again, wild with frustration, Jony looked down in despair at the red mask of that shrouded form, and the rod. He had no time to search those other boxes—no time!

Once more he ran his hand down the length of the box. If he could only locate some join, some sign that there *was* an opening! Then—

Jony stiffened, jerked his hand away. He stared at the box in wild astonishment. Just as his first touch against the palm of the stone woman had informed him that he had tapped an unknown source of energy, so had he now gained a similar shock.

Tentatively he leaned closer, using just the tips of his fingers to trace a space immediately above the mask which covered the unknown's face. There was something there, no fissure. No, his fingers told him that what he could not see was an area shaped like the hand of the woman.

He marked its outward edging by the tingling response of his own flesh. To his eyes there was no evidence of any such marking. Jony reached forth his hand, poised it above that unseen space which seemed attuned to energy. Was this the lock of the box, so different from the cage locks he had been able to handle long ago?

"Spread out!" Once more the order rang in the helmet. "Under as much cover as you can."

No more time! Jony brought his hand down on the place over the mask.

A charge of energy flashed back from that contact, into his body. Was this a protective device to make sure that the sleeper was not disturbed? It was too late for fear now; he could not withdraw his hand, even when he put his full will and strength to do that. Rather, there came a sensation of his flesh and bone being firmly entrapped, being drawn down into the clear substance of that cover. Yet his eyes assured him that was not so.

Instinctively Jony countered with that very personal weapon of his own talent. He concentrated his full will on the opening of the box, the freeing of his hand.

Now! Suddenly a network of fine cracks ran out and away from where his fingers rested. Those merged, as more and more appeared, becoming thicker, shattering so that splinters dropped away from their cleavage to lie on the sleeper. Then Jony was free as the whole portion he had touched gave away.

Only that did not end the crackling of the protective cover. The breaks still ran on and on, until they reached the stone rim. All that clear substance fell away in small broken bits, some as fine as dust. There was a puff of air, cold, smelling of acrid liquids, which Jony vaguely identified with the lab.

He had no time for any exploration or examination. Nor did he want in the least to disturb the mask on the sleeper's face. Instead his freed hand grabbed for the rod, drawing it out of that light grip. If only the rod still worked!

Without another glance at the sleeper, Jony descended in two leaps to the floor of the wide-walled den. He leveled the button, pressed, not quite daring to hope until he saw the results.

Flame answered. The boxes were gone!

He kept on raising and lowering the weapon of the unknown, working with wild haste to clear the floor of all those boxes the spacemen had brought out of the storage place. What still lay below there must be completely destroyed also, though he might not have time to do it now.

"Captain—there ahead! Who's that?"

Jony instinctively dodged behind the nearest tree of stone. He had accomplished this much. Now he had to face the invaders and carry out the rest of his impossible plan. He swung up the rod. The energy which had disposed of the boxes might now blot out men!

Only he found he could not press that button. He raged inside at this unexpected inability to blast into nothingness his own kind. Instead he groped for the stunner.

There were four—no, five of them—slipping from the shadow of one pillar to the next. They all carried arms held at ready. But two (he could not tell them apart with their heads all encased in the bubble helmets) had weapons which were different, probably more potent than stunners.

Jony aimed at the first of those. The figure buckled slowly, fell face down, his weapon skidding out of his loosened grip along the floor. Jony saw the others whirl at the sound of that fall.

One of them darted toward the weapon. Jony used the stunner again.

"Stay back!" That order was sharp. "Whoever he is, he's over there. Use the laser, Mofat!"

A beam of eye-dazzling light sped, to wreath the pillar behind which Jony had sheltered for his second shot. As if the stone were a tree struck by lightning, it blazed up. Heat scorched Jony's hand as he crouched in what he knew now was not a safe hiding place.

"Must have fried him, captain!" the second voice was exultant.

But what the captain might have added to his first command was lost. There was a sound throughout the whole den—not one that the ear could pick up, rather a vibration which filled the body. And Jony's mind! He put his hands to his head, tore off the helmet. His brain! He . . . what was happening to him?

Dimly now he saw those others reel into the open. They, too, were tearing at their head coverings, throwing them down, as if to wear those protections was a torment they could not bear.

And the den was no longer dark. There was light from the glowing pillar. Also there beamed radiance from another site: the box in which the sleeper had lain. All those bits of colored glitter about its sides were on fire, brilliant enough to affect one's eyes. And the shrouded form which had lain within was rising, but not as a sleeper leaves his bed; only the masked head lifted slowly on stiff and unbending shoulders.

The sleeper stood erect now. However, nothing about the shrouded form suggested he was alive. There was no rippling movement in any of the limbs, no turning of the masked head; nor did he attempt to leave the box.

From the air about them thundered sounds, words that Jony at first could not understand. But then—the pain in his head was gone. At that moment he was filled with an exultation, a sense of power which lifted him beyond all weariness of body, all confusion of mind.

He stood up. *This was the Awakening, as had been foretold*—by whom, asked a part of him who was still

Jony—*but he had no time for questions now. He mus:
make sure that all was safe.* Without fear, Jony steppe
into the open, toward those others who still twiste
and moved feebly. He raised the rod.

*Danger must be swept from the place of the Gree
One . . .*

No! That was not right. Jony shook his head tryin
to clear it. He felt as if he were now two people—bein
swept first this way and that. *Use the force. Blot or
those who came in anger and greed.* No . . . proteste
the other Jony.

He could not think straight. *Kill*—no! *Destroy*—n(
The two orders contradicted each other with a risin
need for action. On the next "no" he fired—with th
stunner.

The intruders crumpled. *See—they were safely qui
now. The Great One was safe. He must approac(
make ready the return of . . .*

Jony moved with swift strides up toward the stan(
ing figure wearing the blank metal mask. The rouse
sleeper was as stiff as the stone woman. Stone Womar
Gulfa of the Cloud Power. A name floated out of som
where into his mind. *Gulfa, who would never die b(
cause of the forces sealed within her. But this was n(
the hour of Gulfa. This was the Hour of the Retur
. . . the Awakening which was designed to be—*

Jony climbed the steps, moving to face the maske
one. As he went he mouthed words he did not kno
nor understand. *Gulfa had rightly entrusted him wi(
the power to rouse the sleeper. Now he must use it.*

He put out his hand. *The mask! Draw aside the ma.*

*the Great One could breathe, could live again. For
is one act alone had he been born, been schooled—
e half-memory, the purpose which had flowed to him
om Gulfa's touch was strong.*

However, in him now struggled that same queer
oubt which had kept him from first using the rod to
stroy those who had come unbidden into the place
the Great One. There was another fear. He must
ot take the mask from that head. *That was untrue,
is was his great mission: to return the Great One to
e world.* No . . . yes . . .

No!

Jony came aware, fully conscious, as one might
ake from sleep. This was his once dreamt nightmare
terror. He was himself, Jony. He was not tied to this
ing of dread rising out of a broken box!

He swung up the rod, pressed the button.

There was a far-off sound, like a thin scream of ut-
rmost despair.

Nothing stood in the box. Jony lurched closer to
ok within. Nothing lay there now. Somehow he had
en saved from a danger he did not understand, but
hich he sensed was greater than any this world or the
acemen had ever threatened.

Shuddering, he turned around. The bodies of the in-
ders lay on the floor. He did not know how this thing
d come to pass; but he had won this part of the bat-
against double odds.

Jony descended to inspect his prisoners. They were
unconscious. From them he took their weapons,
thered these into a pile, and used the rod.

Now—for the ship.

He found the flyer easily enough. They had left guard; but Jony's helmet, his ship's garb, gained h the entrance. Once more he disarmed and destroyed weapon, letting the guard see plainly what he d Under the threat of a similar raying, the spacem flew him back to the towering ship.

Jony stood below the star-pointing bulk of the sh gazing up its side into the heavens where dawn h already broken. A ship which never returned—it wou not be the first one lost on such exploration. This par had come here purely by chance. The only records what they had discovered were on board. Those wou never be delivered now to the distant authority w meant to make this world theirs.

Perhaps, in time, there would come another ship by chance. But then the People would be warn ready. Jony would see that this story would be ke alive so that they would know what must be done that did happen.

Men of his own kind had built this ship, had had t courage to take it into the far reaches of space. could understand their pride of achievement when looked upon it. Only, in truth they had not achiev very much. Things they could make: machines obey them—to set them among the stars—to live new worlds. But they had other machines which th took pride in using. Jony grimaced at what he had se in the lab—Yaa in the grip of equipment set to tear secrets of her life out of her.

Perhaps the men his act would leave here for the rest
their lives would never understand. Perhaps some
them could learn—in time. Jony did not care, or
ow. He was only aware of what he must do.

Men were not "things." Nor were "animals" things
to be used, discarded, experimented upon. All had
e-force in common and that life-force was a precious
t. Man could not create it. If he destroyed a ma-
ine, as Maba had destroyed the one in the lab, that
uld be rebuilt. But if the invaders had destroyed Yaa
ring their ruthless quest for knowledge, who could
ke her live again?

Men, the Big Ones—all the arrogant kind who be-
ved that their will should rule . . .

Slowly Jony began to walk around the ship. Geogee's
ormation had been sketchy, but the older boy had
rned enough to guess what he must do. He had
stroyed the motor power of the flyer and stunned the
ot before he had left it. Now this larger craft must
 in turn.

With the rod of the Great One, Jony took careful
n at the casing above the fins on which the ship
lanced. How many levels above lay its motor power
was not quite sure. But he was going to hold the rod
his target until he had done all the visible damage
could.

Under the glare of the ray a hole appeared raggedly
the smooth casing of the ship. Through that Jony
ntinued to pour the energy he did not understand.
 could feel the pulsation of the power as it left the

rod. There could be no repairing the destruction h
now wrought. Then he turned in a half-circle to c
away the fins, so that the ship crashed to the groun
broken, dead, and harmless. There was still life insid
he could sense that. Men bewildered by his attack. H
had no quarrel with them now. They would be weapo
less, helpless—forced to come to terms with this worl
—not dominate it.

For a long moment Jony surveyed the crumple
bulk. He dropped his stunner to the ground, and d
stroyed that in turn. The rod he must keep—for
while. Until he was sure all danger from the invade
was over.

What would happen to them after this was up
them. If they learned to accept the People, they mig
eventually become one with this world. If they cou
not, then they must exist as best they might.

Jony took the helmet from his head, hurling it awa
He tore at the fastening of the ship garment, dropp
that onto the ground. The wind about his body fe
fresh, clean. He touched his throat once, rememberin
the collar. But he, Jony, was not a "thing"; he was
man. As Voak, Otik, all the rest were men—and wou
remain so.

Turning his back on the fallen ship, Jony began
walk north into a new future.

HEY—LOOKIT THIS! A BOX ALL TORN UP. AND, GEE, ohnny, there's a dead kitten in it!"

"Let's see. Boy, think of someone throwing out a itten just like it was old rubbish or something."

The cat raised her head at the sound of voices. She vas not yet wary or abused enough to fear such sounds. They had always meant food, warmth, comfort. She newed.

"Well, I'll be! Now, lookit here—in this old fridge! There's a cat, and one—two—three kittens. I'll bet hey were all in that old box! What are you doing, ohnny?"

"Doing? I'm going to take her back home. Here, ou empty out this bigger box. Get those rags over here. No, you dummy, don't take those wet ones on op, get the dry ones. There ought to be some still dry nderneath."

"Your Mom is going to have fits if you turn up with cat and three kittens. 'Member how she took on 'bout hat old dog?"

"Sure. But he got a good home with the Wilsons, nce we fed him up and cleaned him, and everything. This is a good cat. See, she likes me. See her rub gainst my hand? Anyway, I wouldn't leave anything here just to die—nothing at all. Sometimes I just don't dig people. They don't care about animals. You'd think they were broken toasters or something. Throw 'em out and forget them!"

"Well, you can't be a one-man army to save all the animals—"

"Maybe not—but I tell you, if *somebody* doesn't start doing something—then someday . . ."

"Someday what? Animals get back at us? Shut us up in cages? Leave *us* on dumps? That what you mean?"

"I dunno. I just have a feeling we've got to learn how to live so everything has a fair chance. There was something I read once, had to learn it for my book report. 'Animals are not brethren nor underlings, but others, caught with ourselves in a net of life and time, fellow prisoners of the splendor and travail of earth.' "

"Huh? What's all that mean in plain talk now—"

"That we're all part of this world together—and—well, we've got to learn to live together in another kind of way. Or else we've all lost."

"You and your books! Come on anyway. I'll give you a hand with the box . . ."

A thousand years later and half the galaxy away, Jony rubbed his throat again. He could scent the camp of the People. He wore no collar, nor did they. No iron cages waited for either of them—alien to each other though they might be. He threw his arms wide, and the feeling of freedom made him almost giddy.